KORGI

CREATED BY

ANN & CHRISTIAN SLADE

top
Shelf
PRODUCTIONS

CHRISTIAN SLADE

BOOK 3

TOP SHELF

ATLANTA / PORTLAND

Korgi (Book 3): A Hollow Beginning © & tm 2011 Christian Slade.

Published by
Top Shelf Productions
PO Box 1282
Marietta, GA 30061-1282
USA

Publishers:
Chris Staros & Brett Warnock

Visit our online catalog at
www.topshelfcomix.com.

First Printing, August 2011. Printed in Canada.

Thanks to Chris, Brett
and the Top Shelf family

Fellow artist friends
Brad, J Pat, Ken, Mike, Ray, and Joe

Janice, Deb, Kandee, Art & Pat, Thyra
and all the corgi people who have
supported my work over the years

Special thanks to my family.
Especially, Mom, Dad, Maggie, David,
Ann, Kate & Nate

Extra special thanks to
Queenie, Will, Wanda, Penny, Leo
and all the Welsh Corgis in the world

Thank you
for helping me find Korgi!

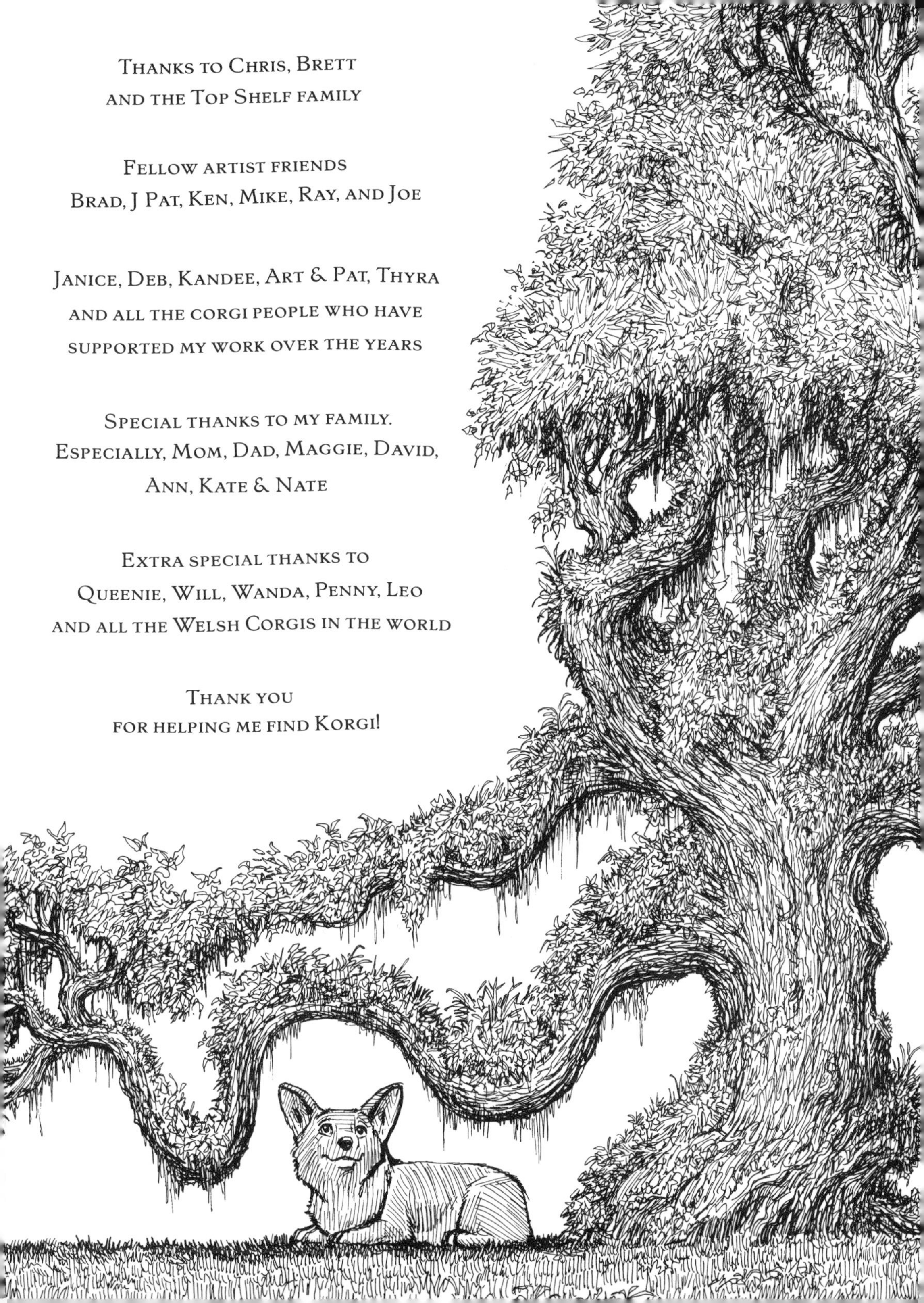

3

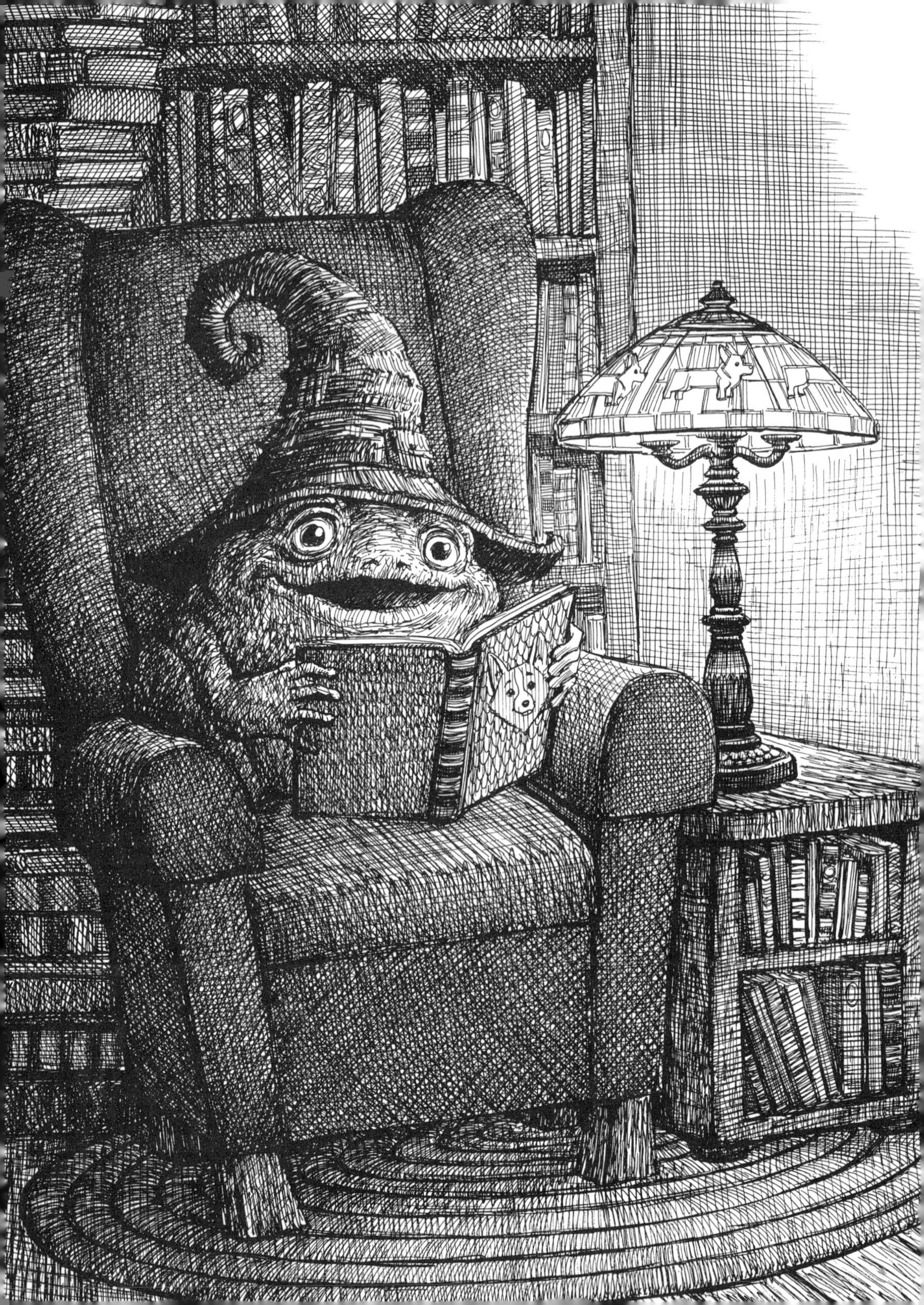

Hello again, curious reader!
It's so good to see you return.

The world is a wonder. And the things that lie within are even more wondrous.

One of these wonderful things that I often ponder is how creatures and places begin. The large giant oak tree was once a tiny acorn no bigger than a flower. Each creature living in, under and above the forest has its own unique spot. As different as we are from each other, we are also the same in many ways. One of the things that binds us is that we all have a beginning. Over the many years I have been here, I have made it an adventure to discover how the magical world around me began.

In this special book, the very beginnings of Korgi Hollow itself will be revealed. For in this story you will find another tale, an older tale, told by none other than myself.

So you'll be seeing me in a short bit. In the meantime, do find your best reading place, curl up with your favorite blanket, and prepare yourself for,

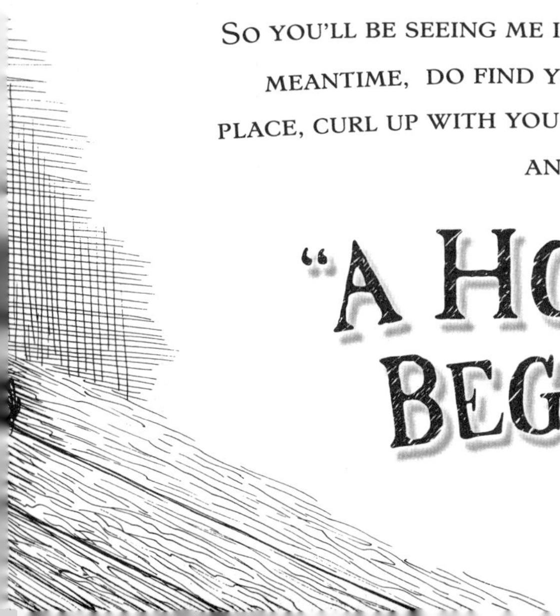

"A Hollow Beginning!"

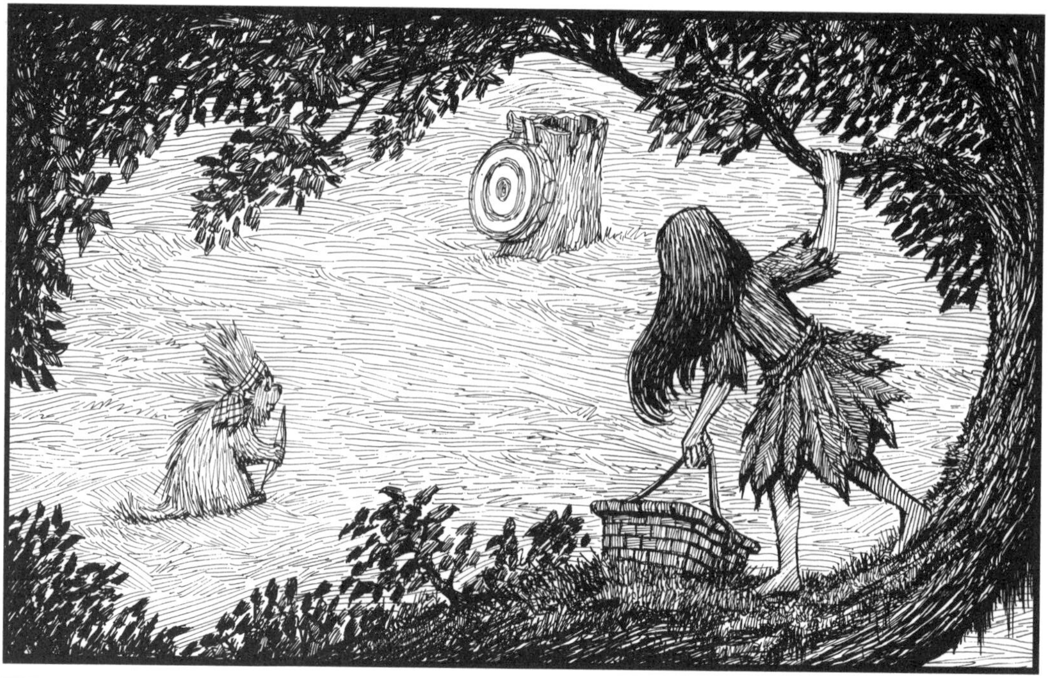

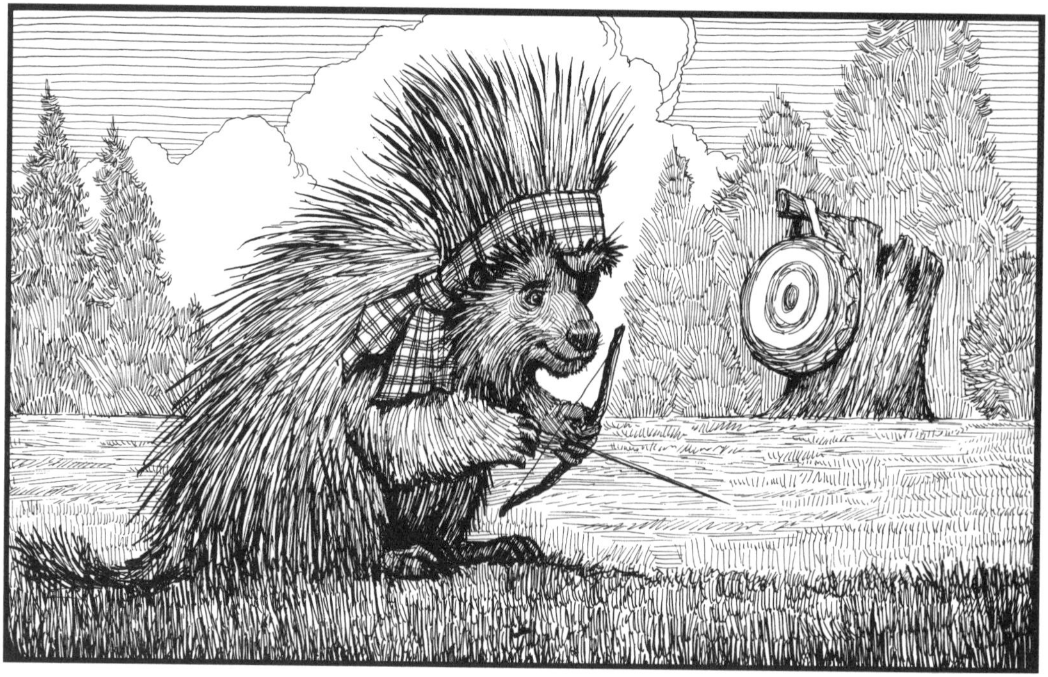

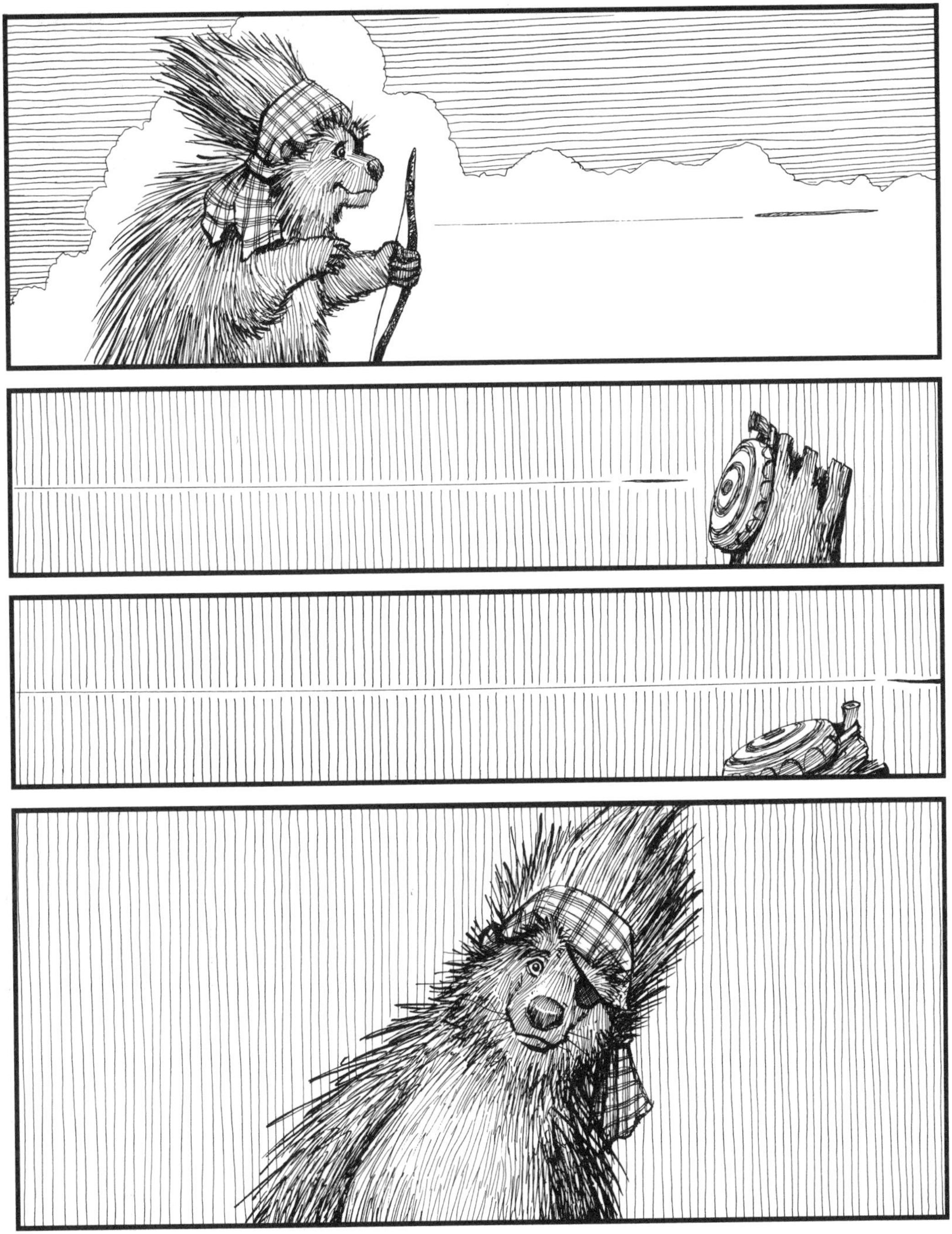

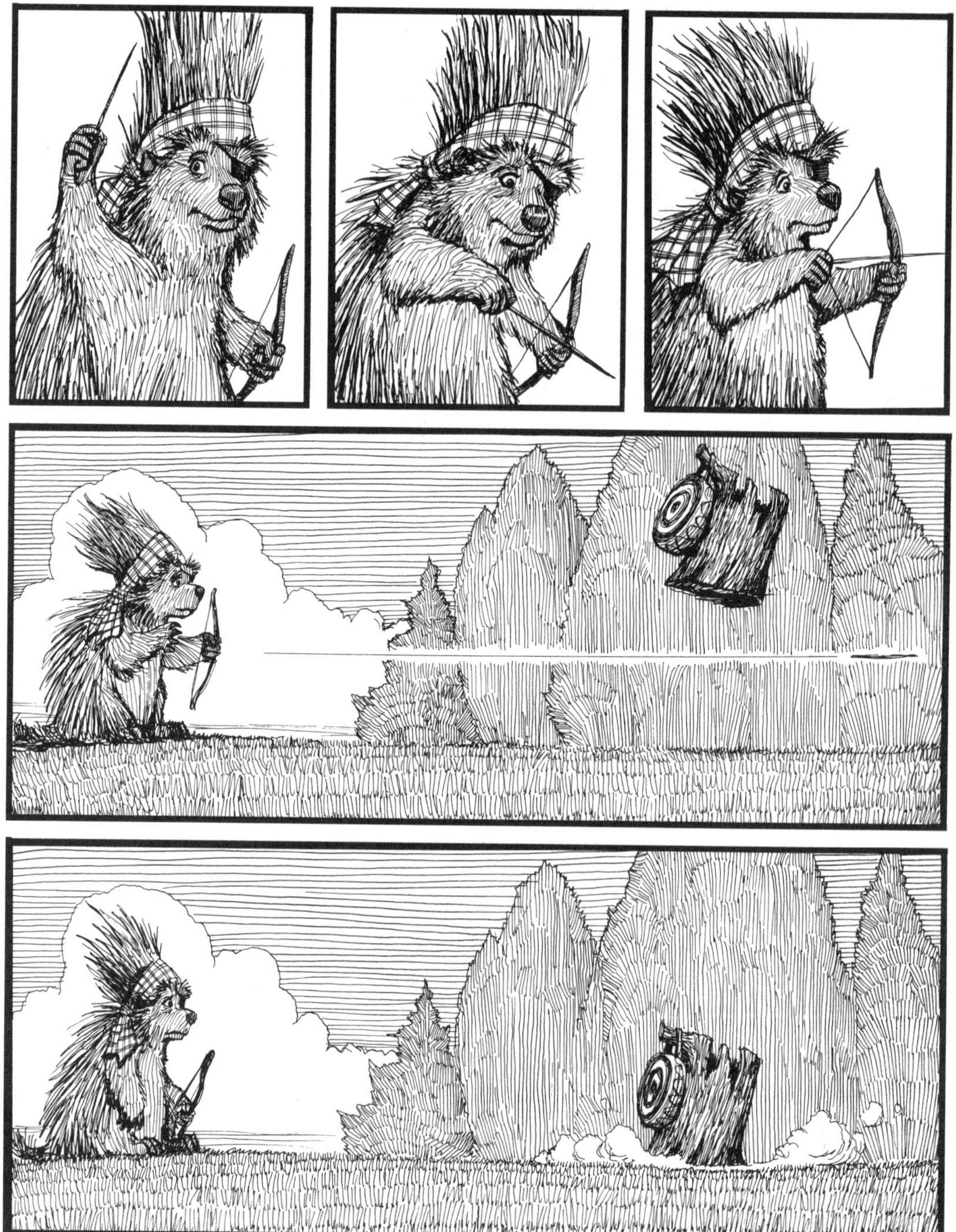

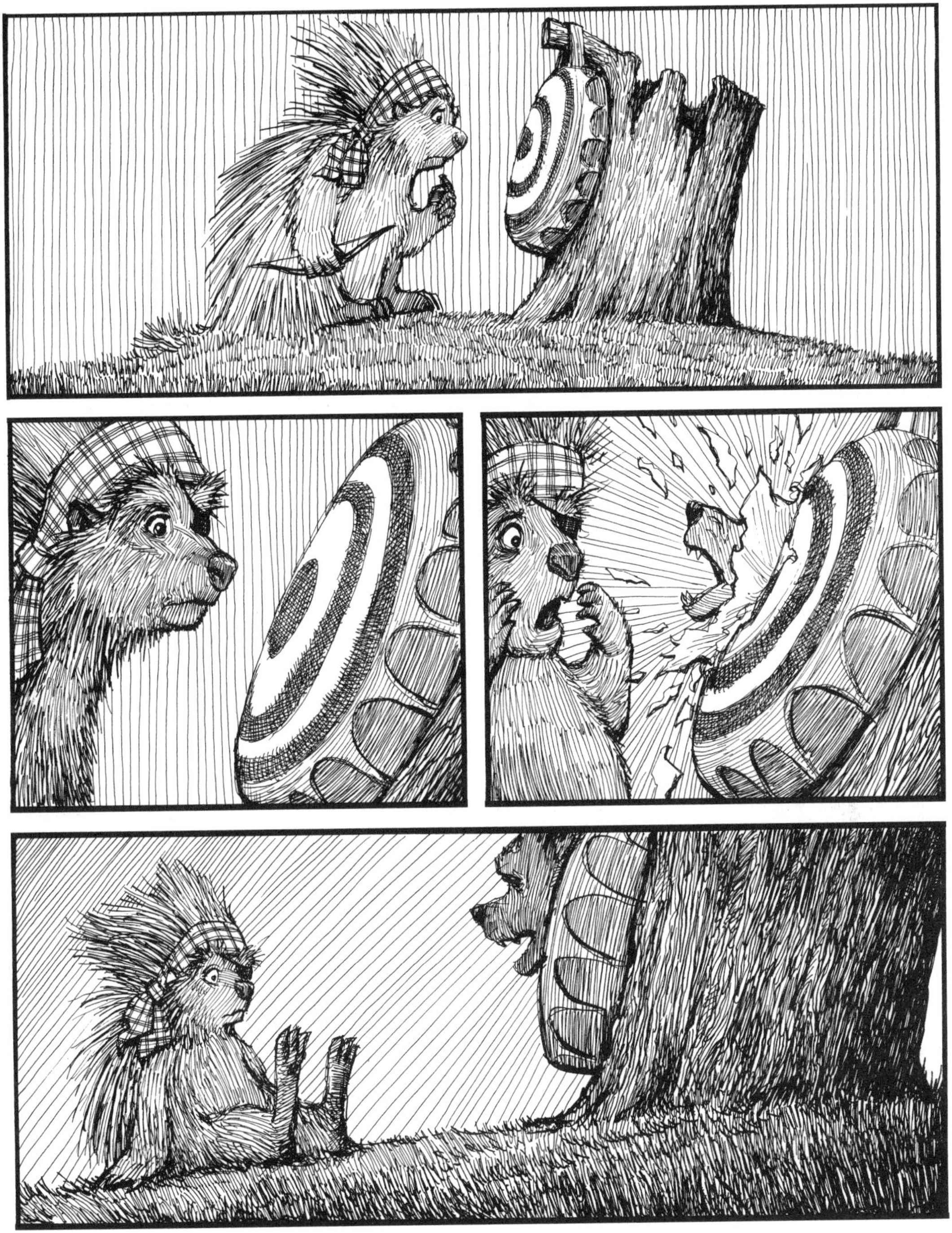

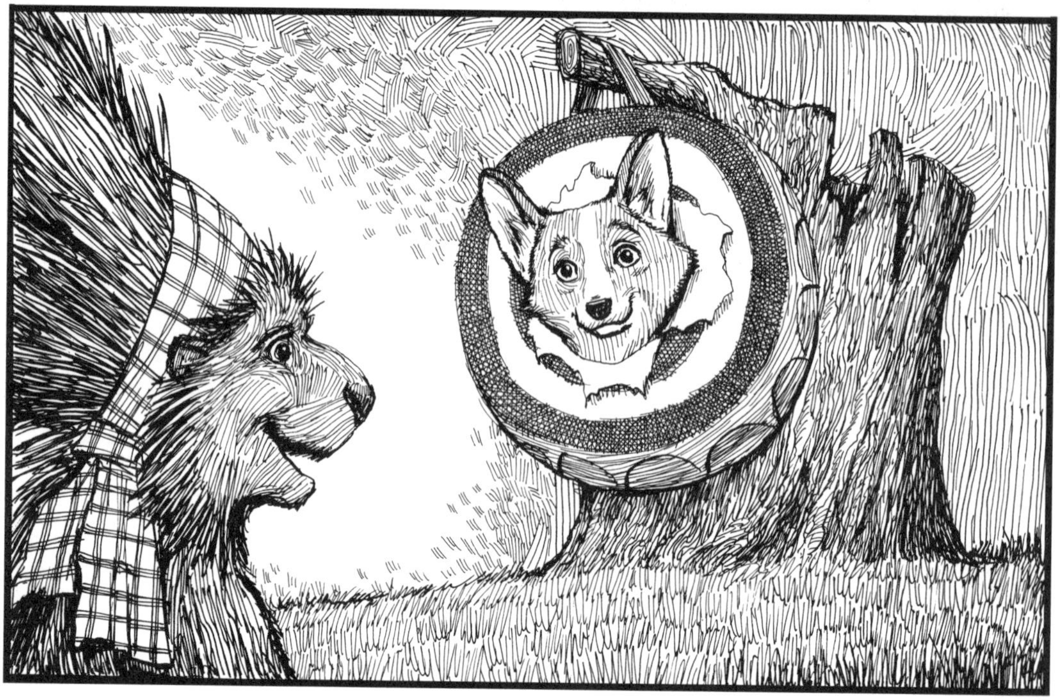

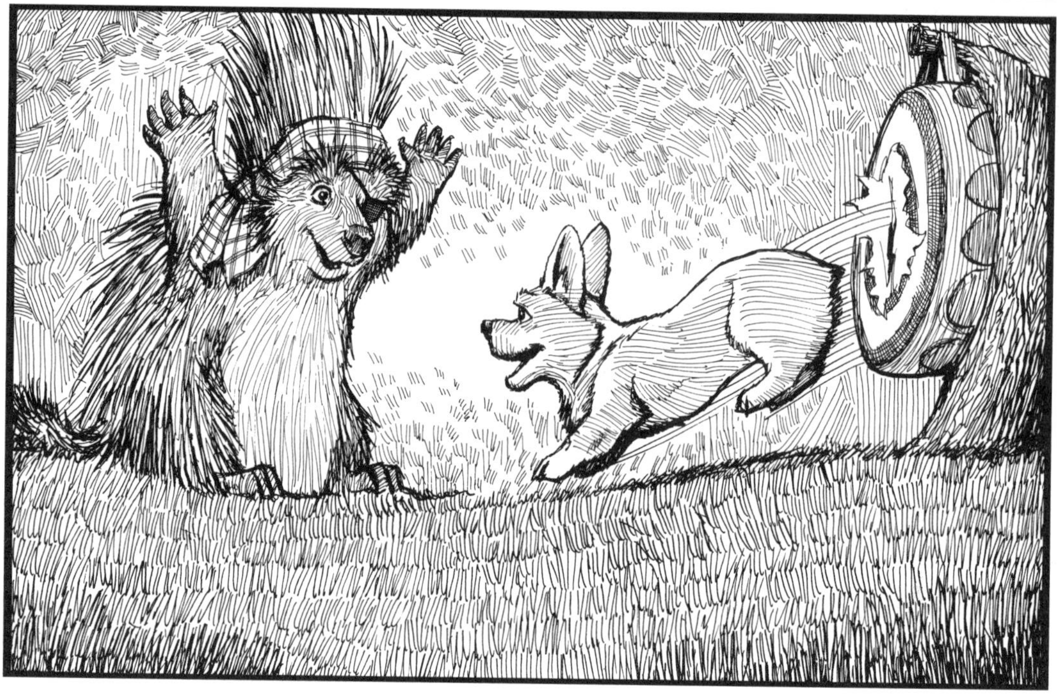

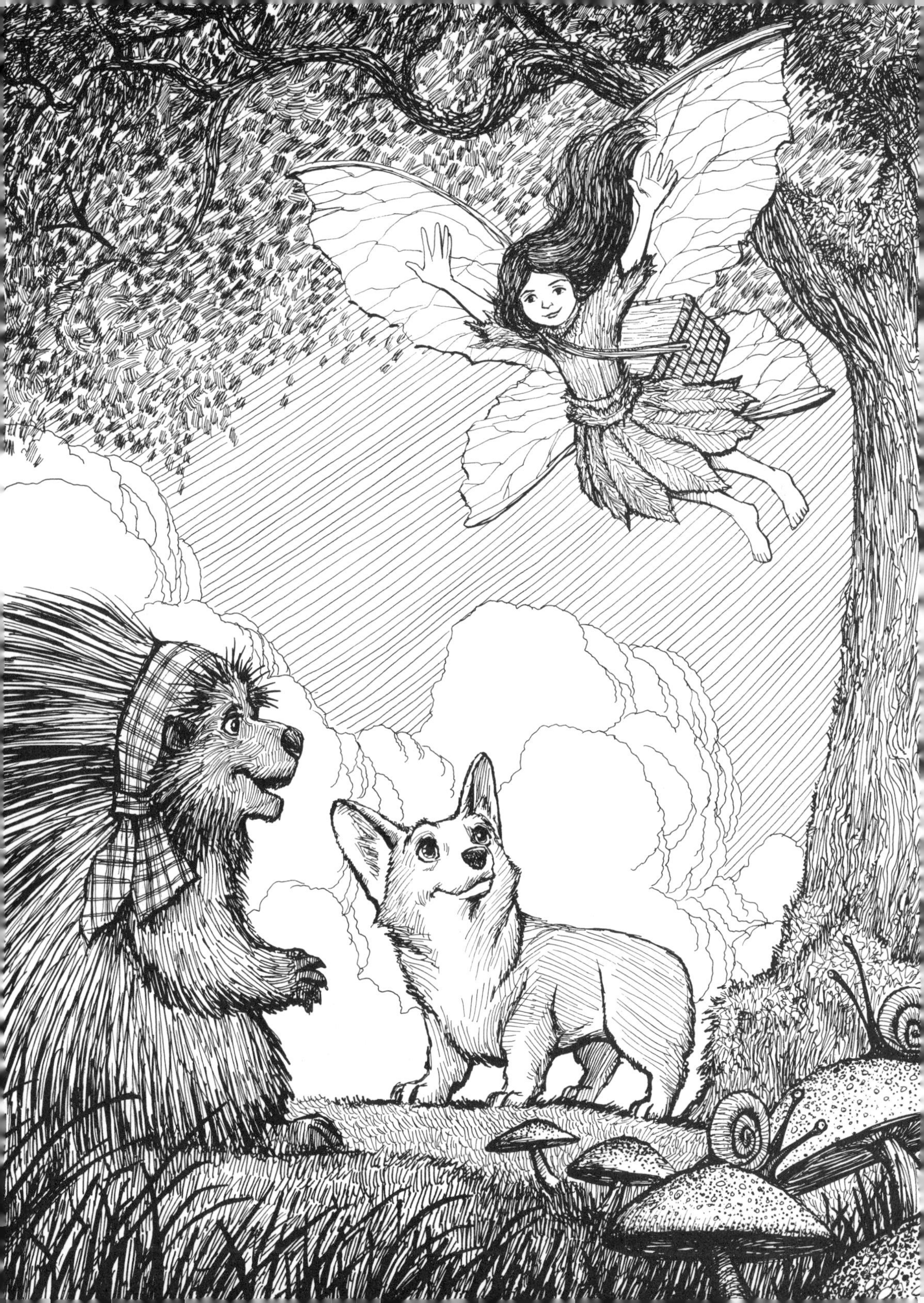

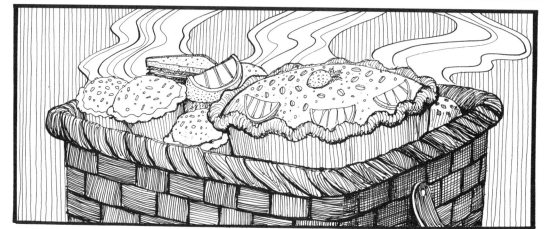

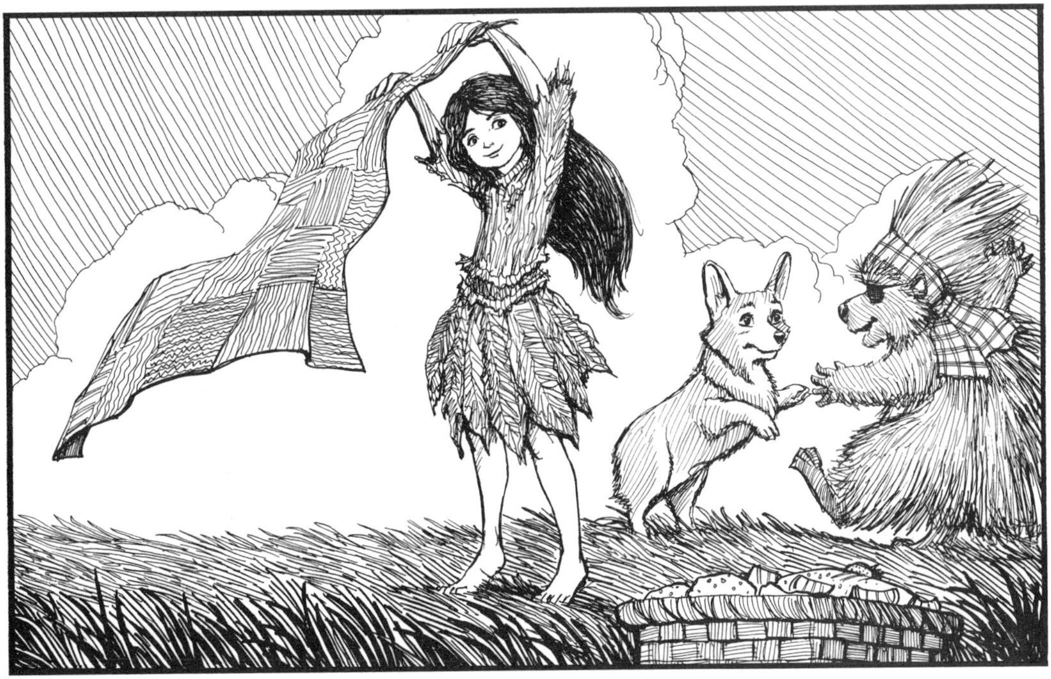

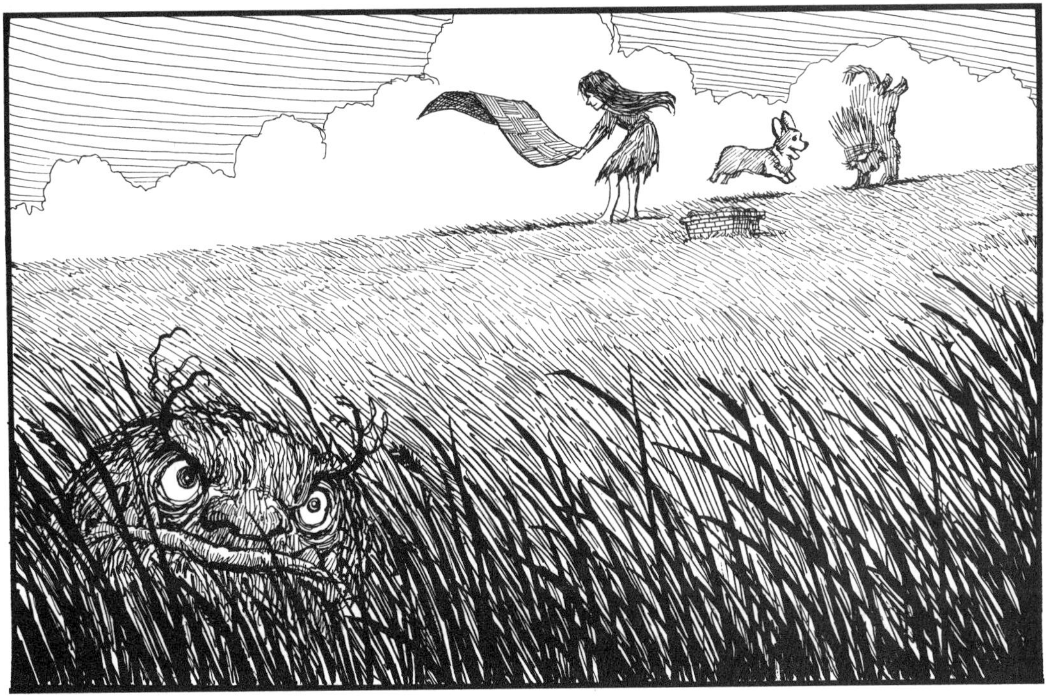

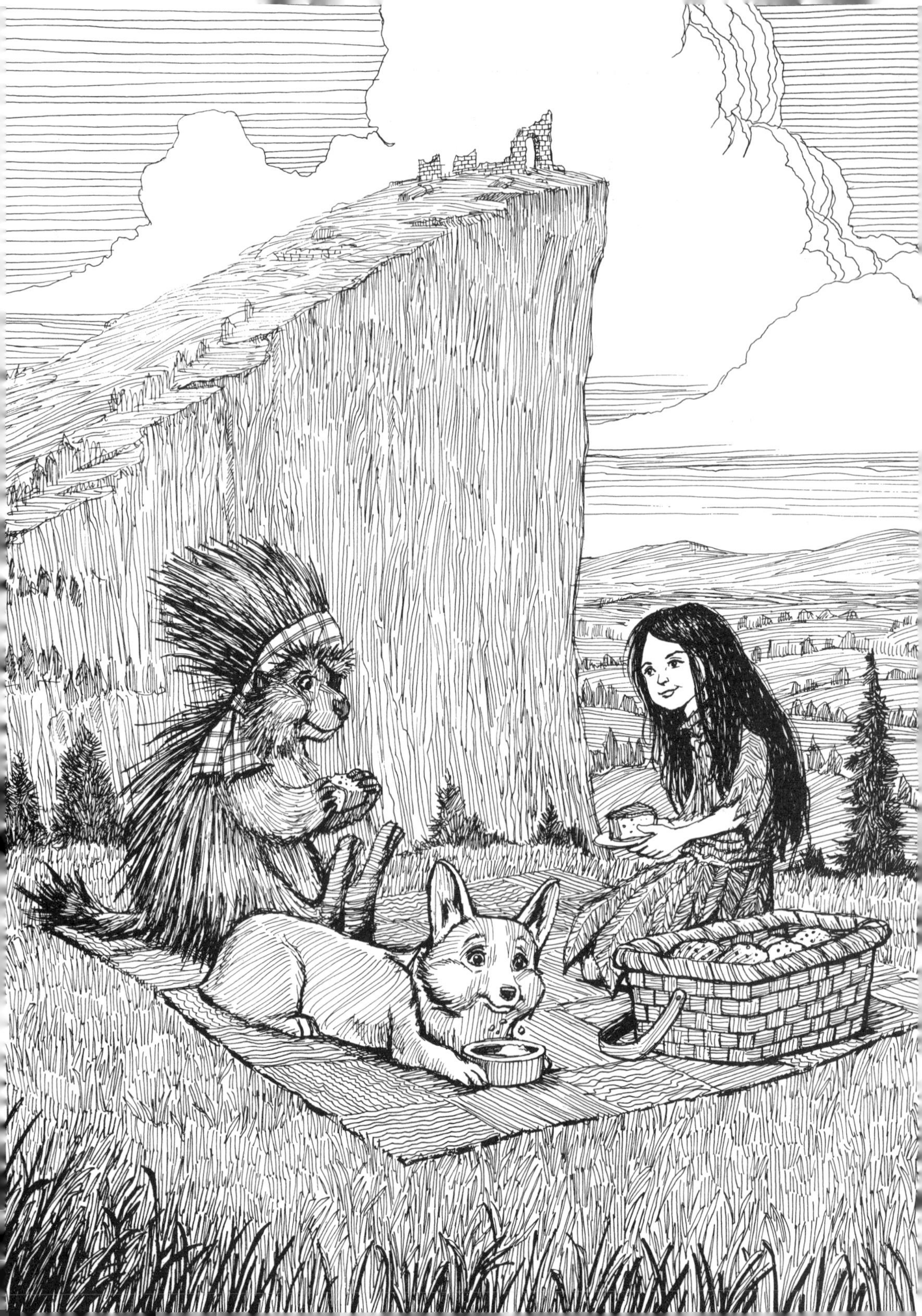

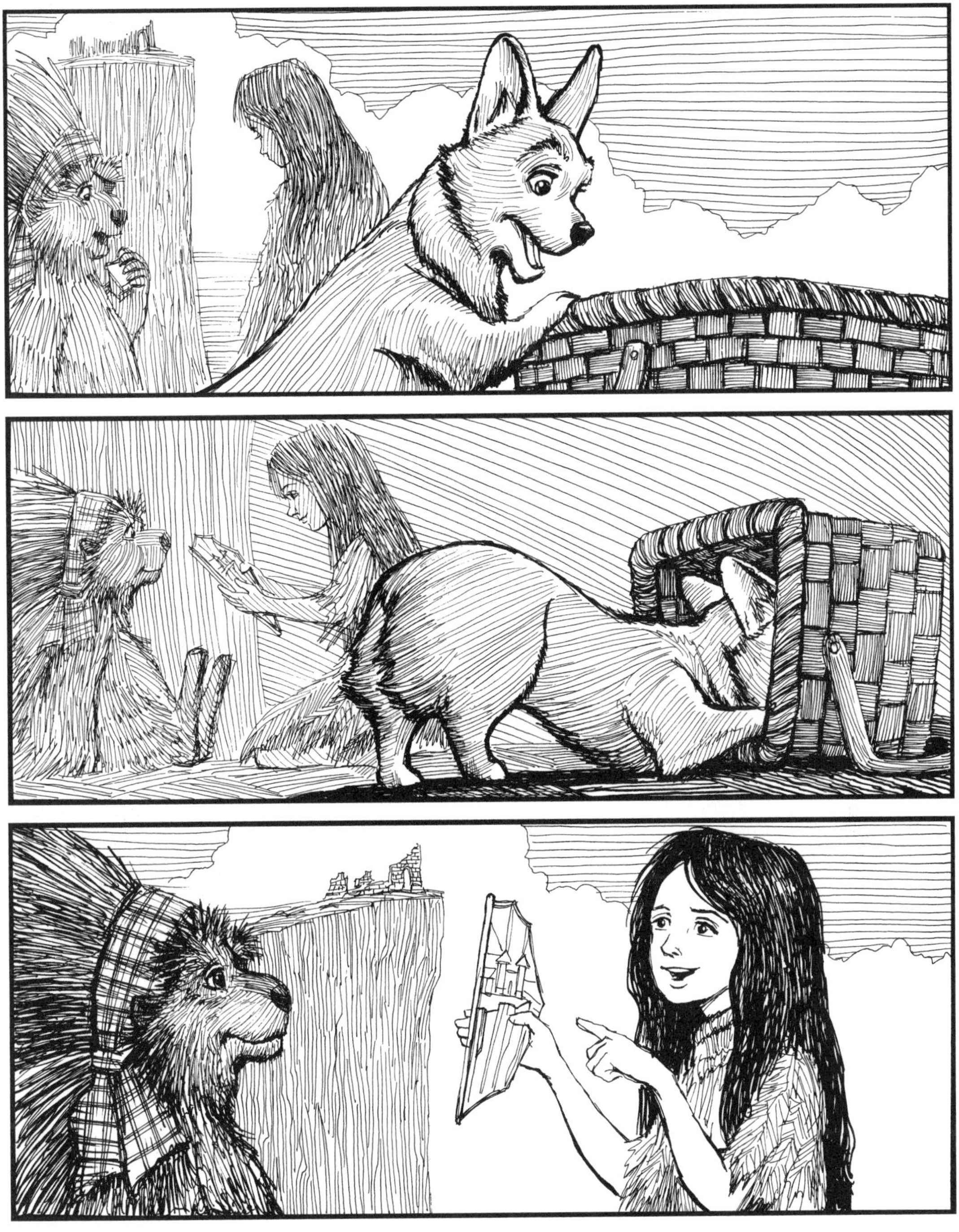

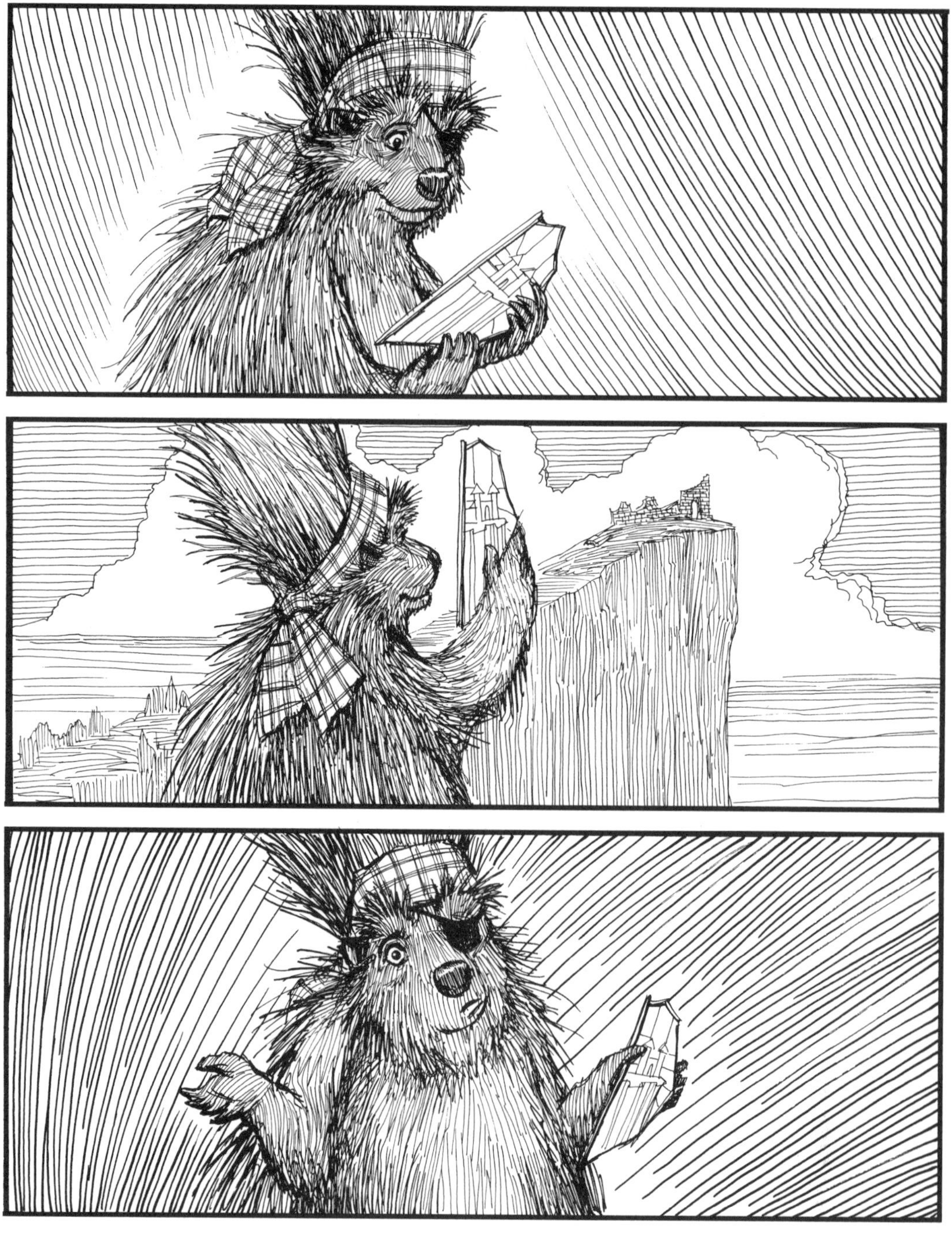

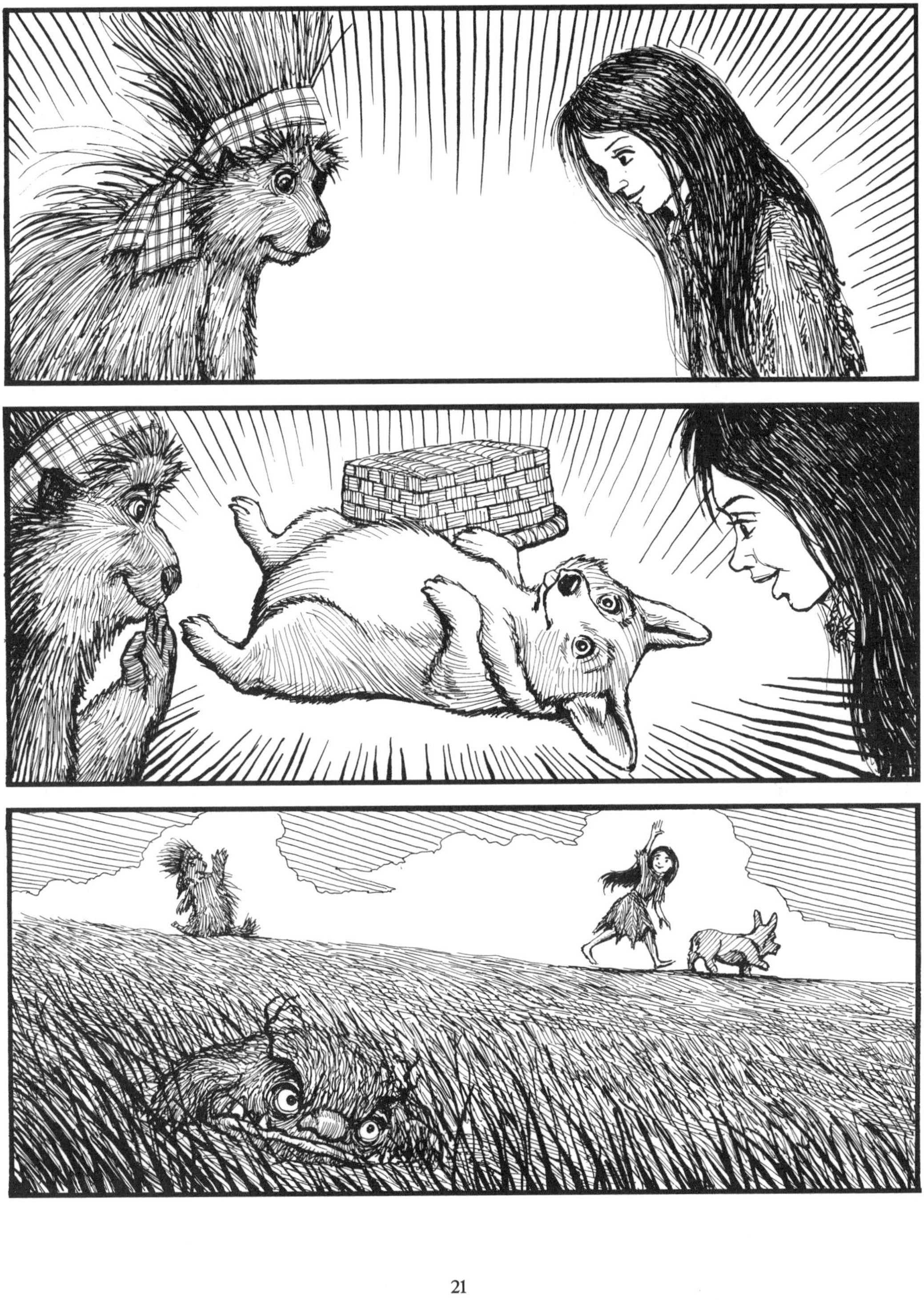

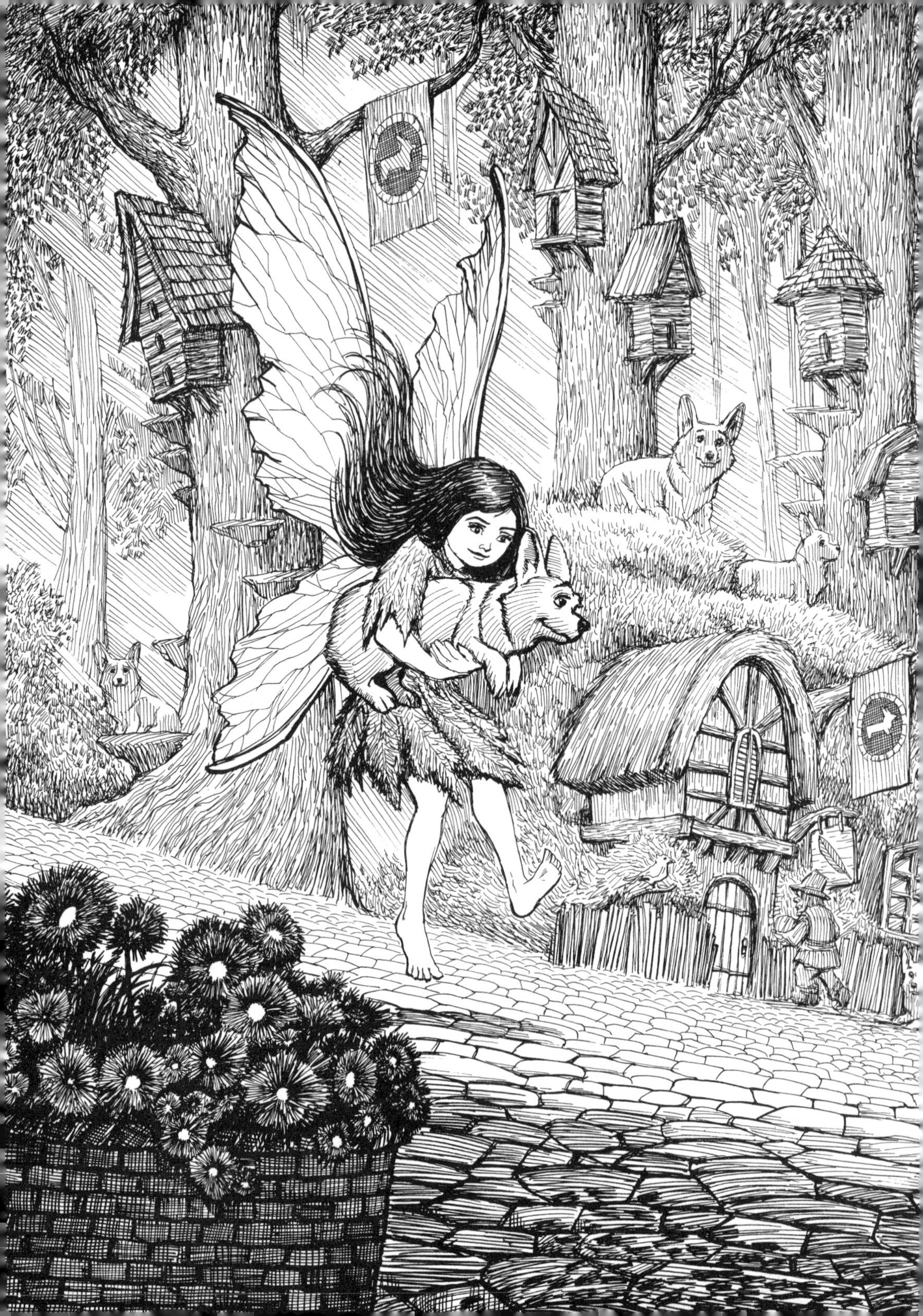

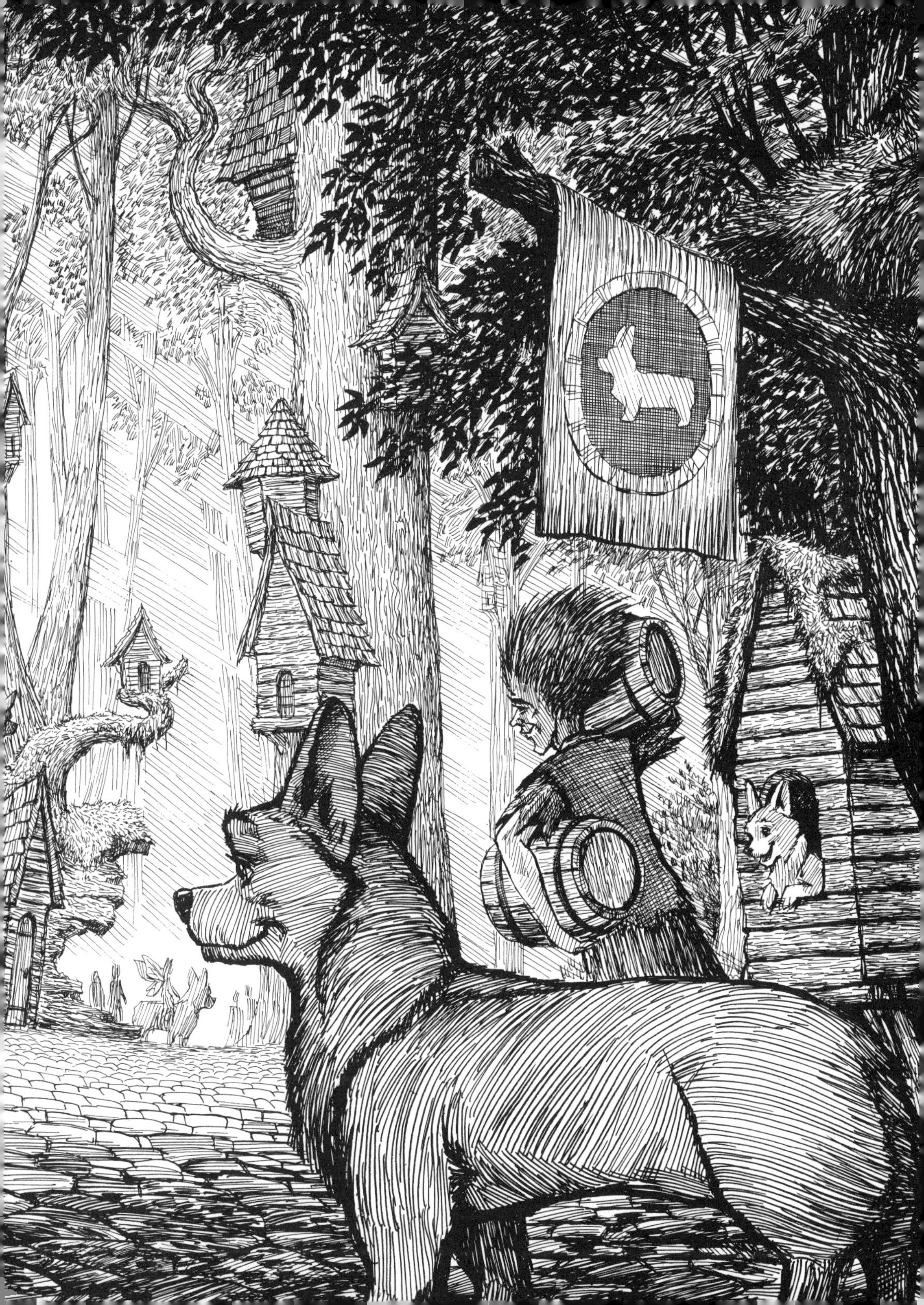

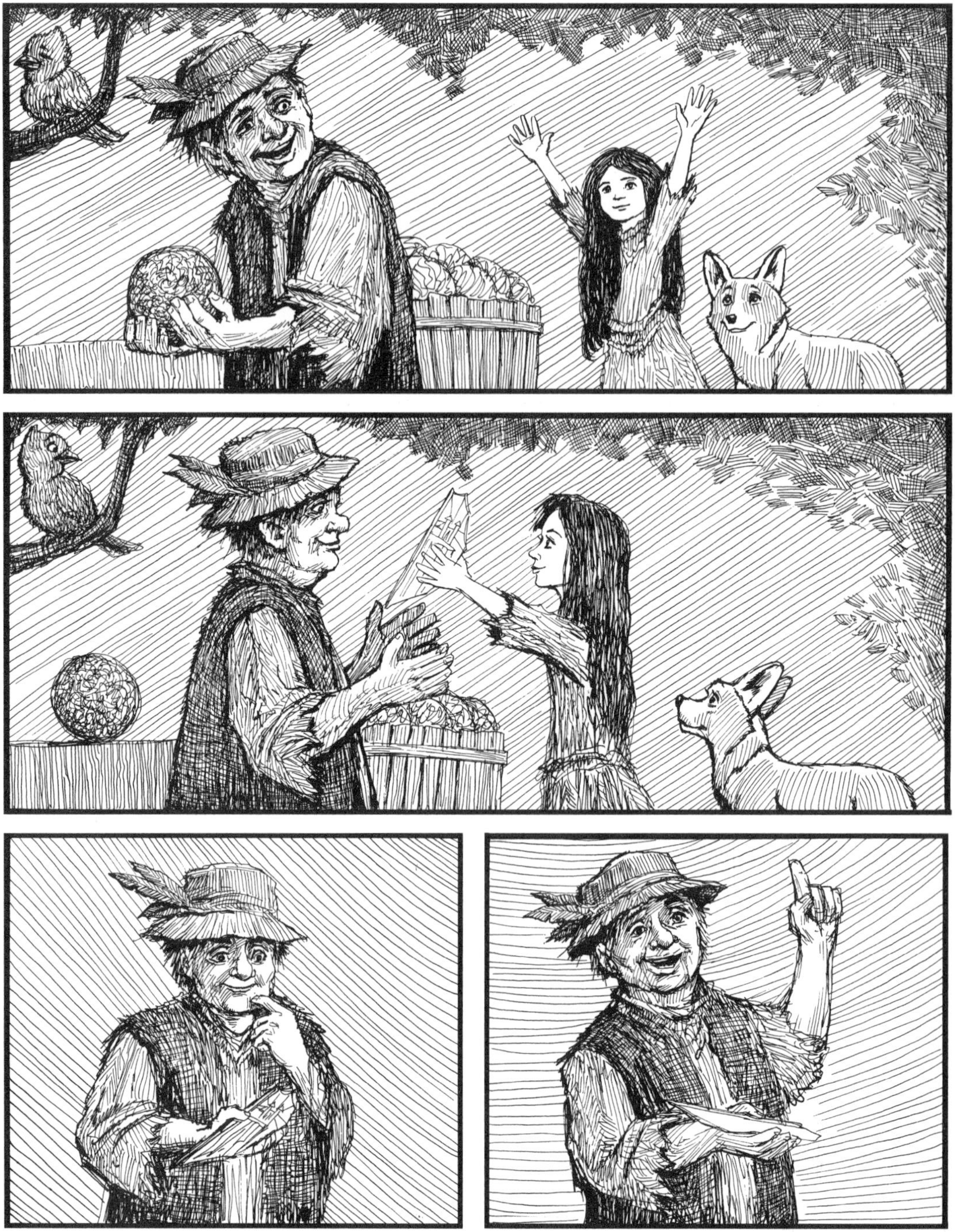

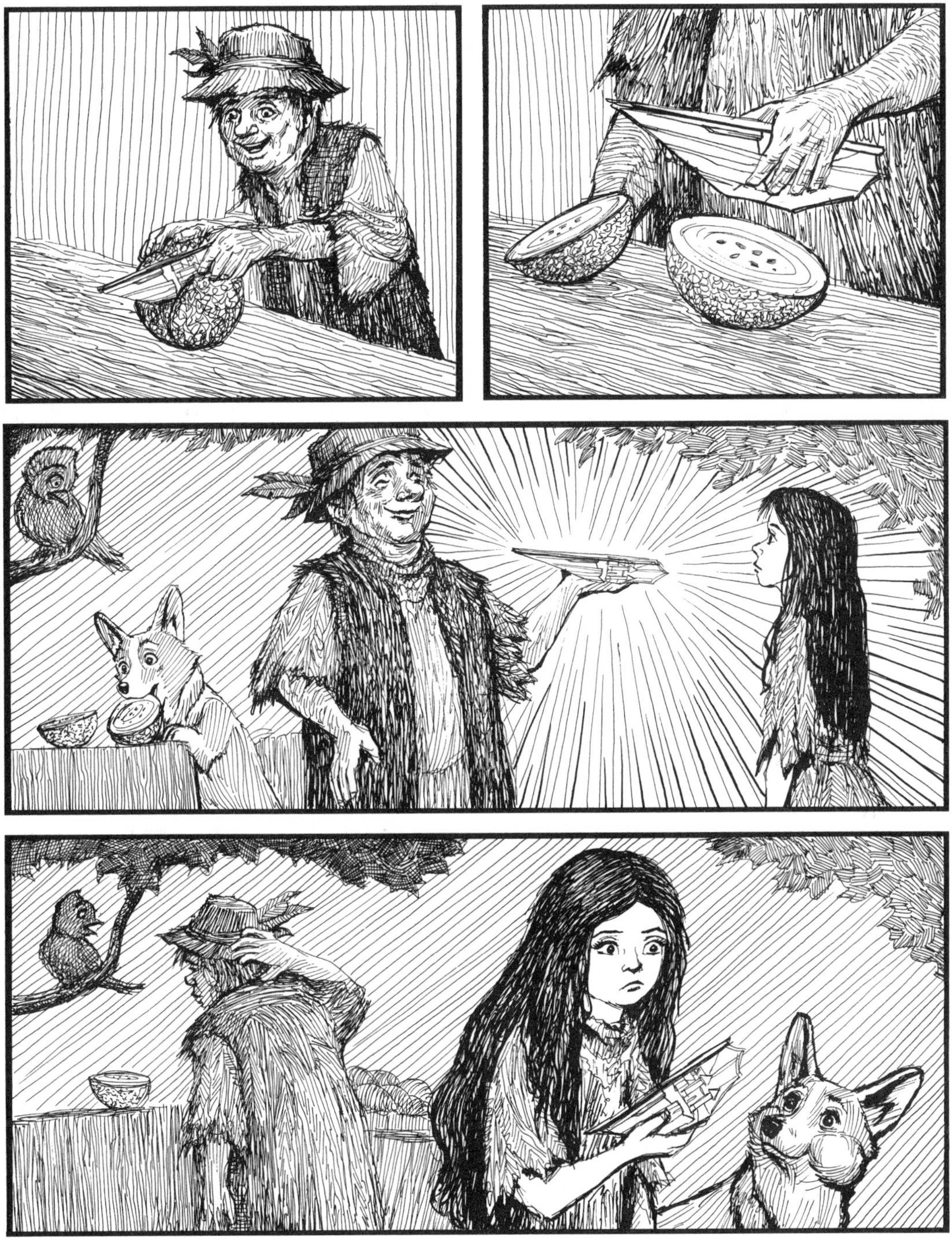

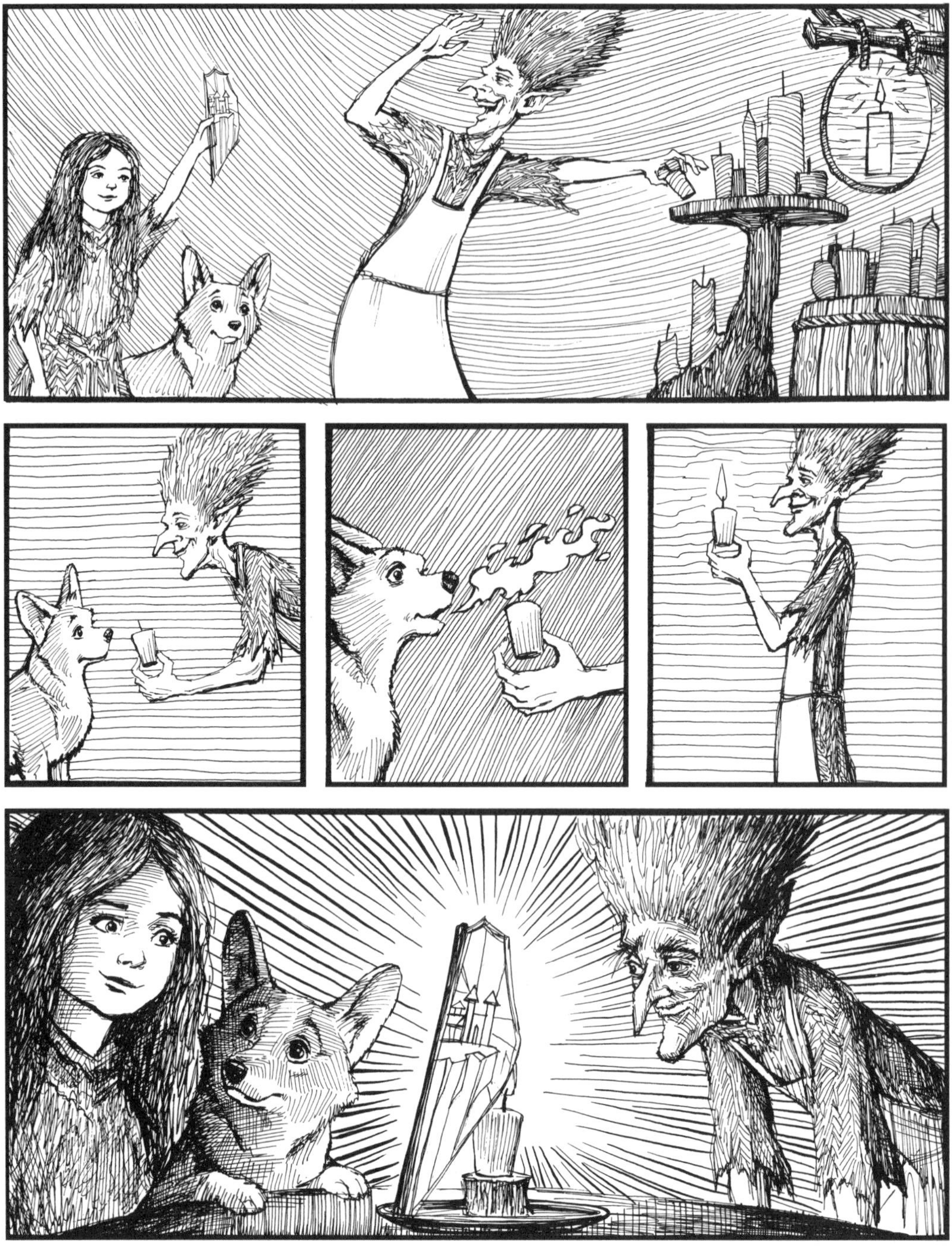

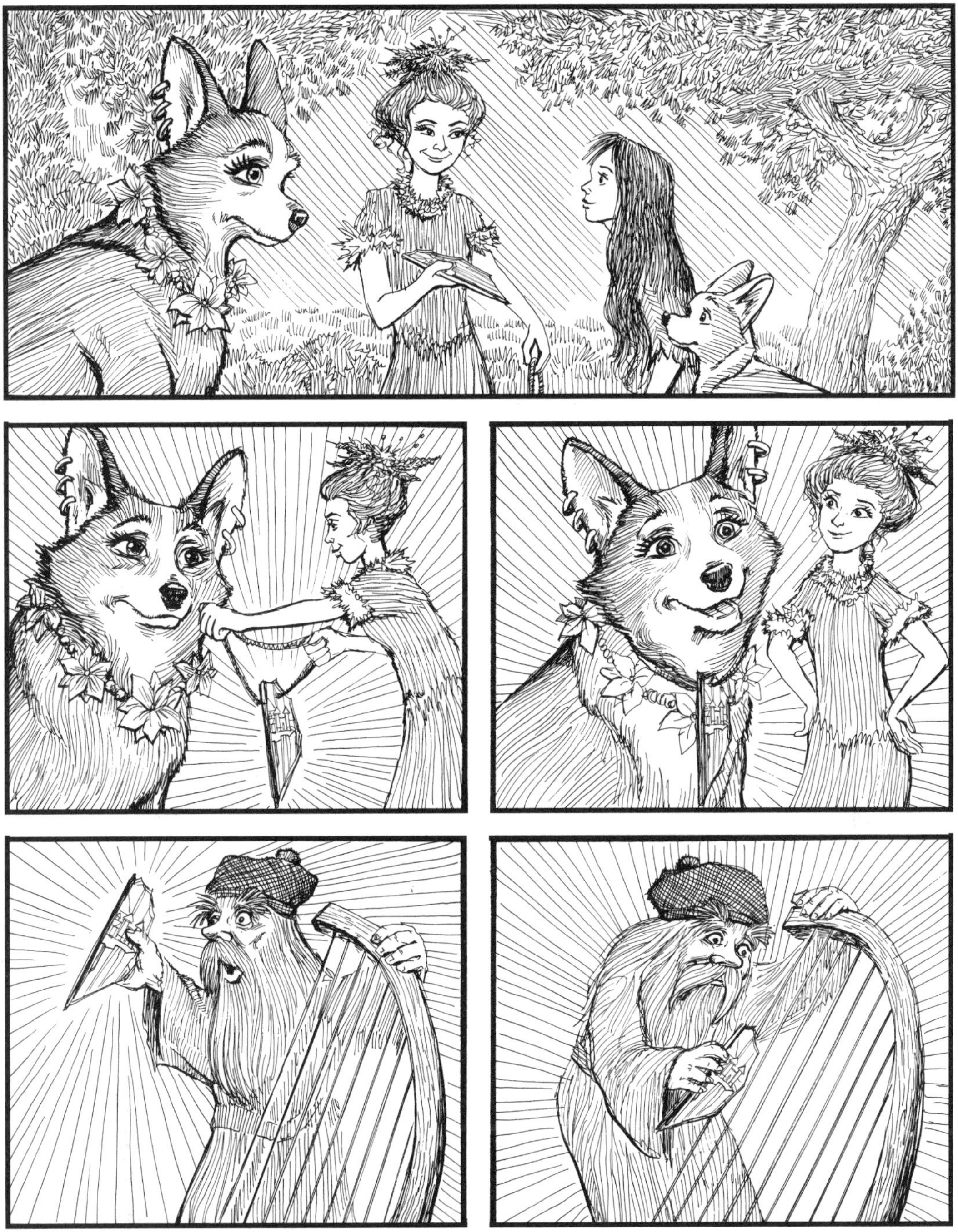

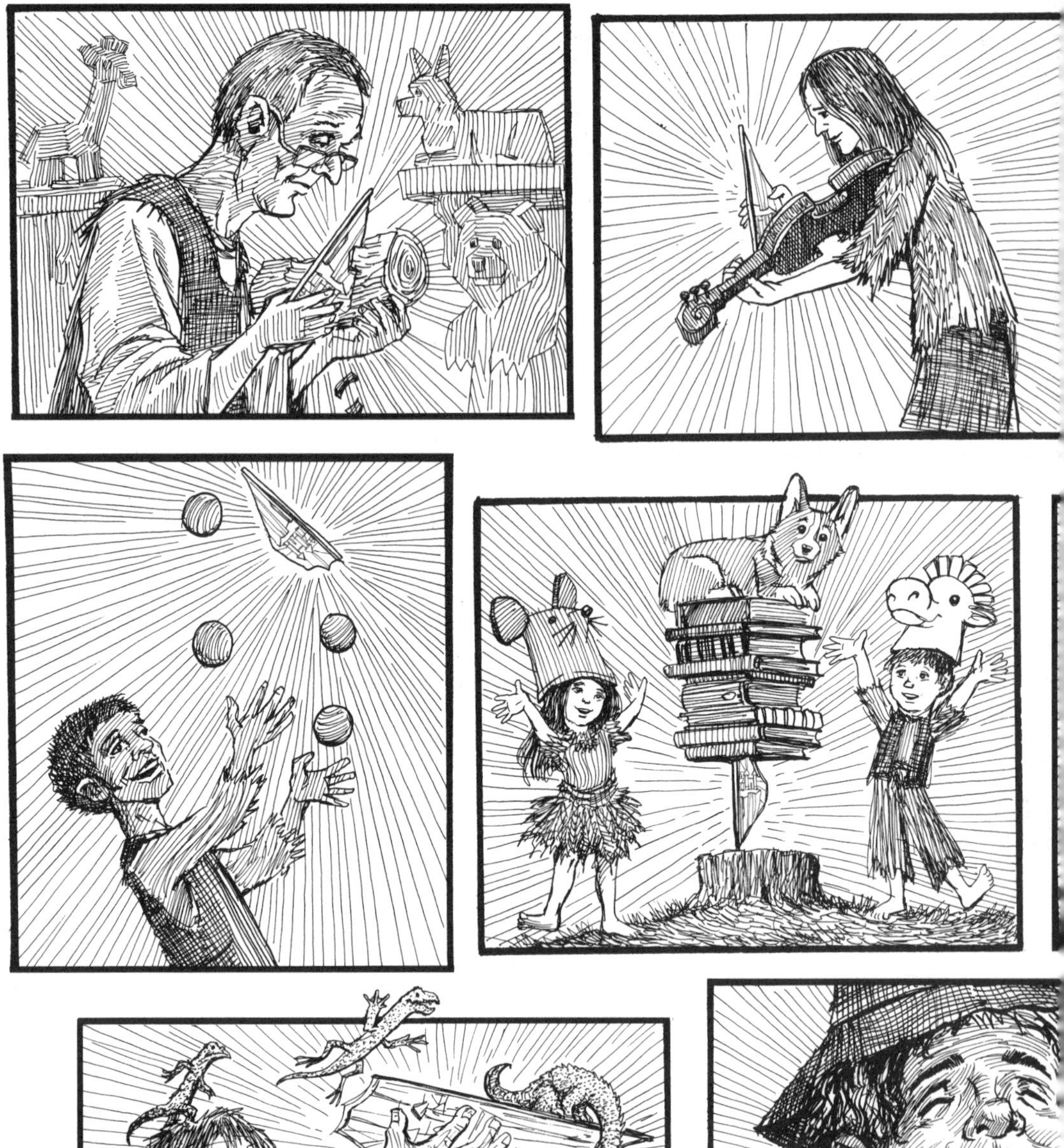

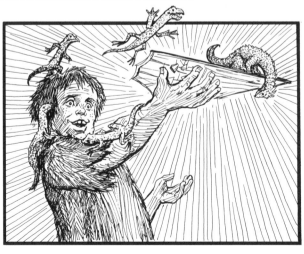

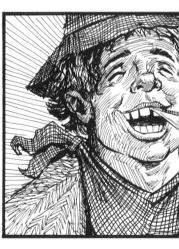

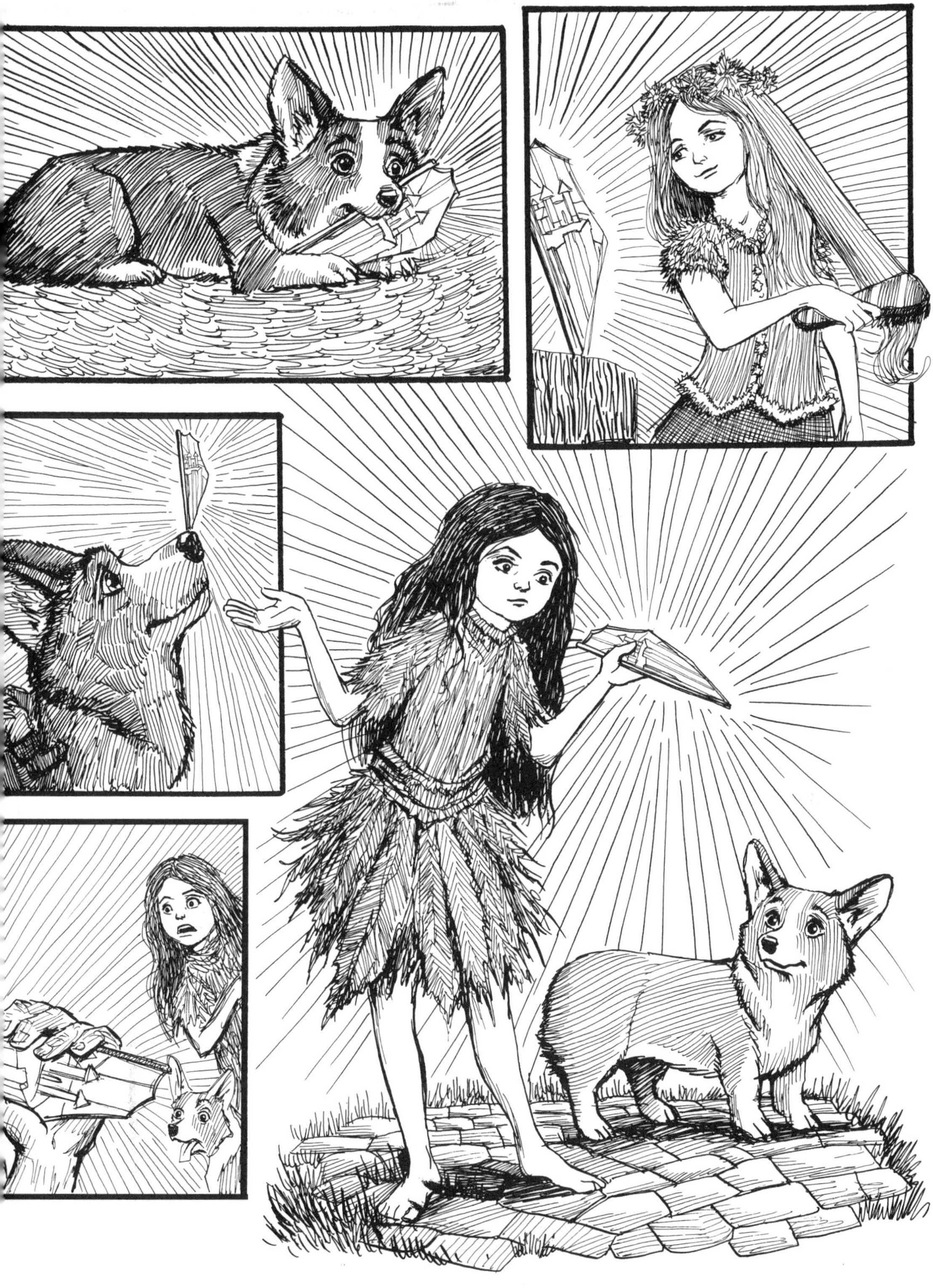

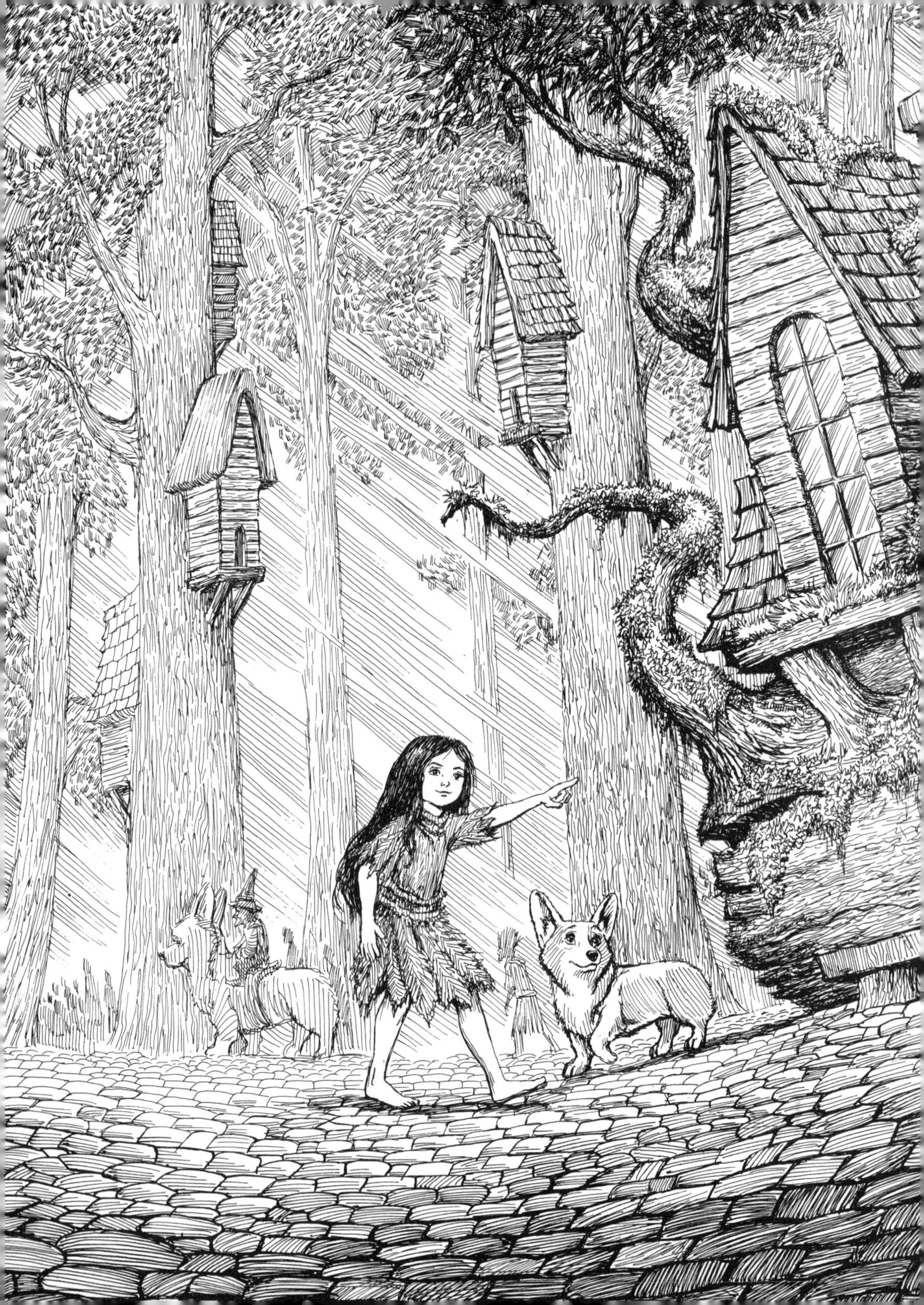

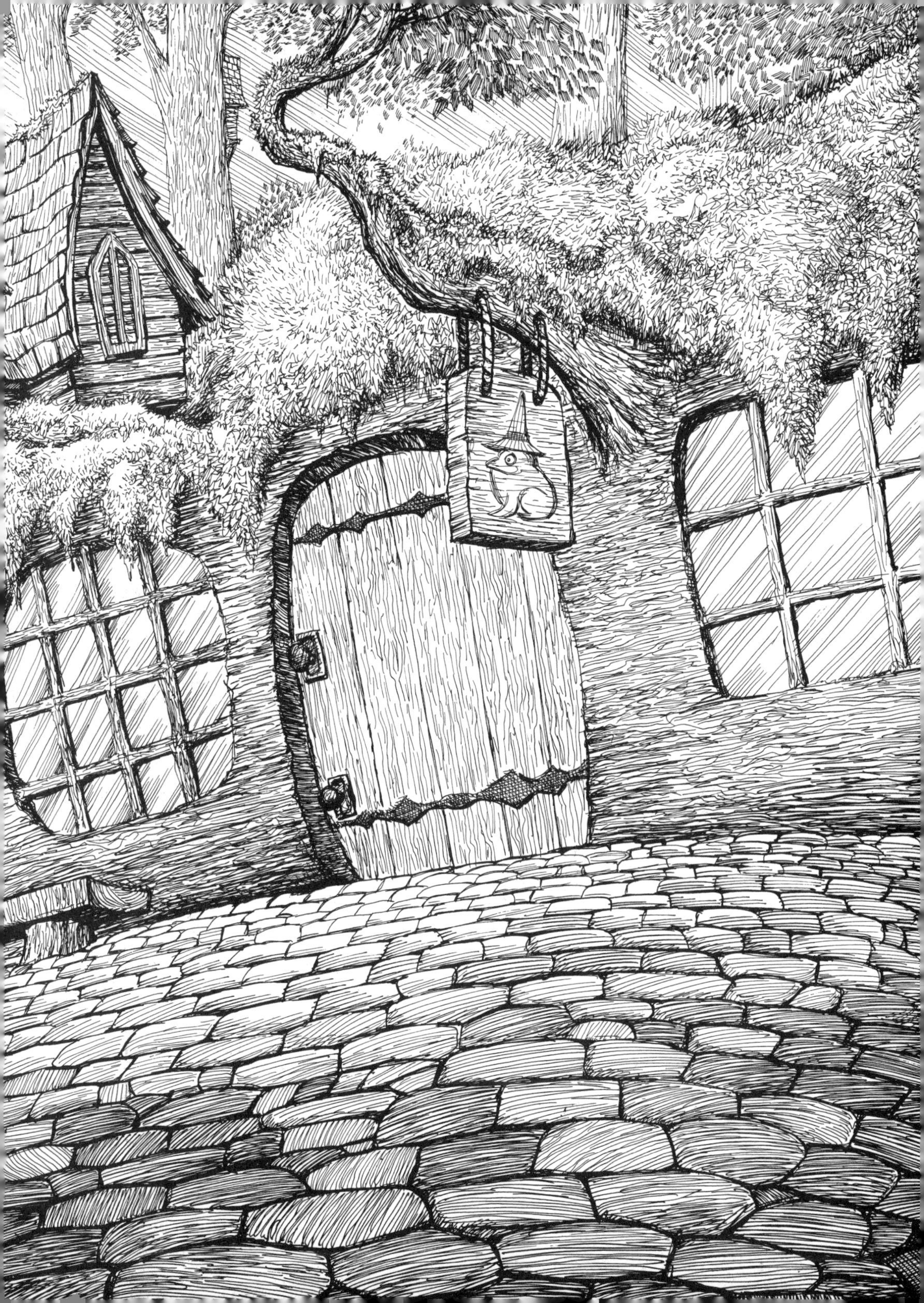

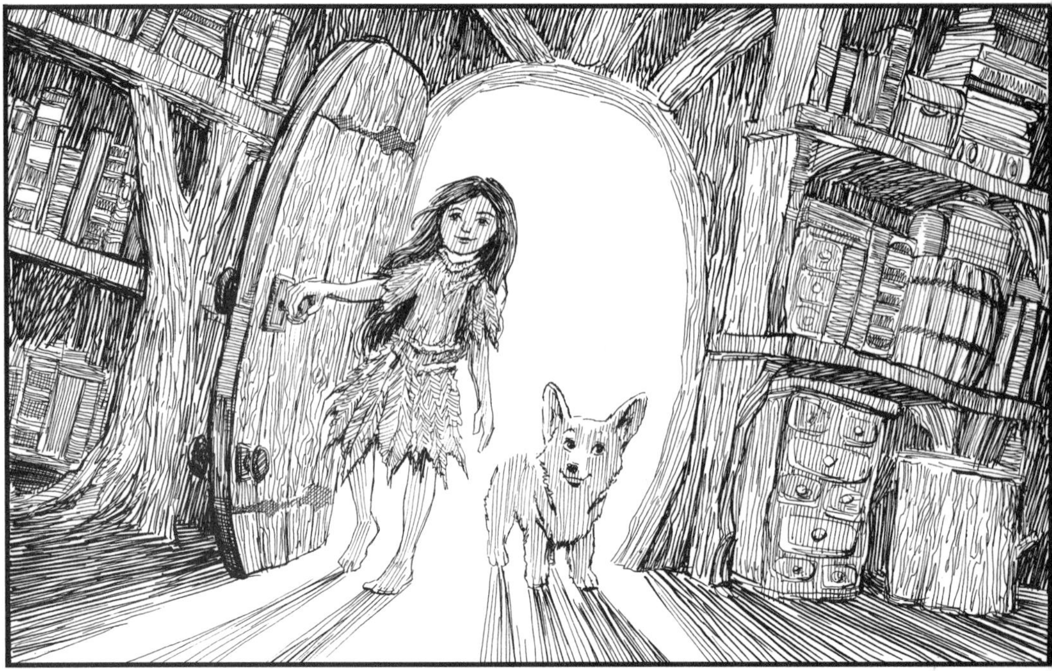

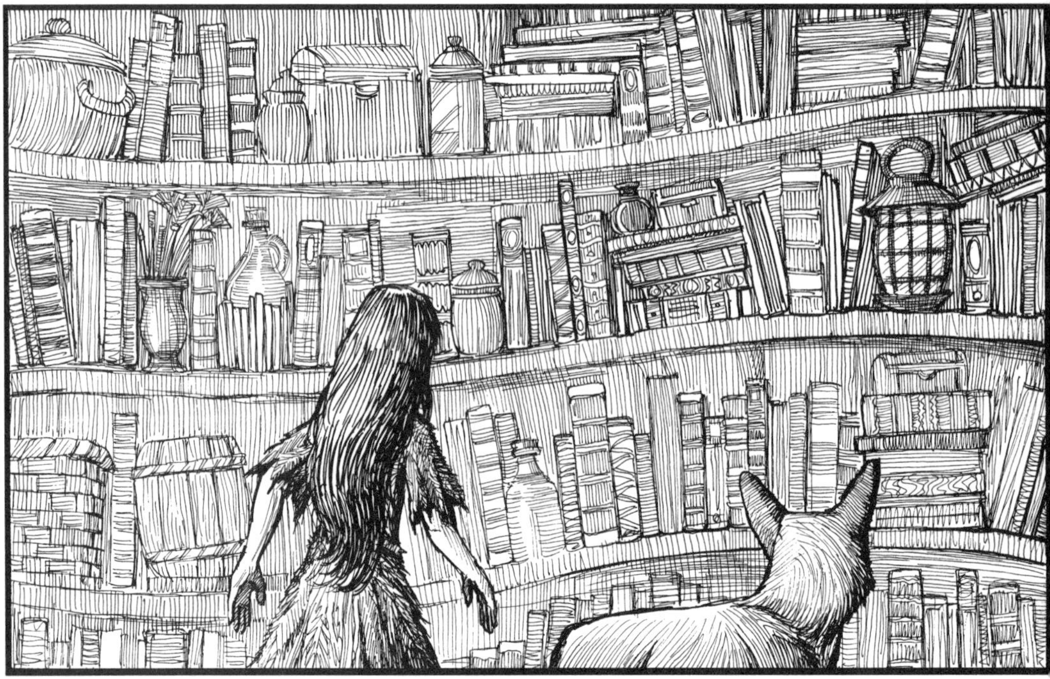

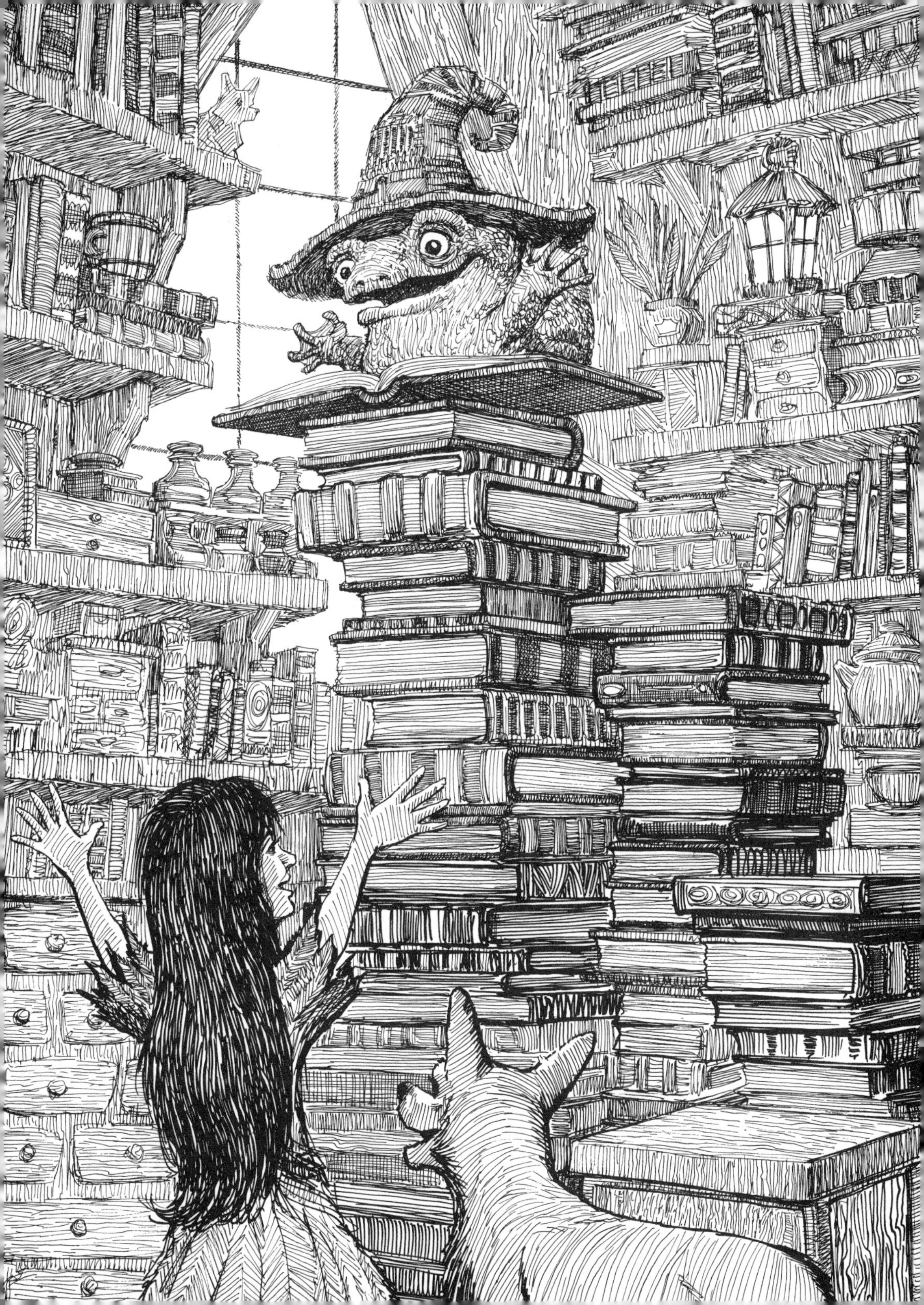

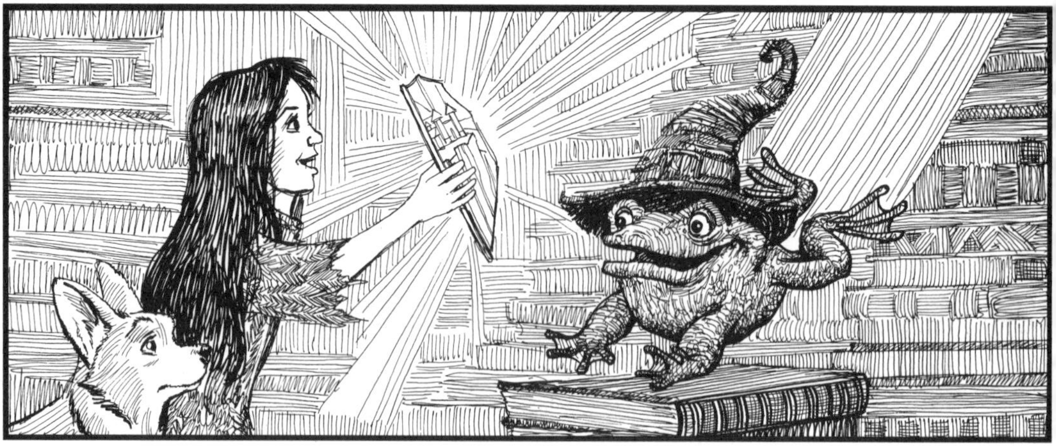

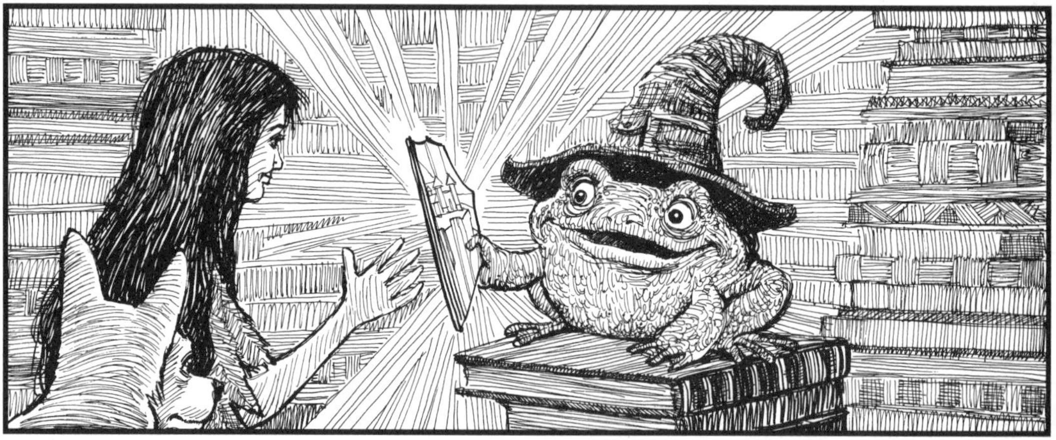

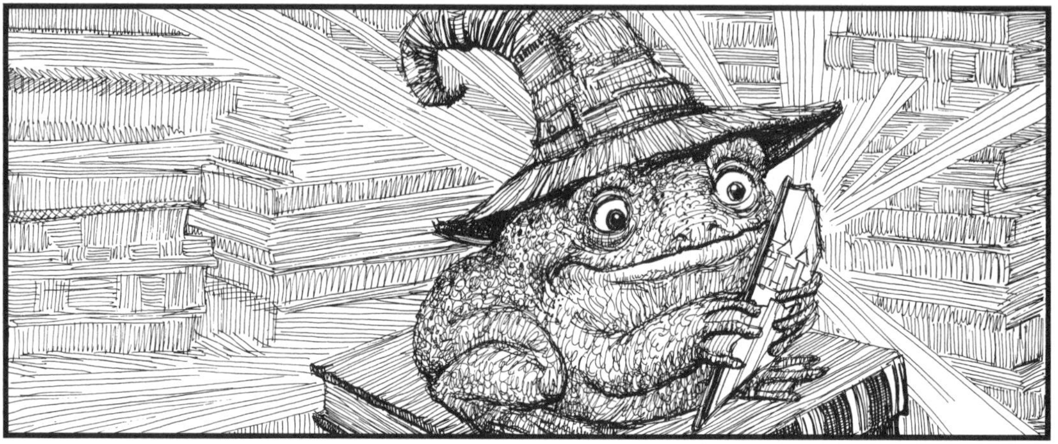

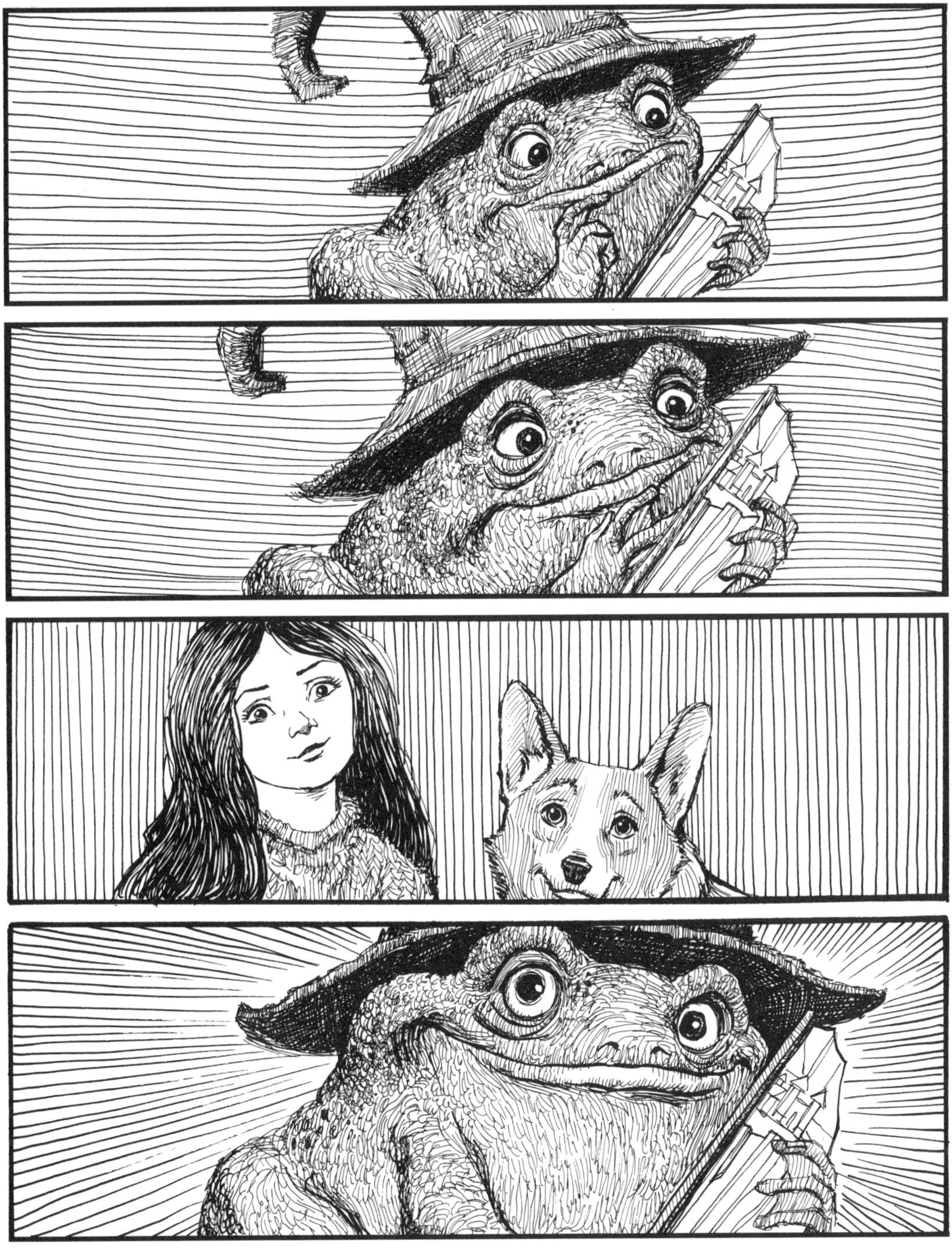

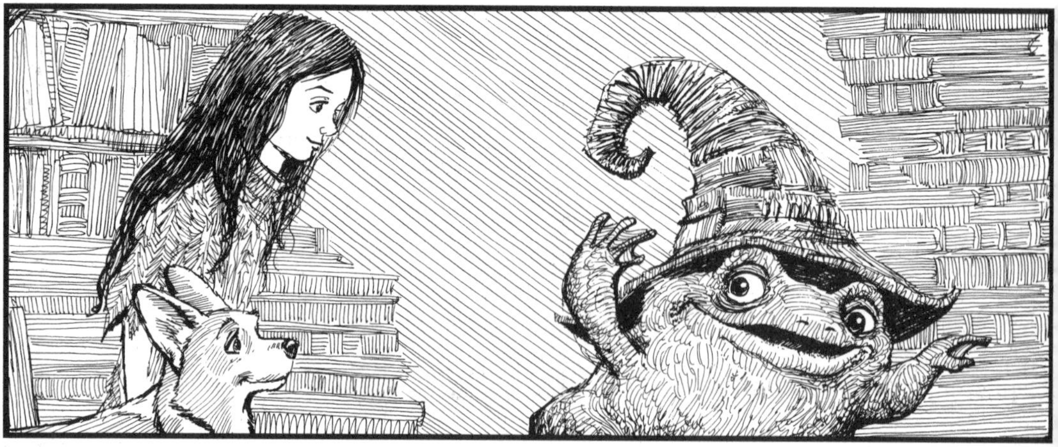

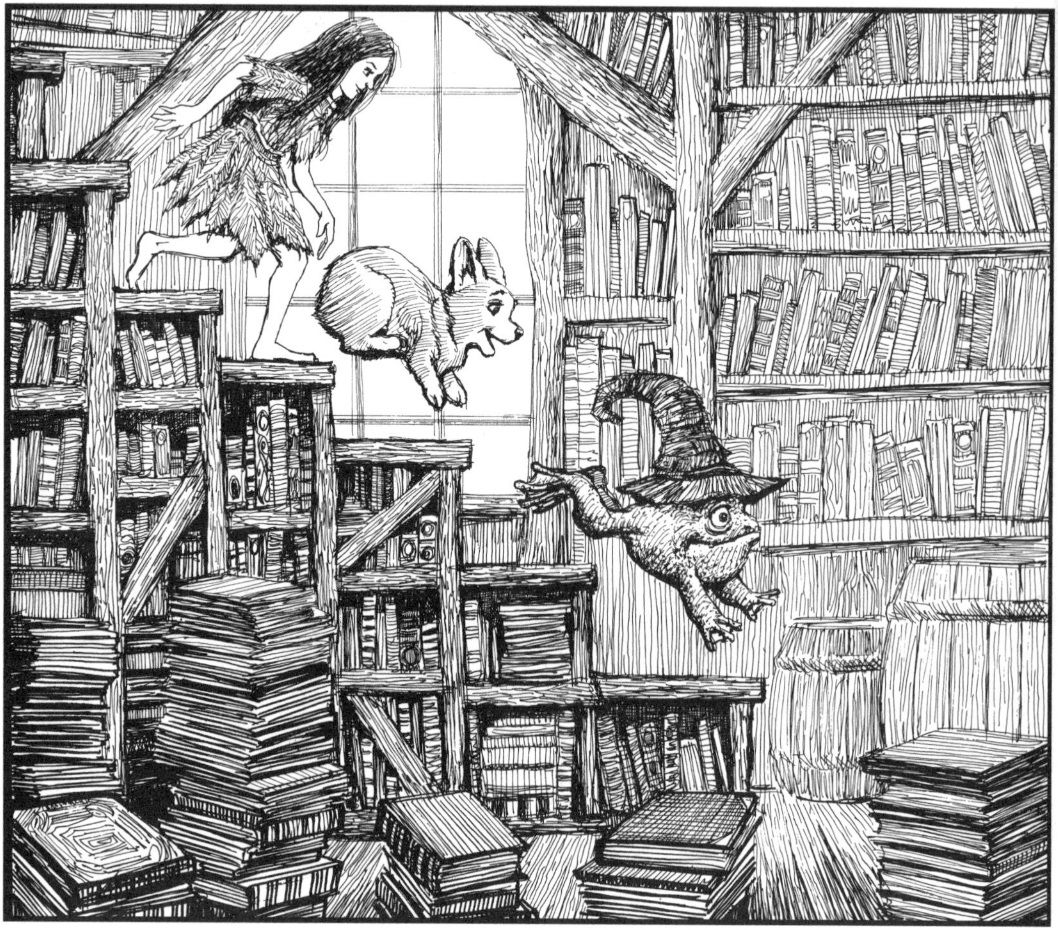

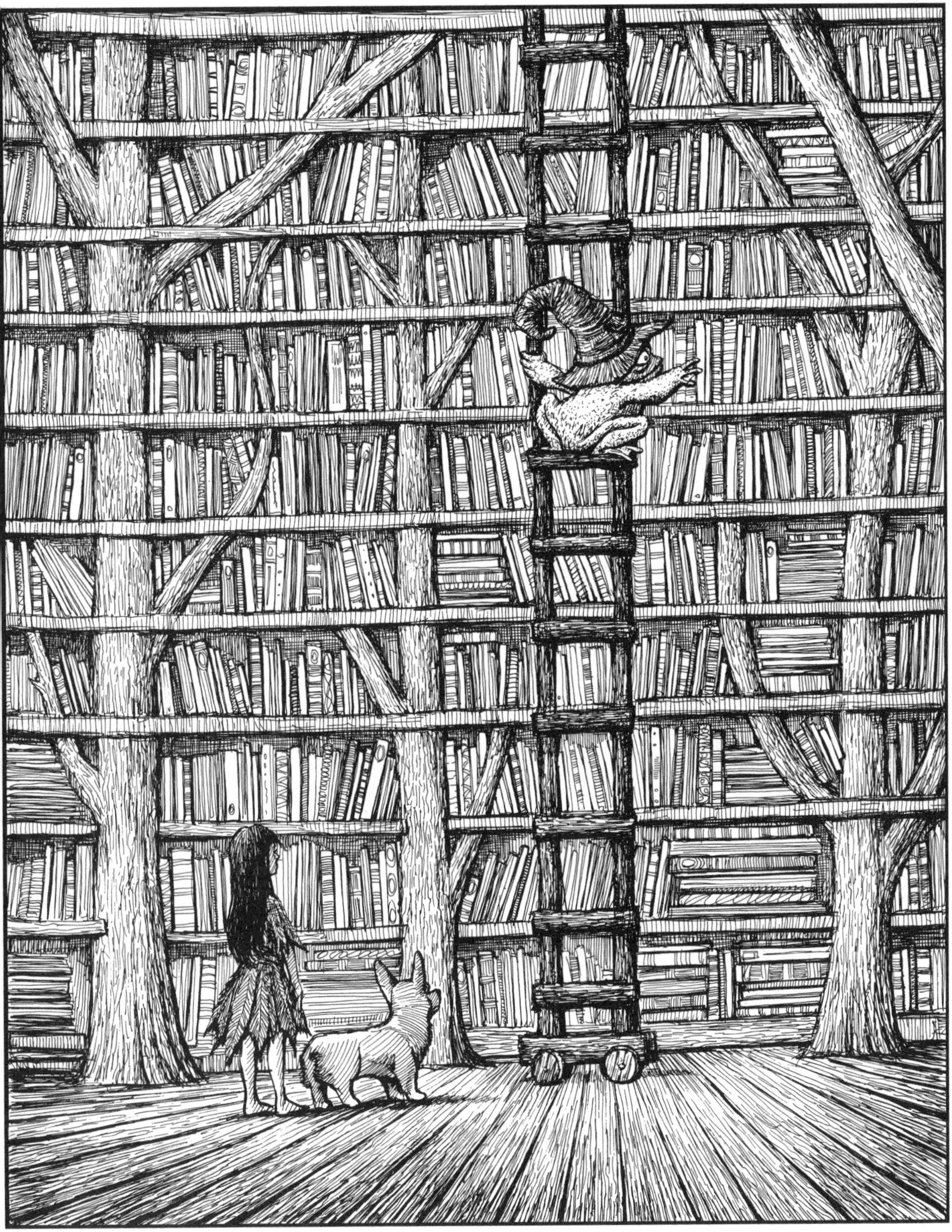

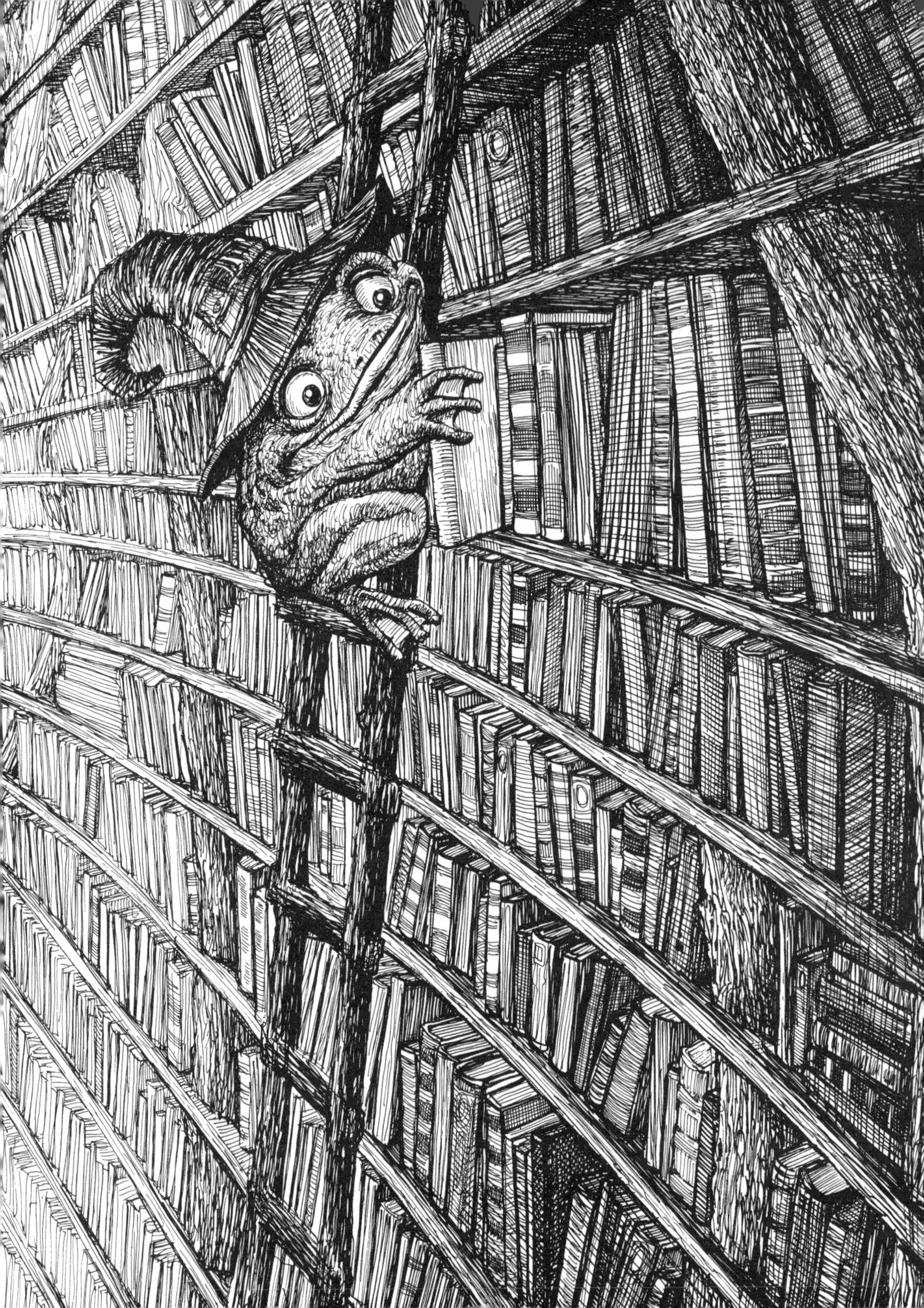

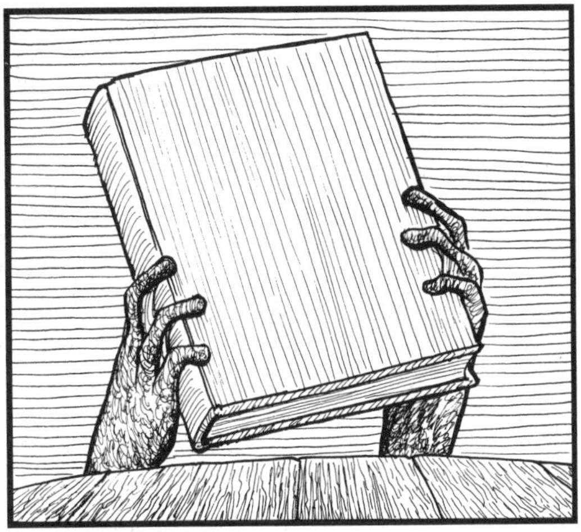

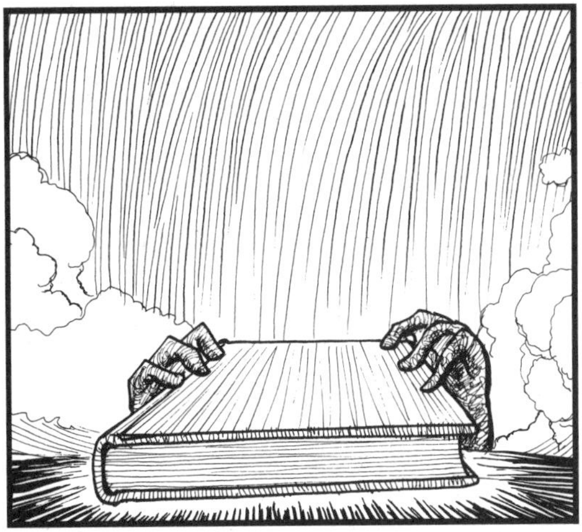

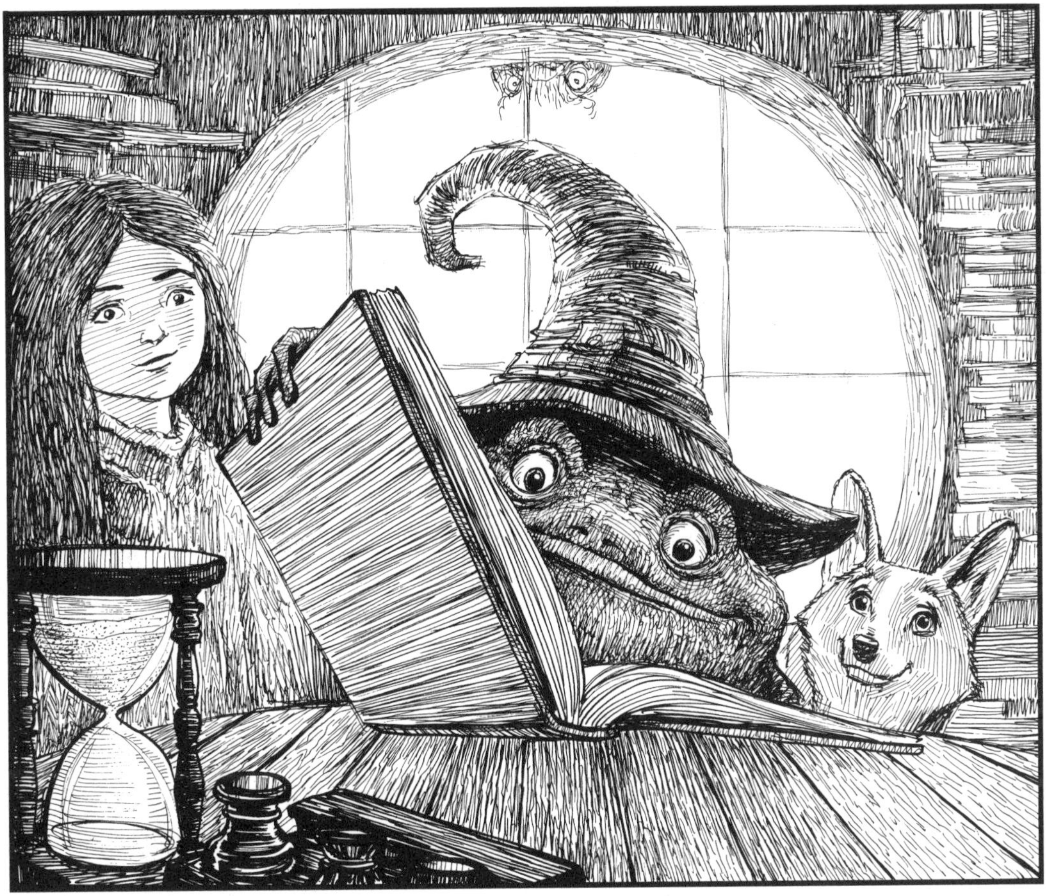

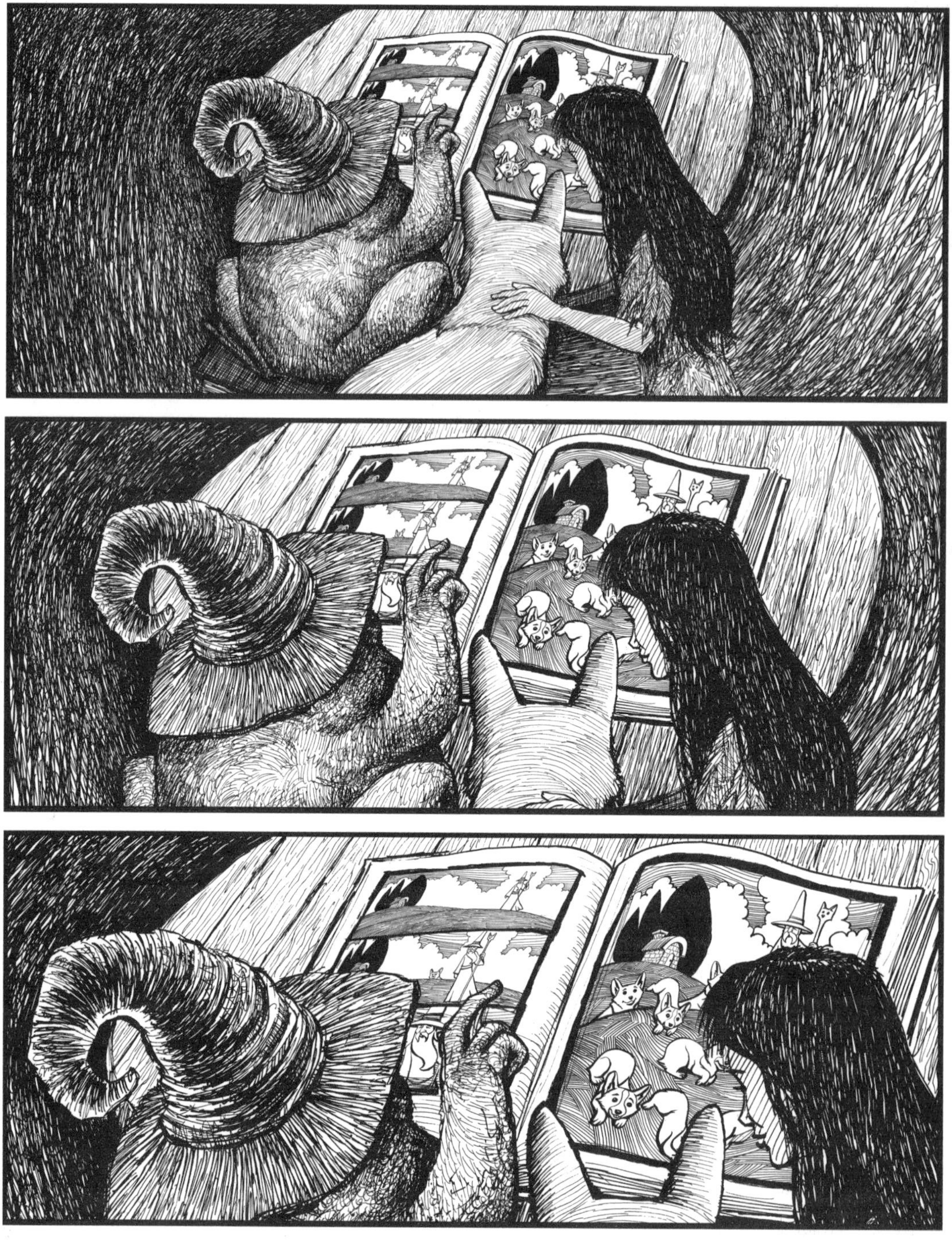

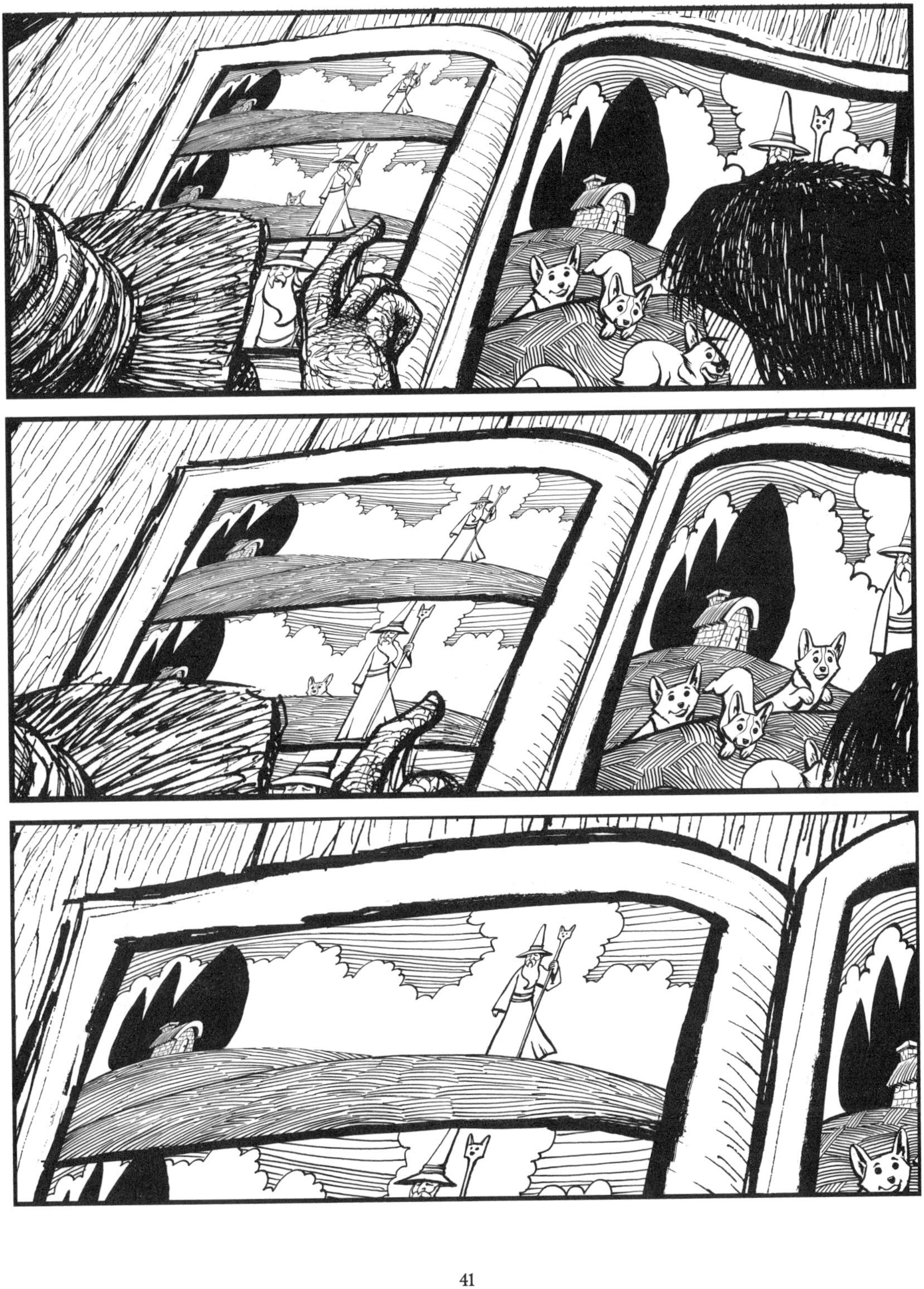

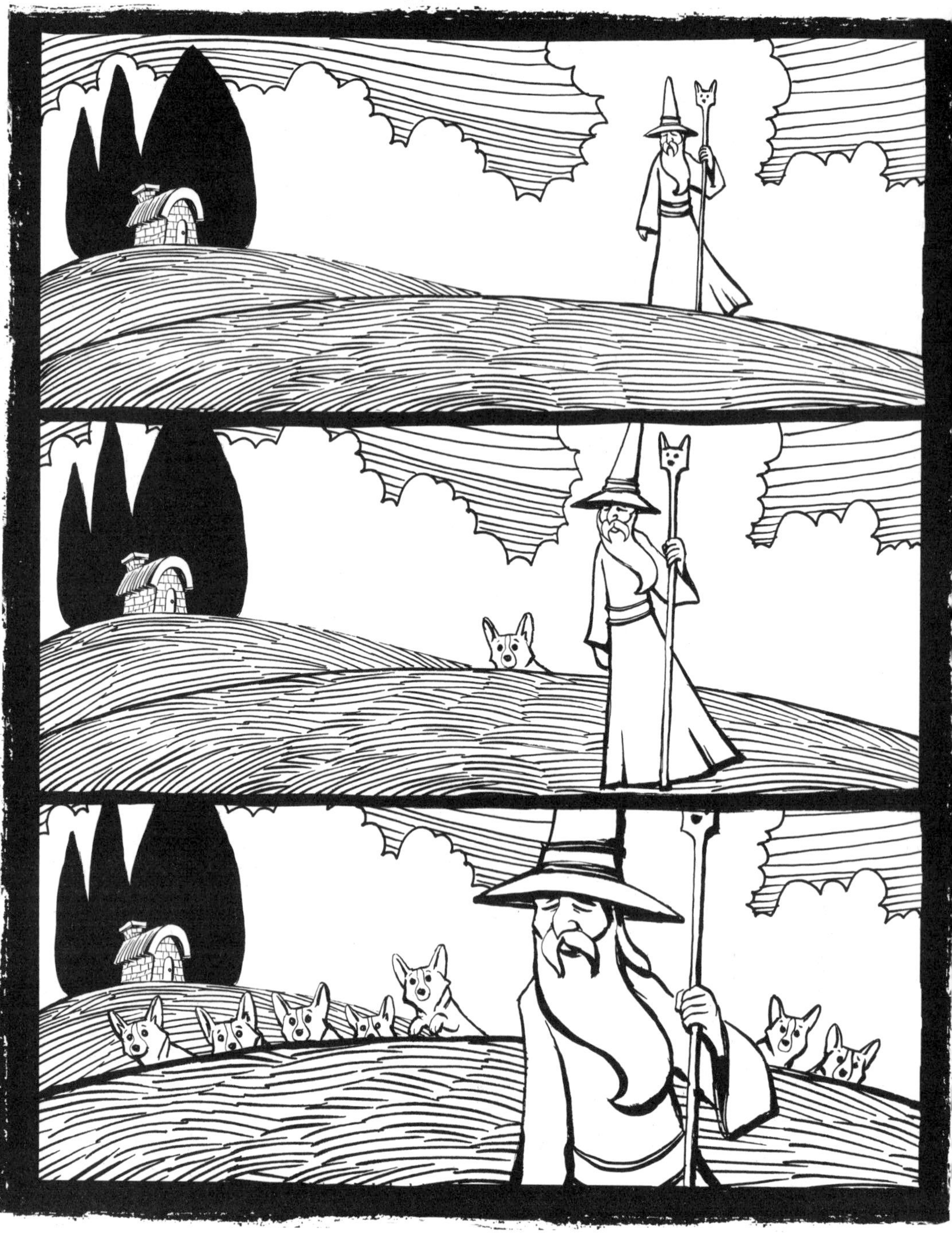

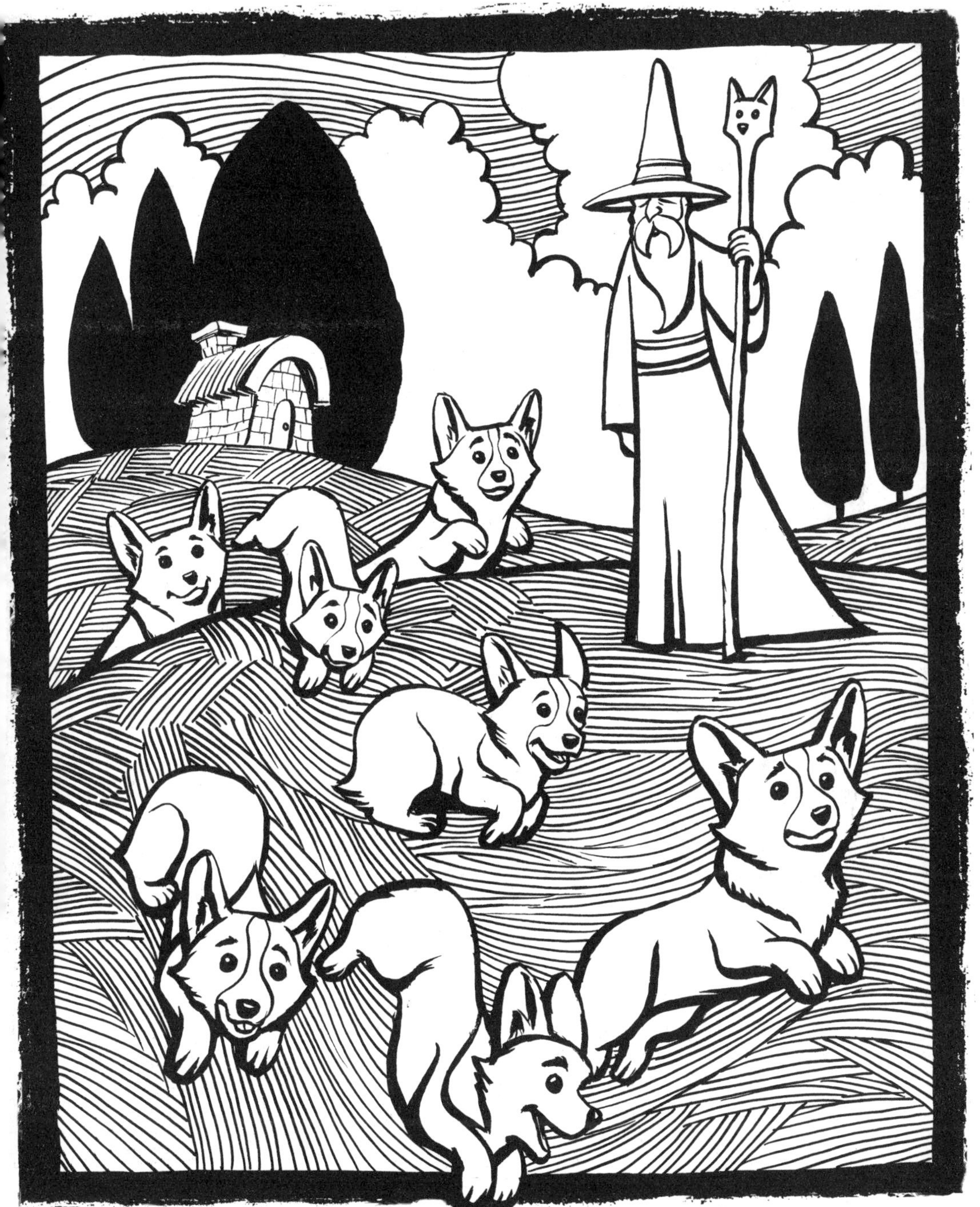

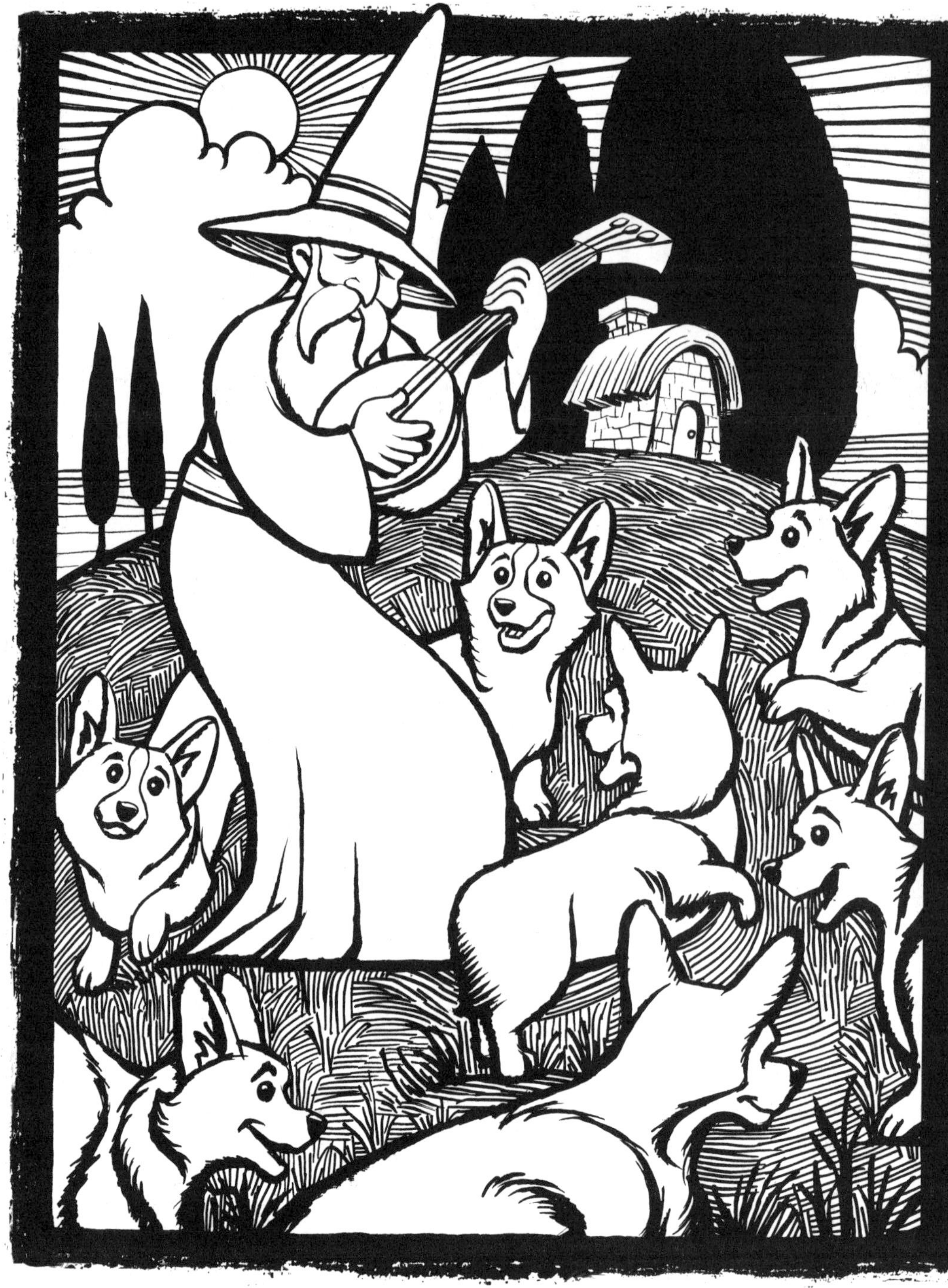

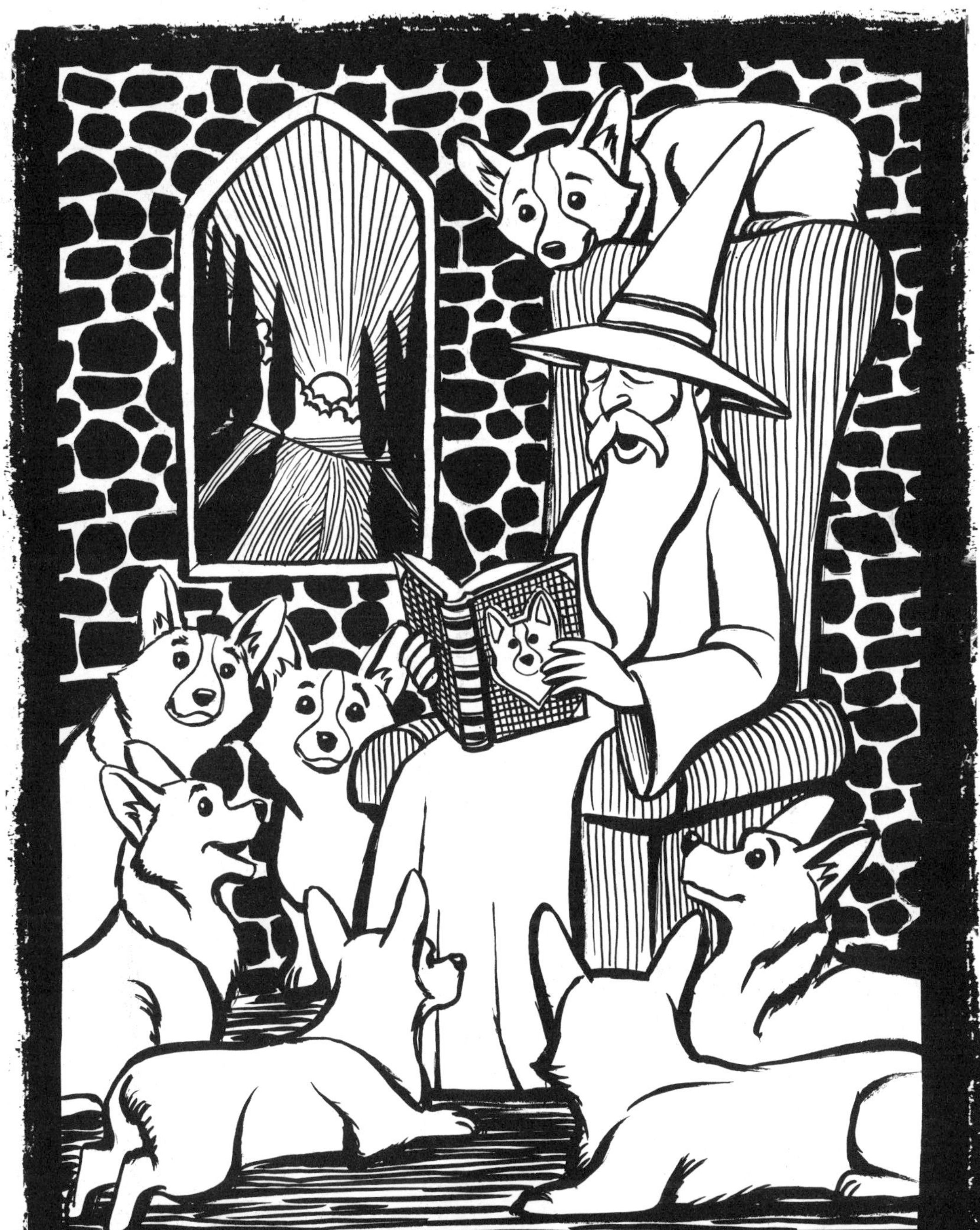

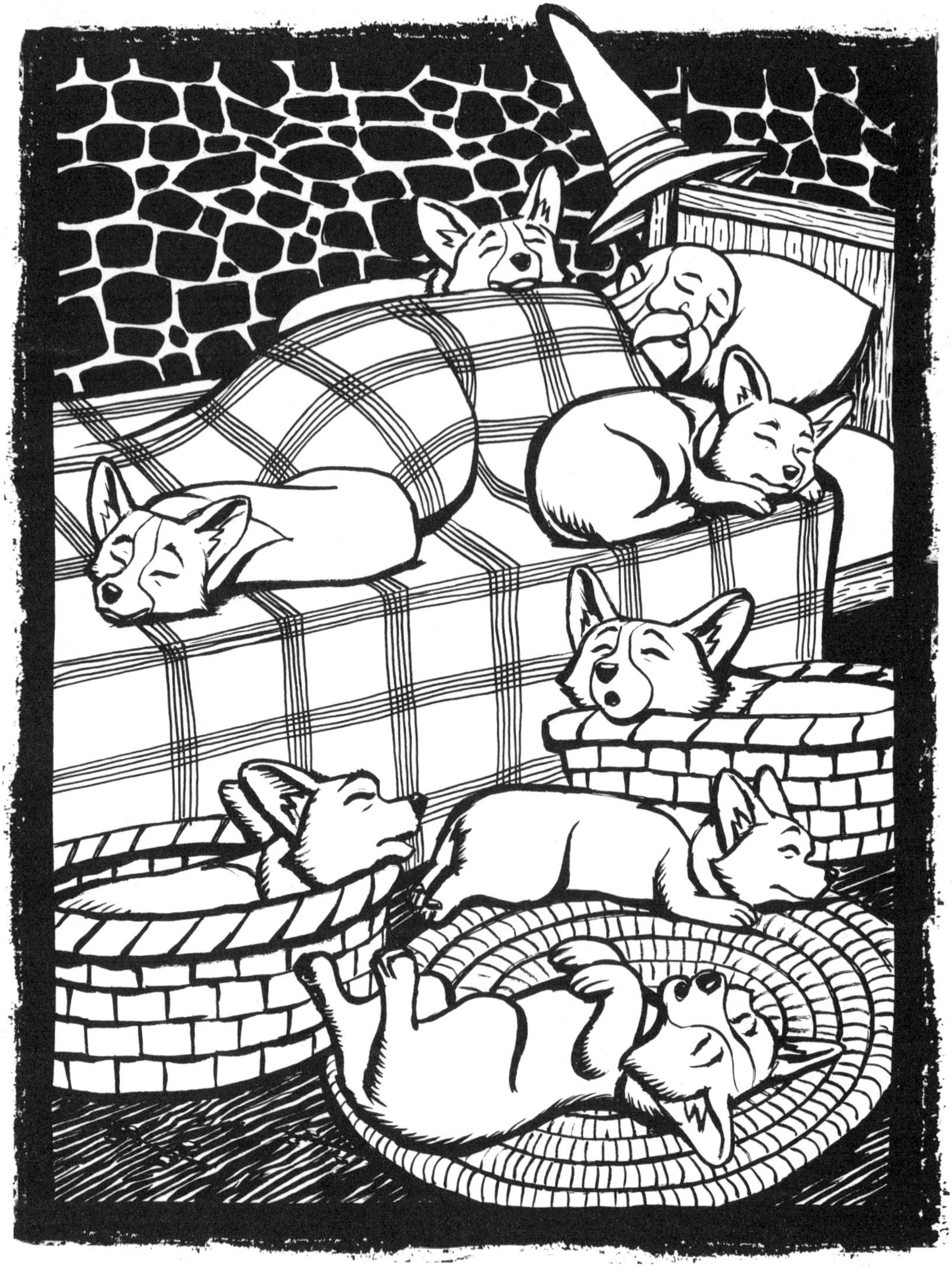

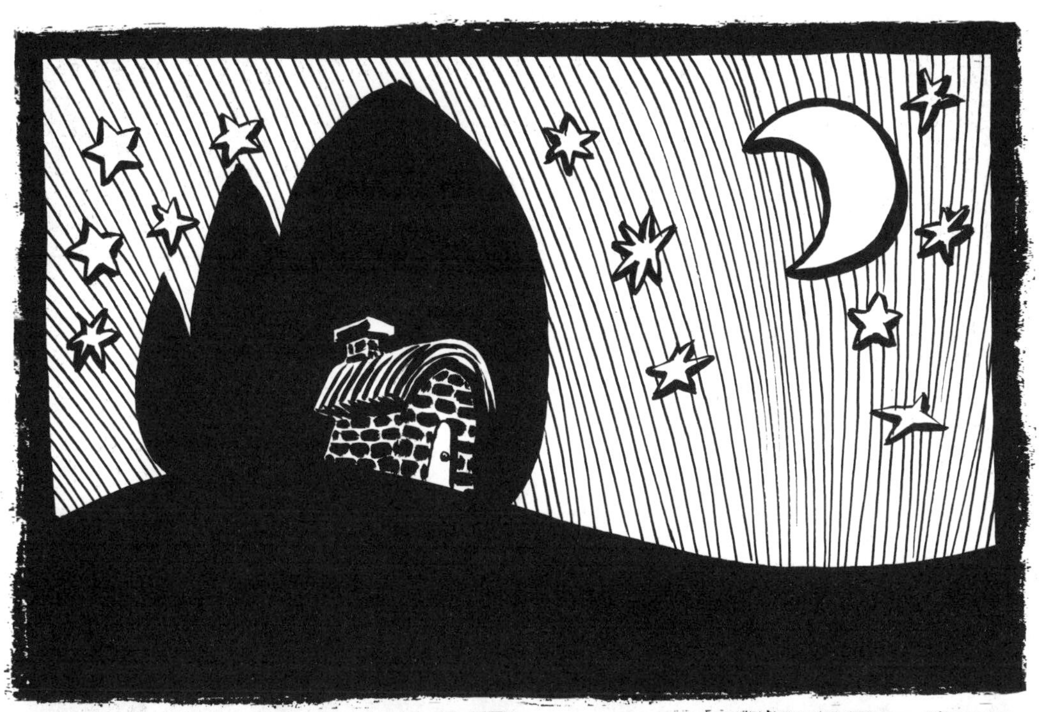

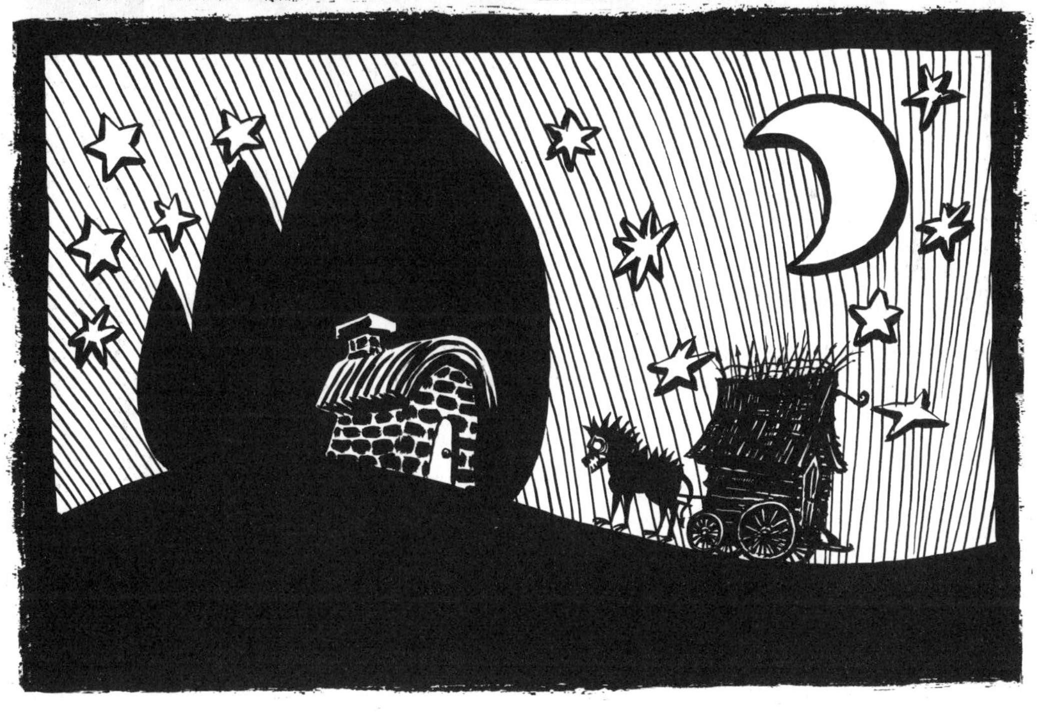

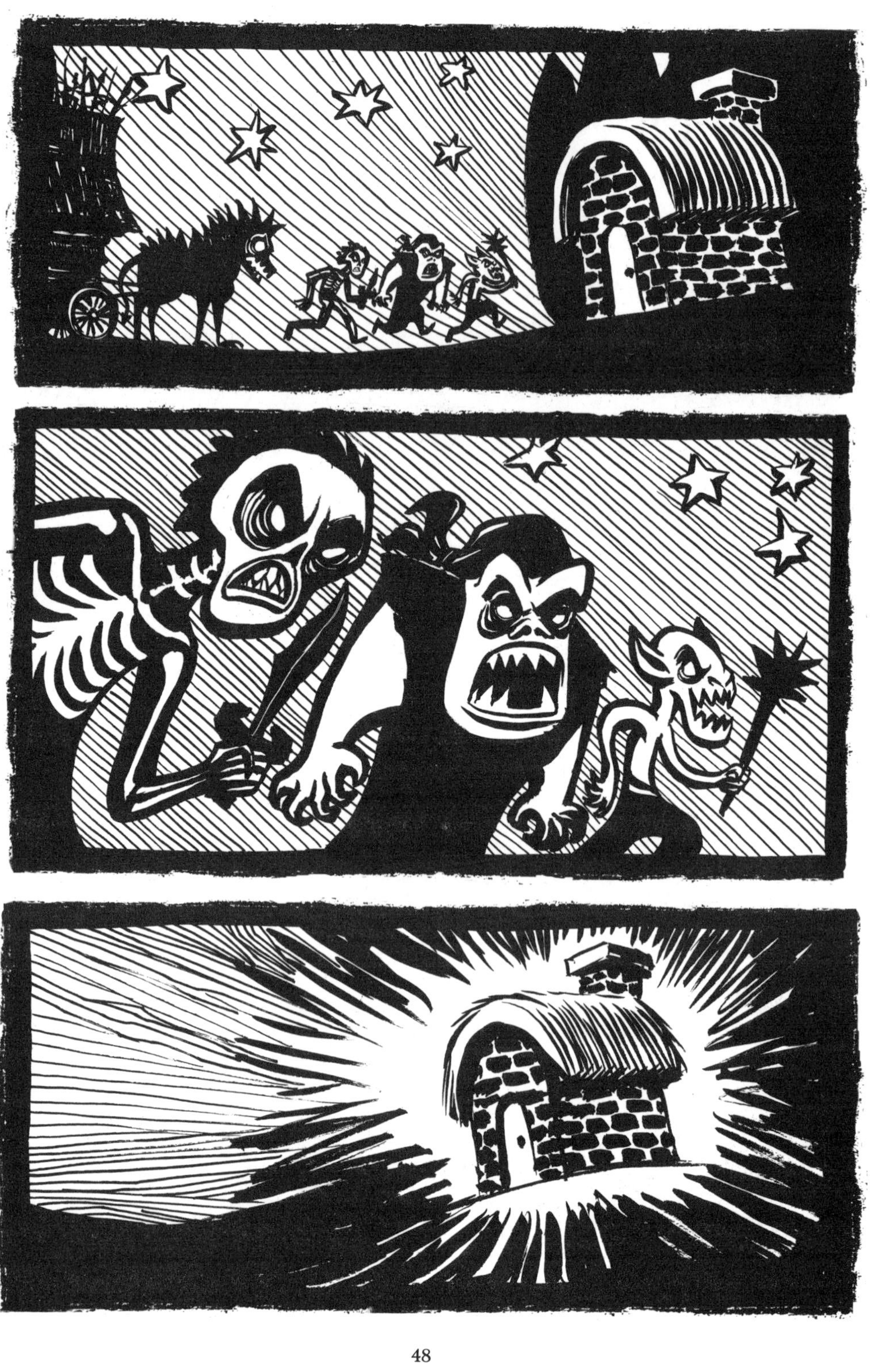

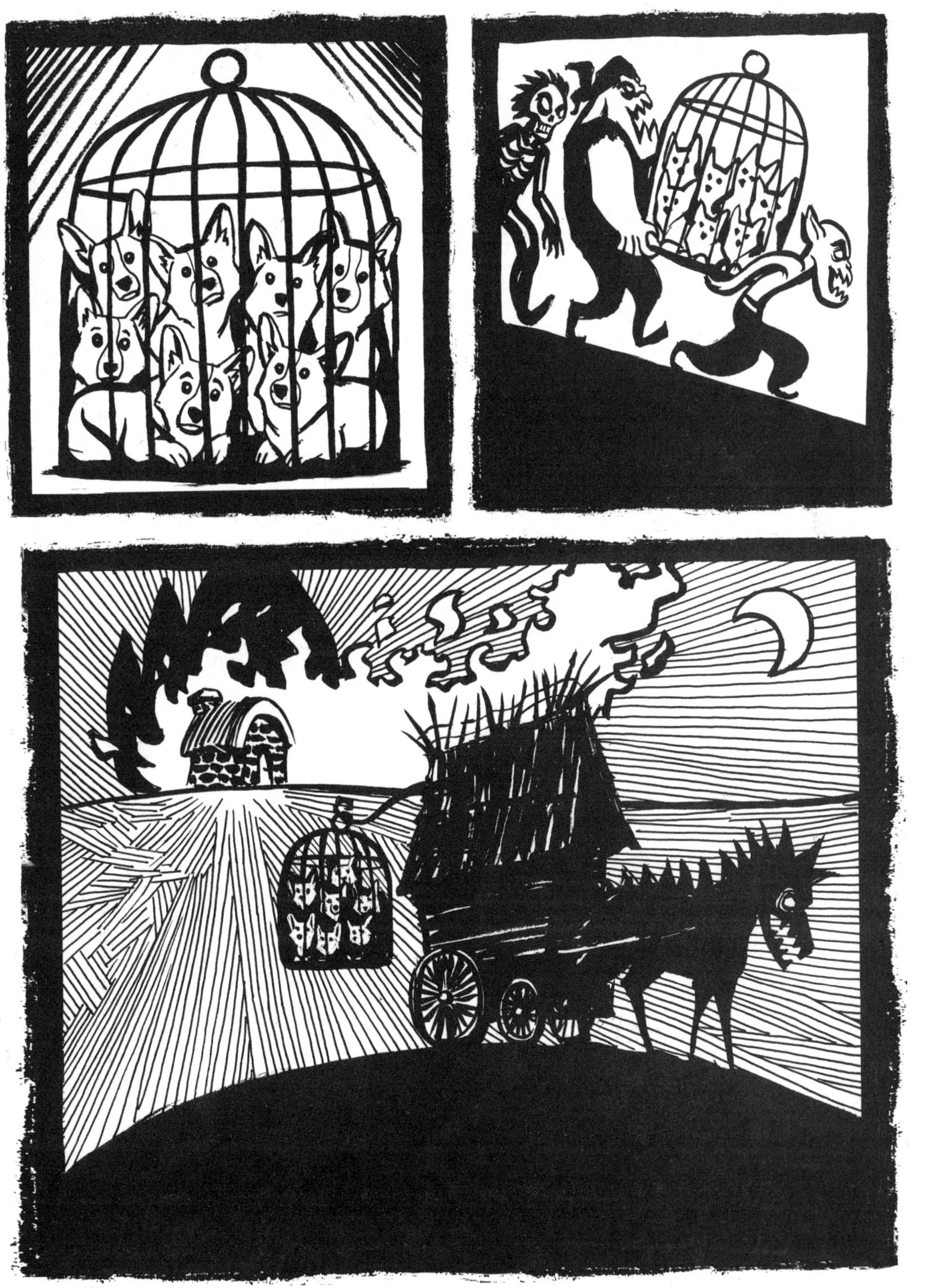

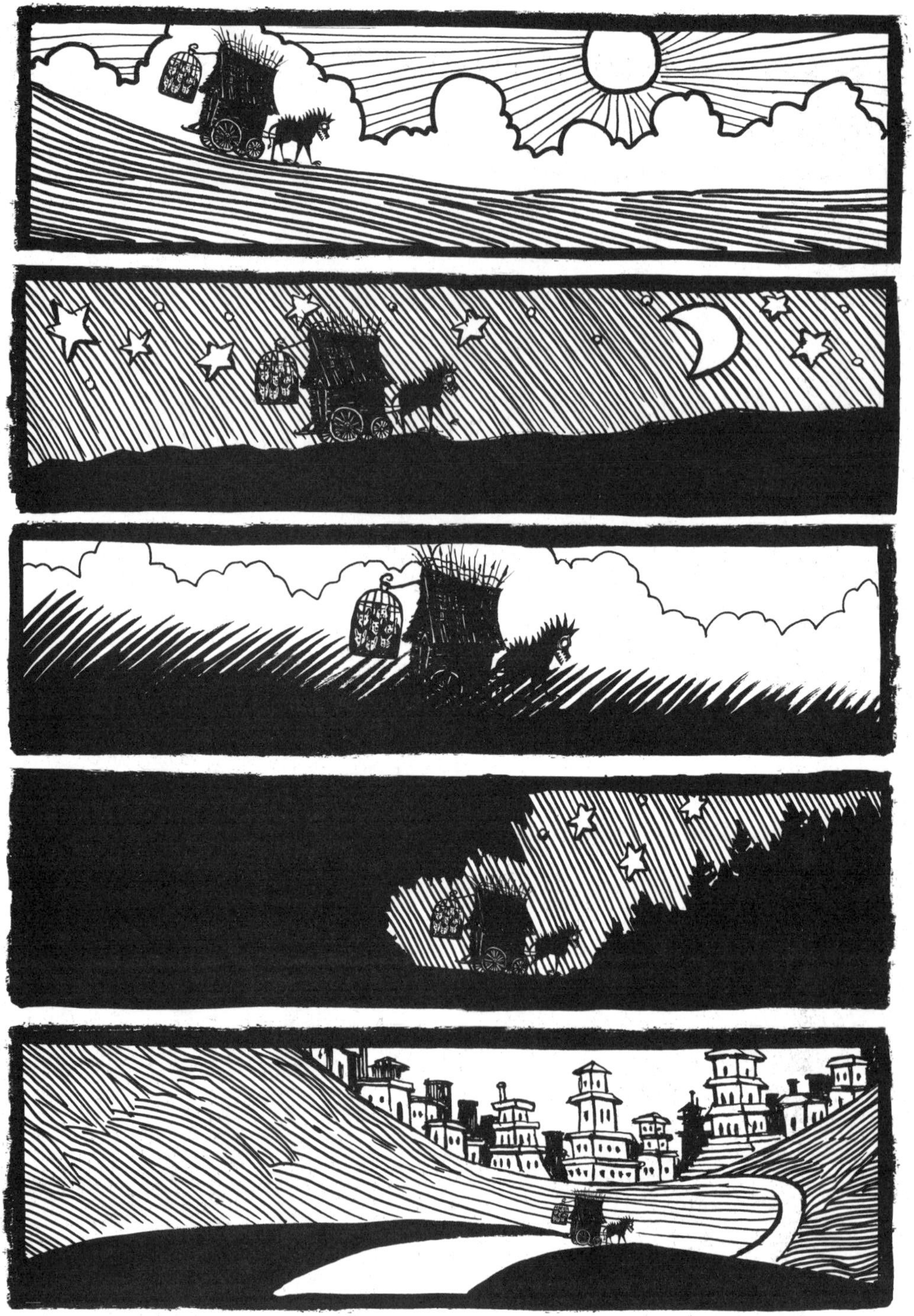

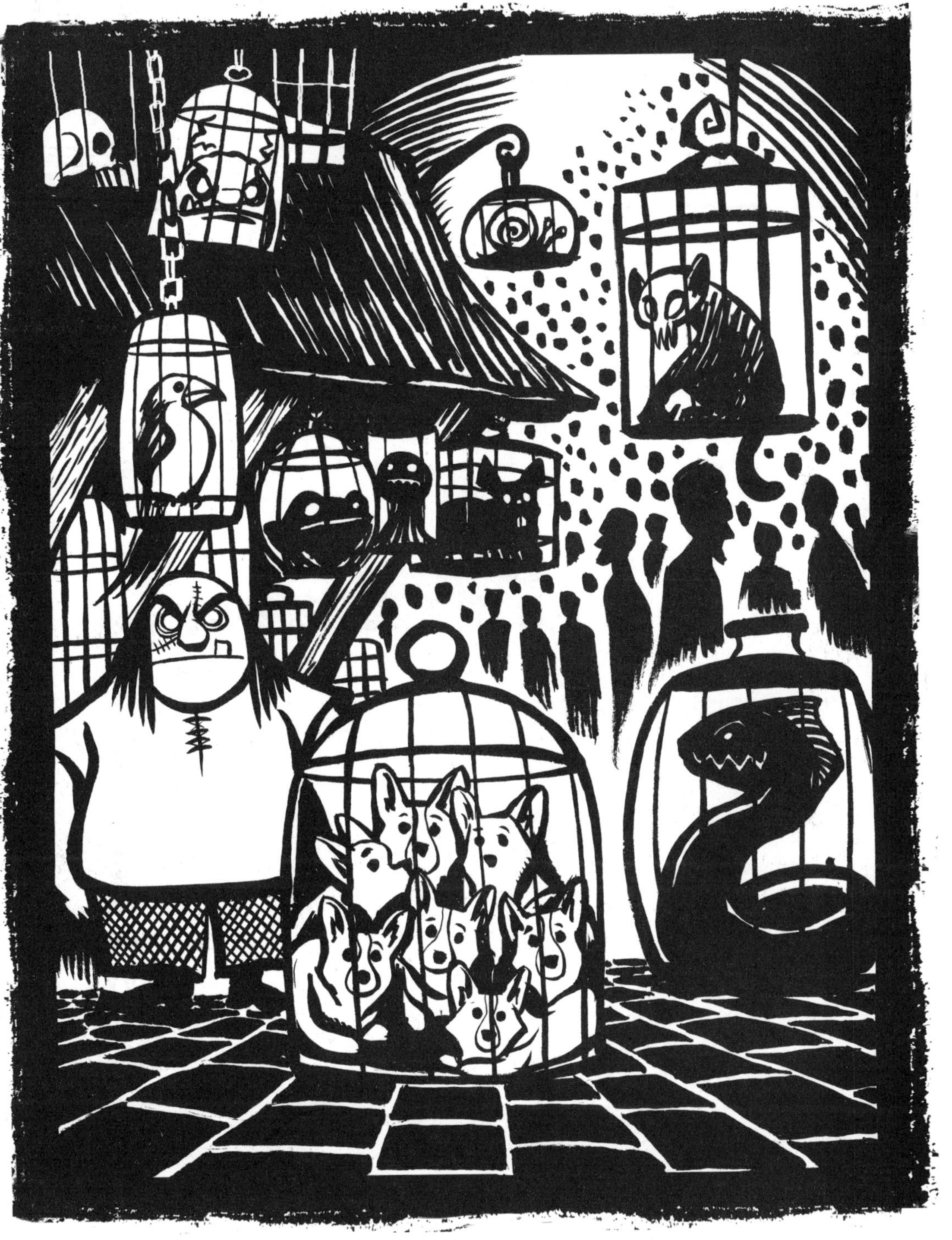

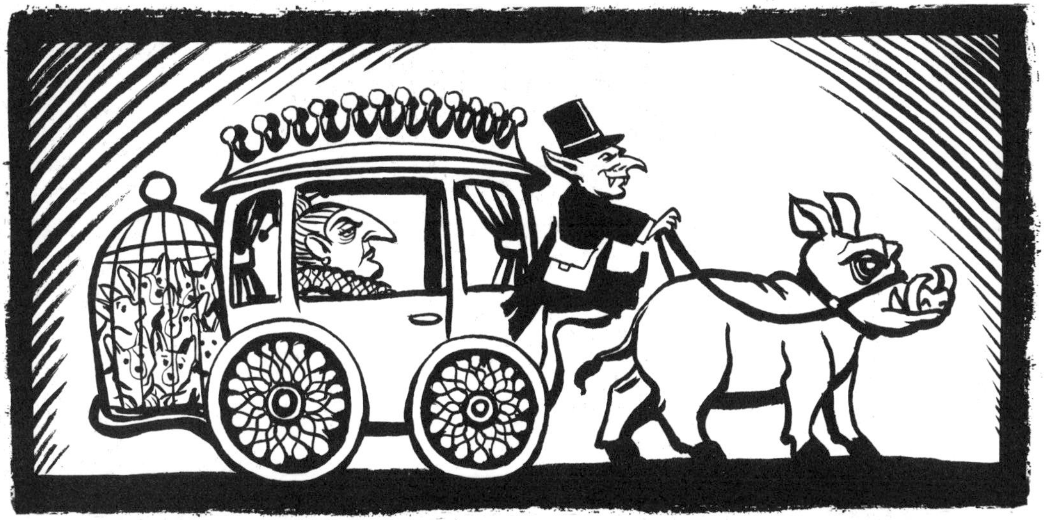

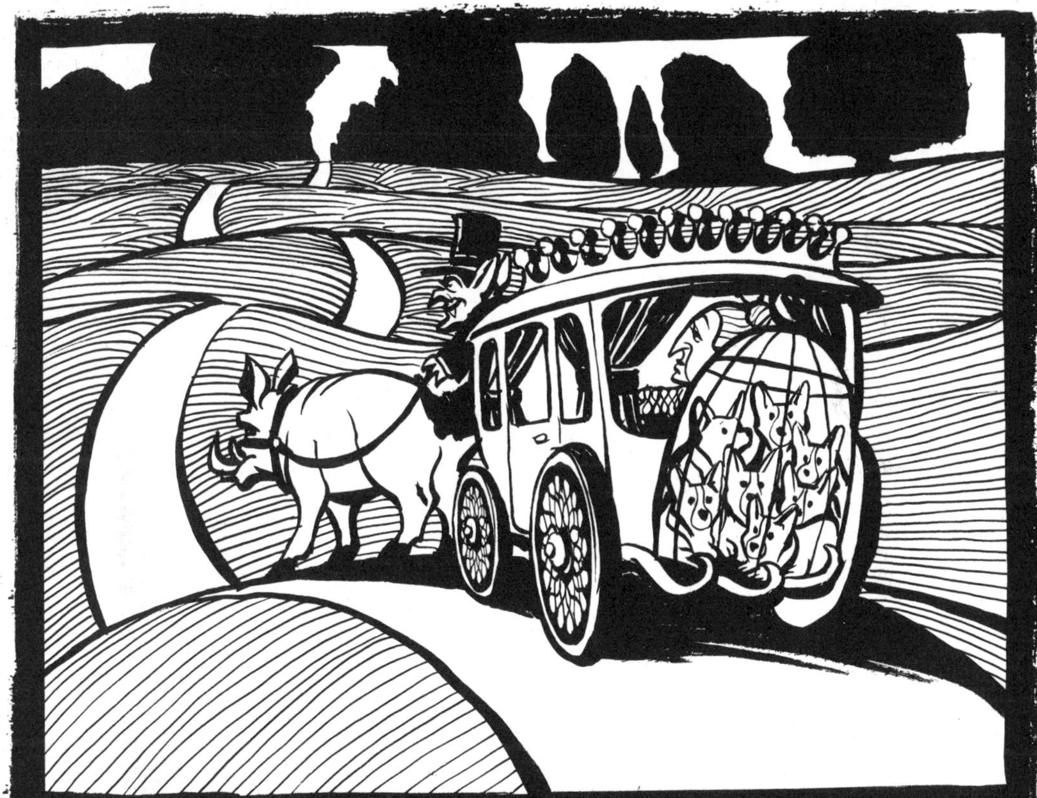

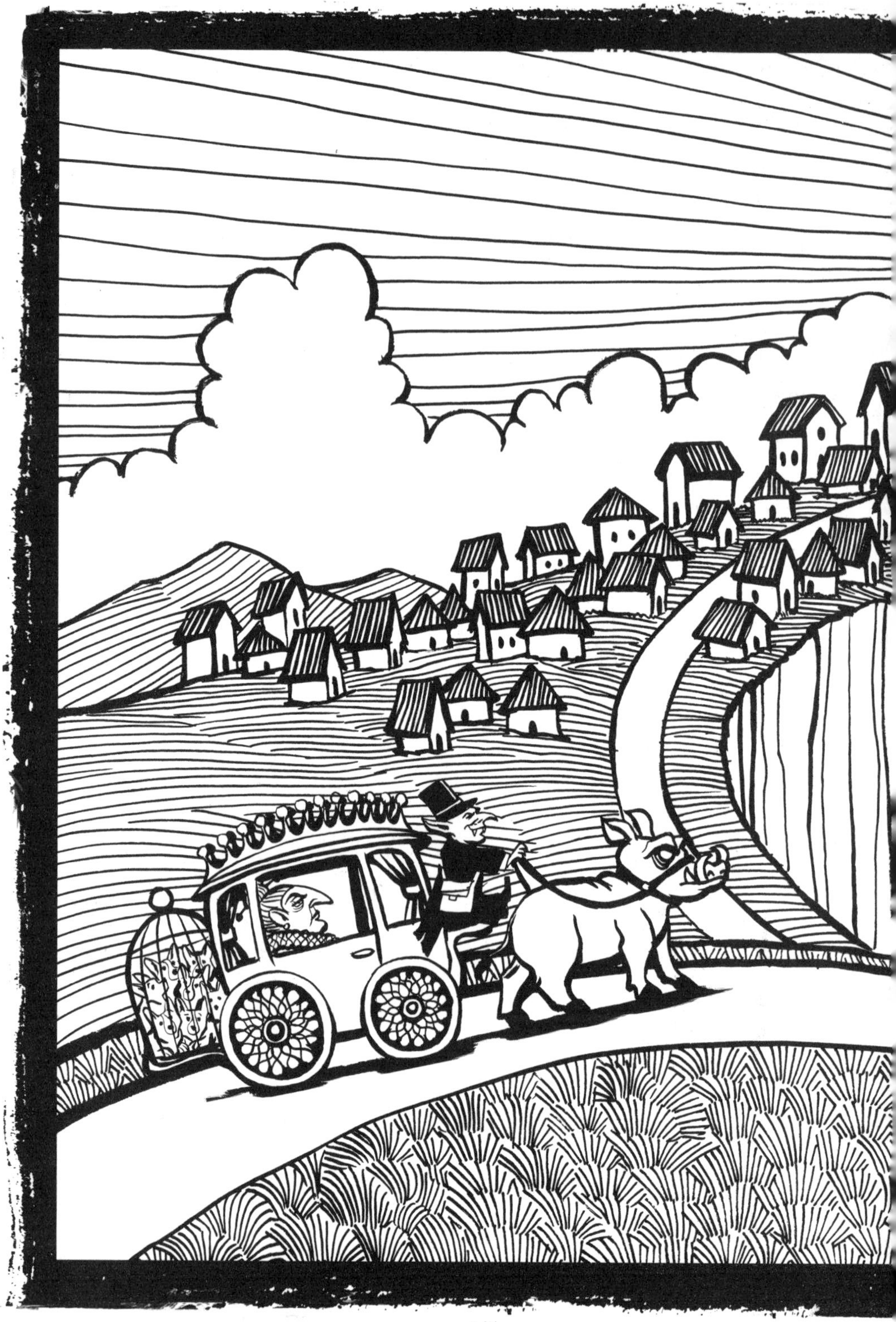

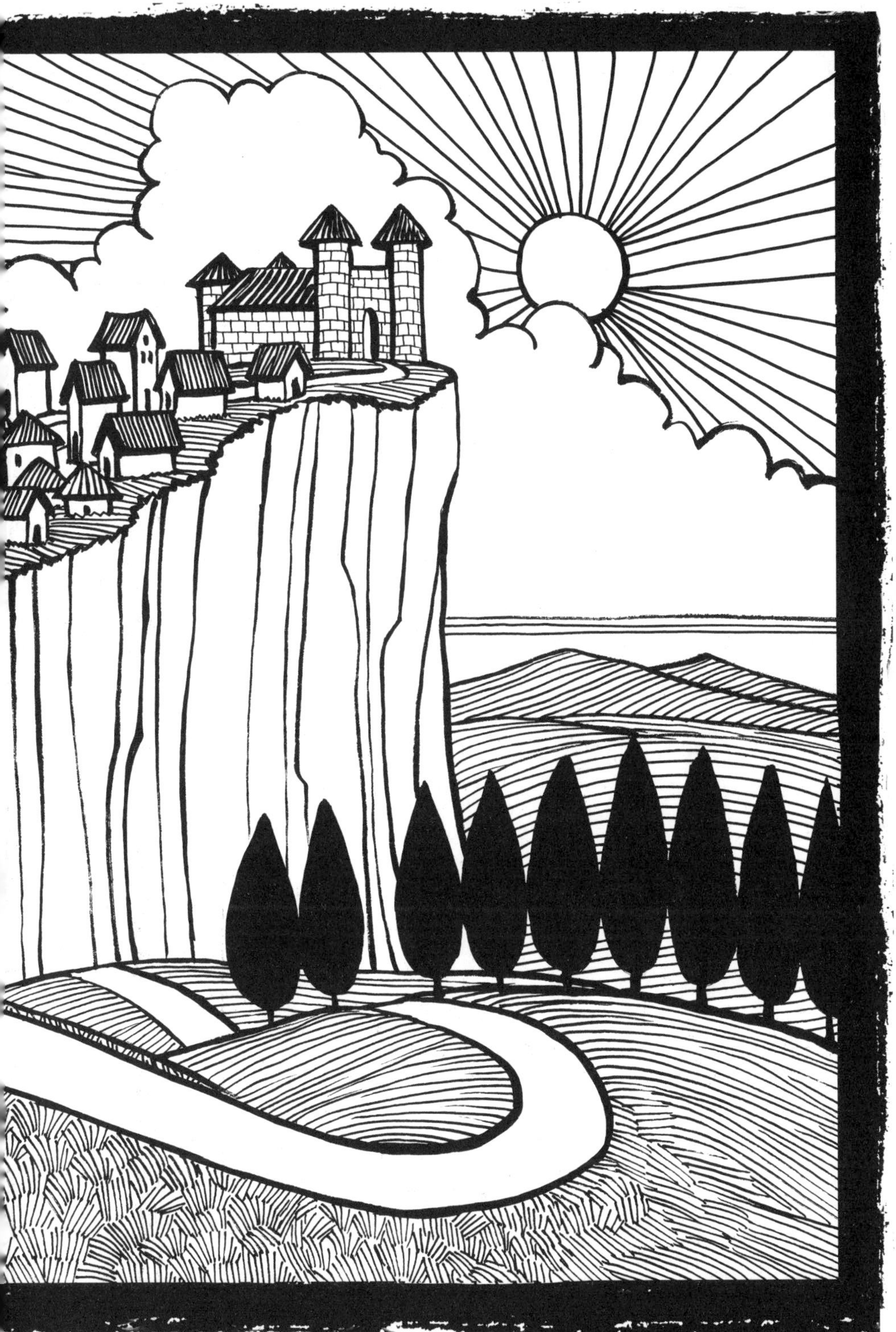

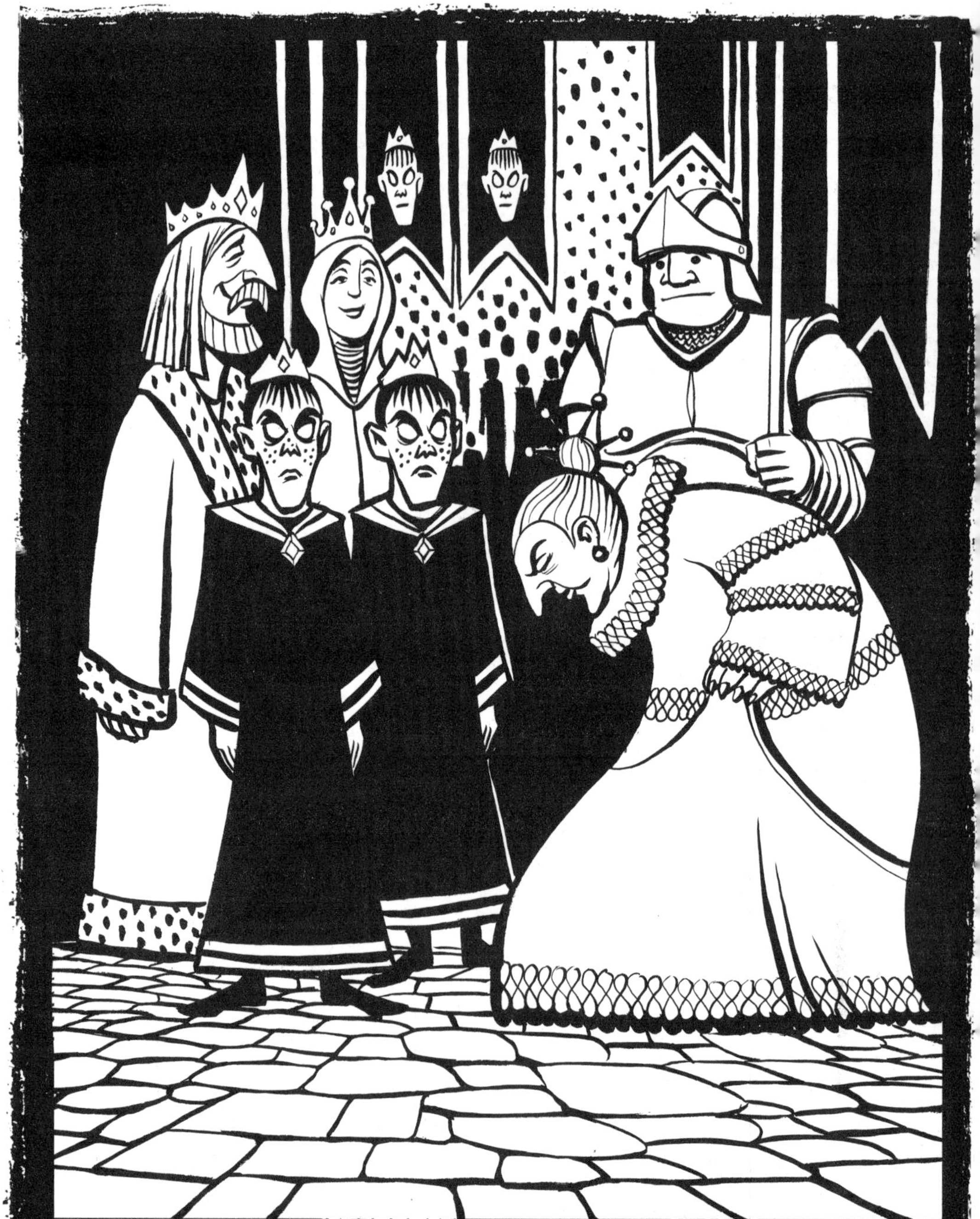

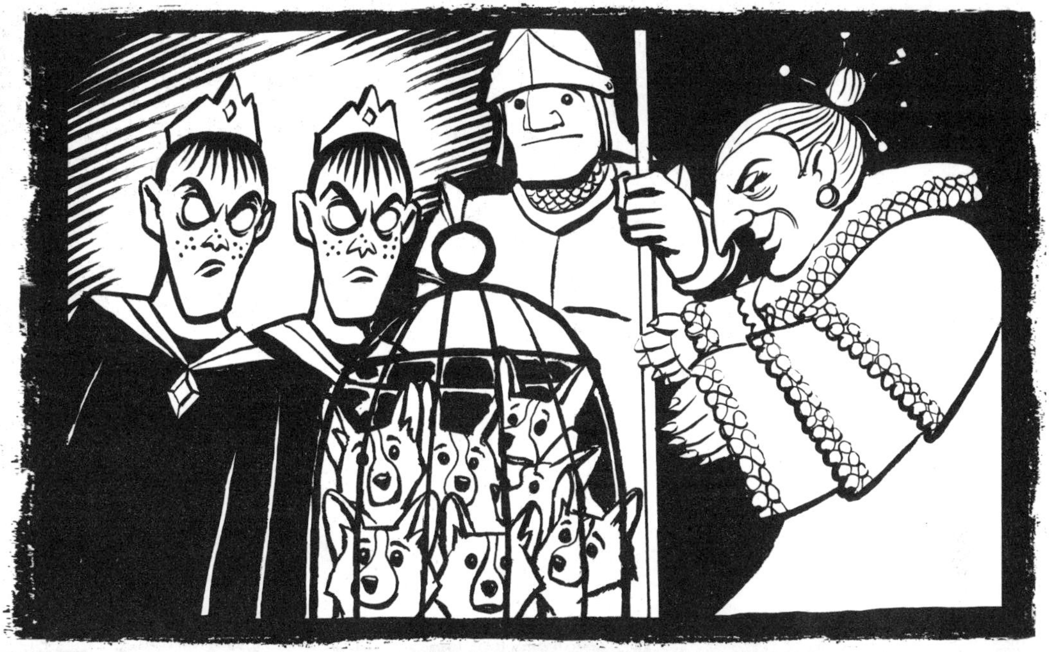

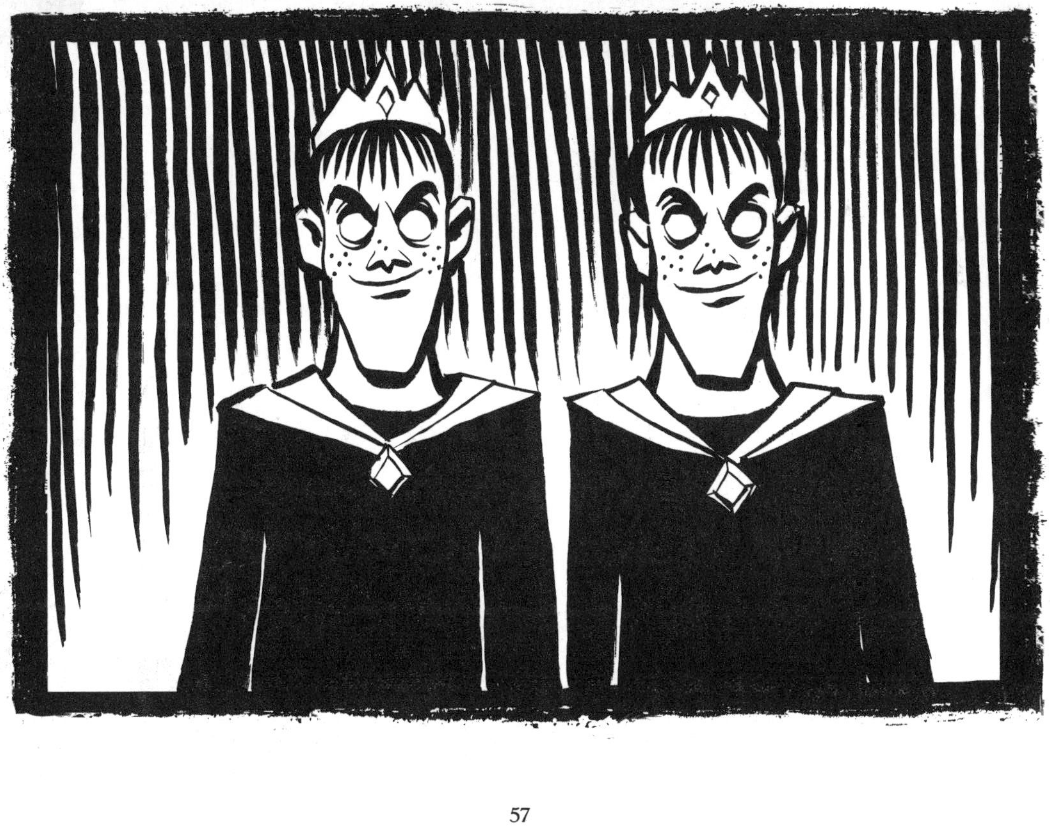

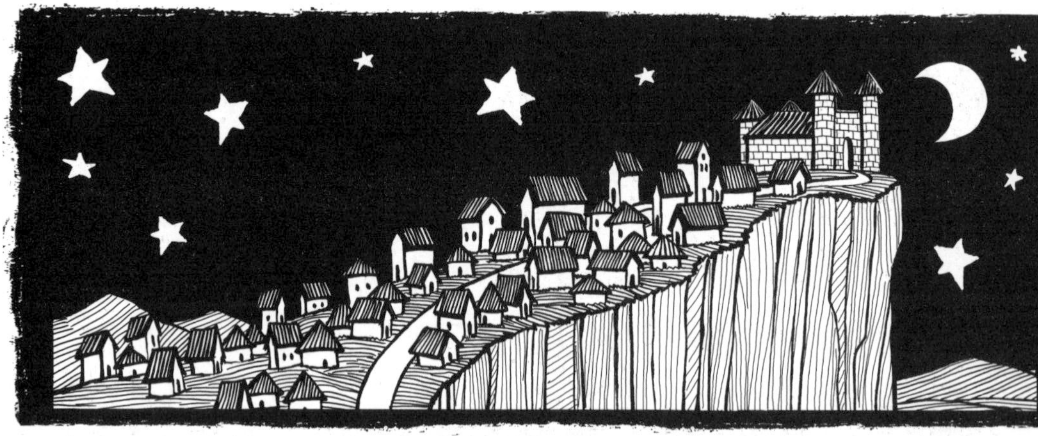

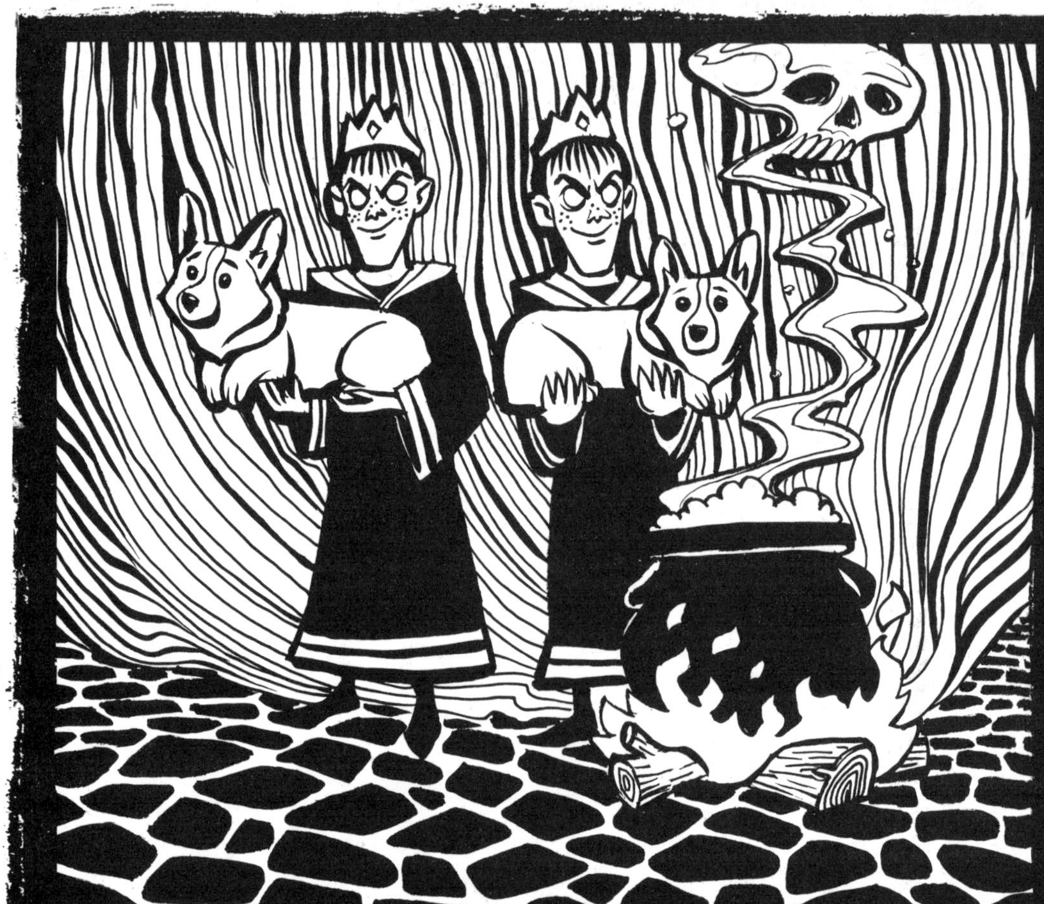

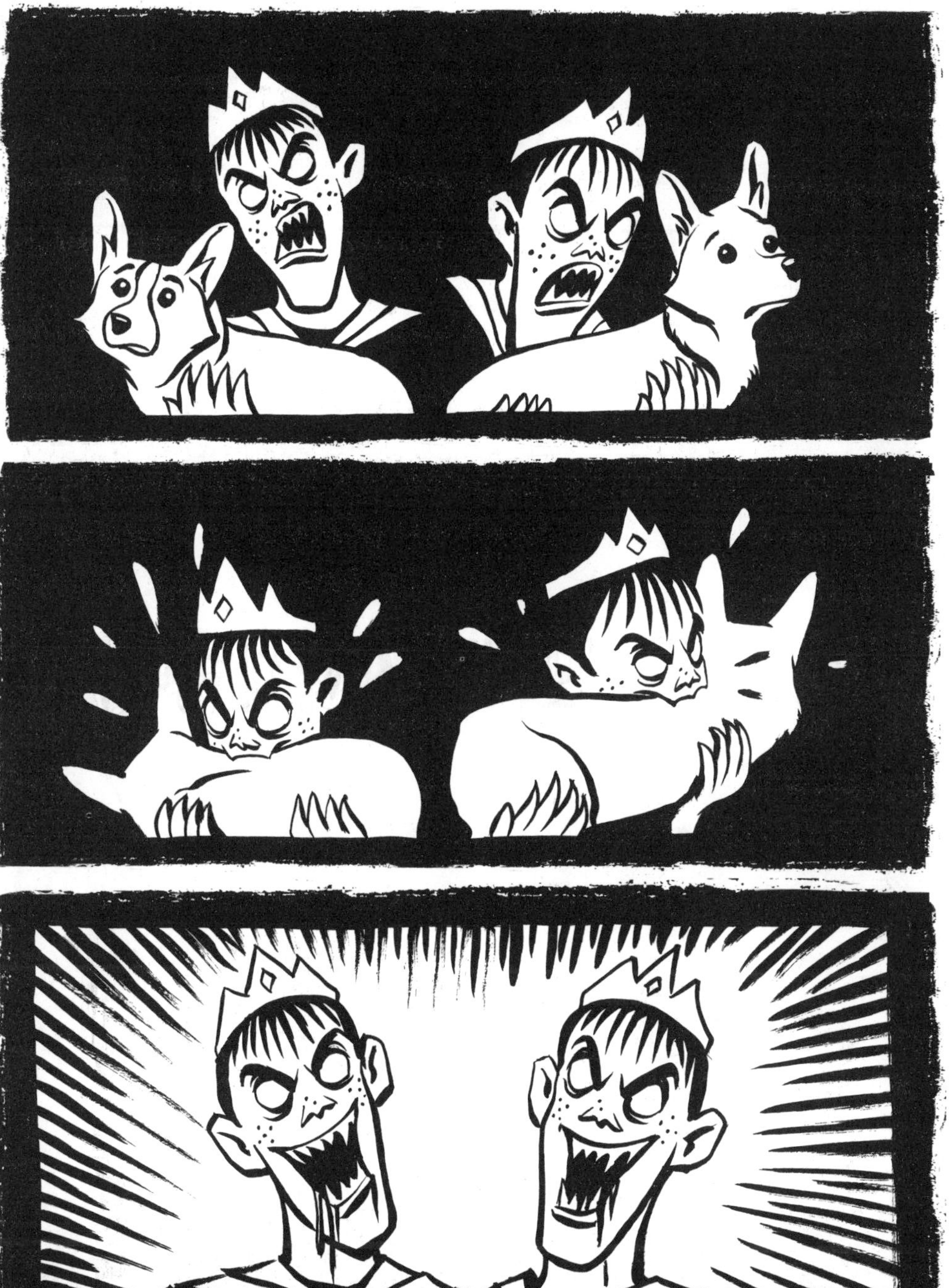

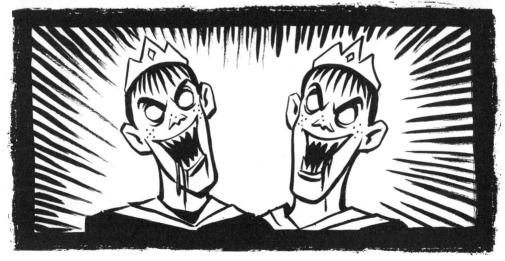

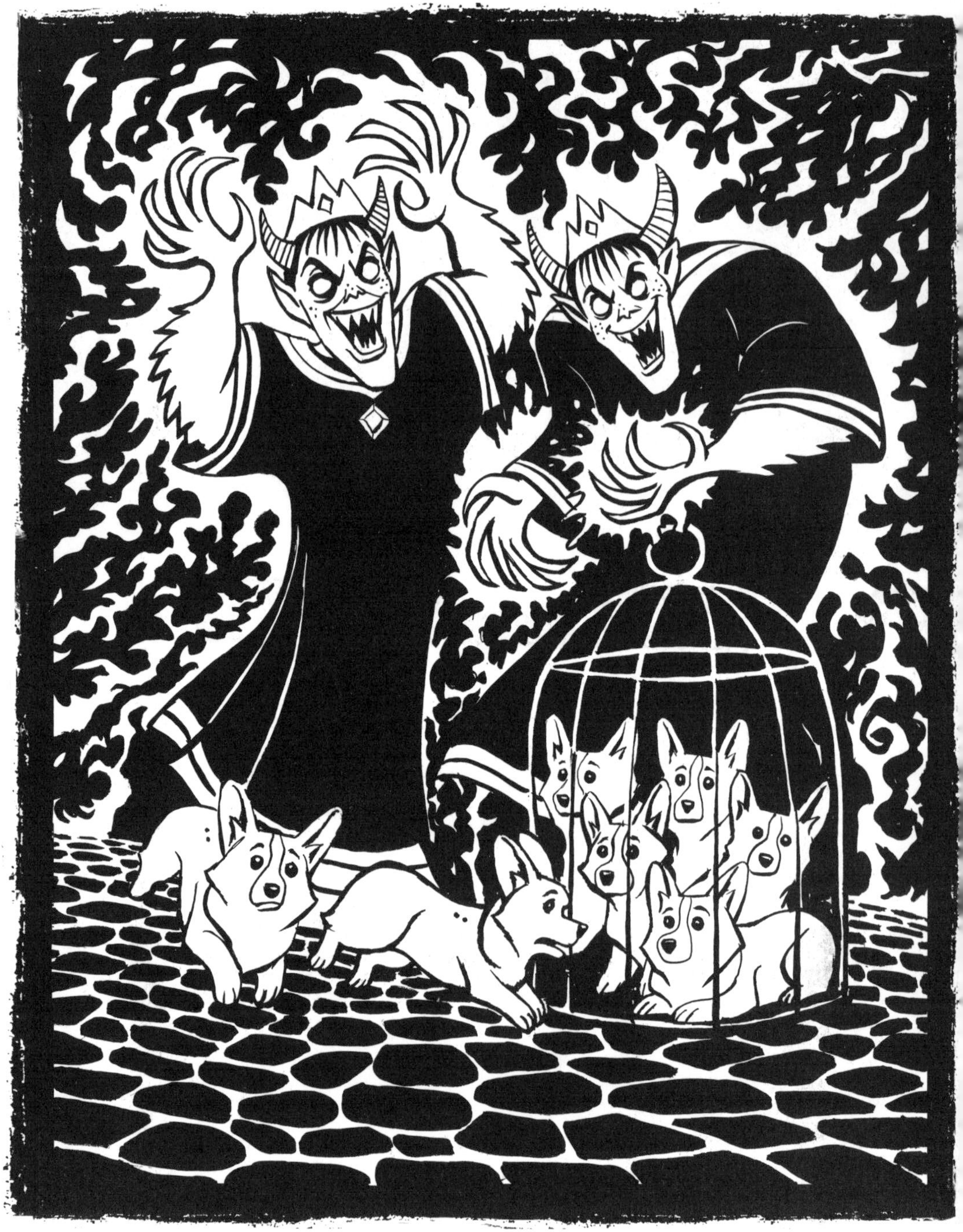

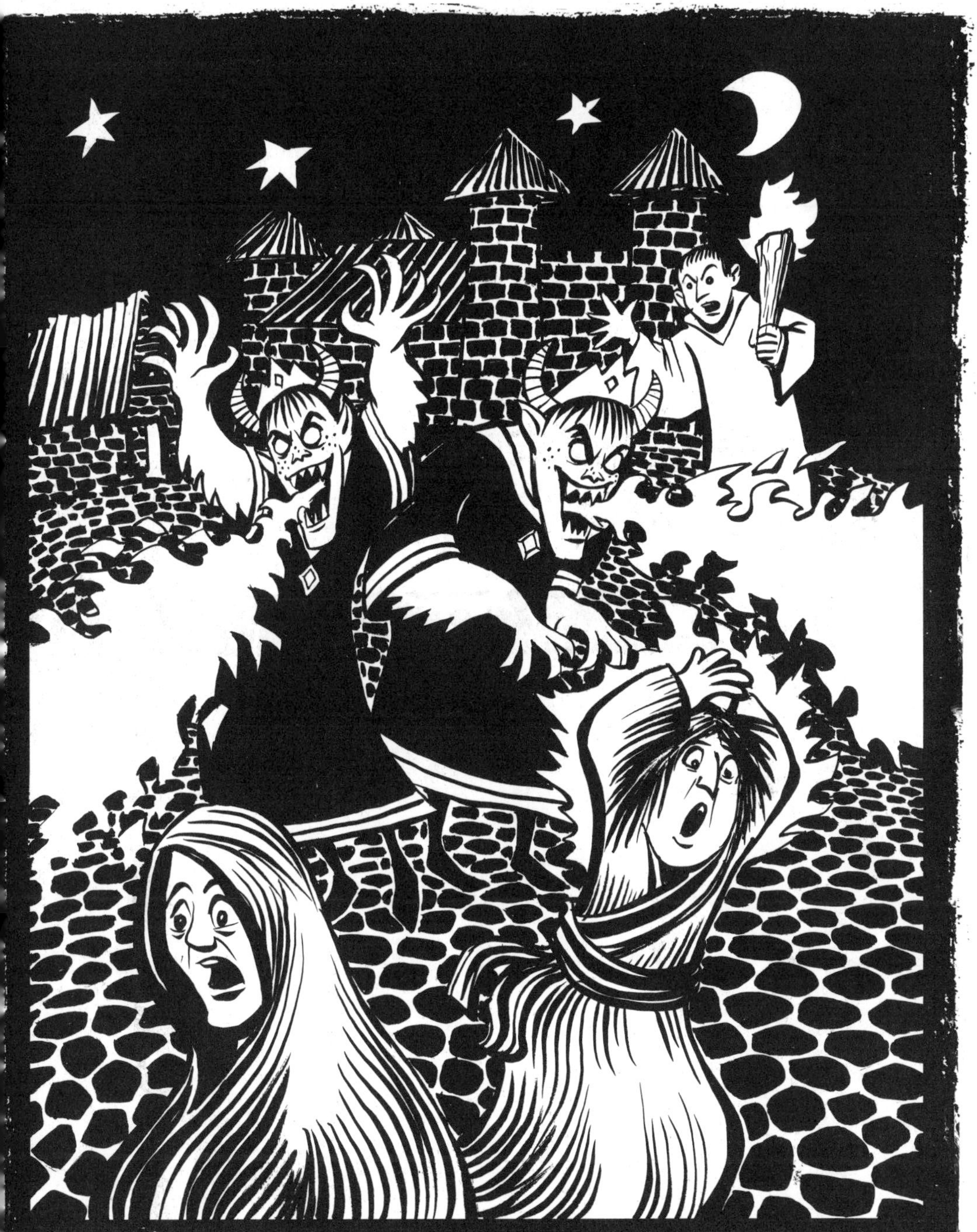

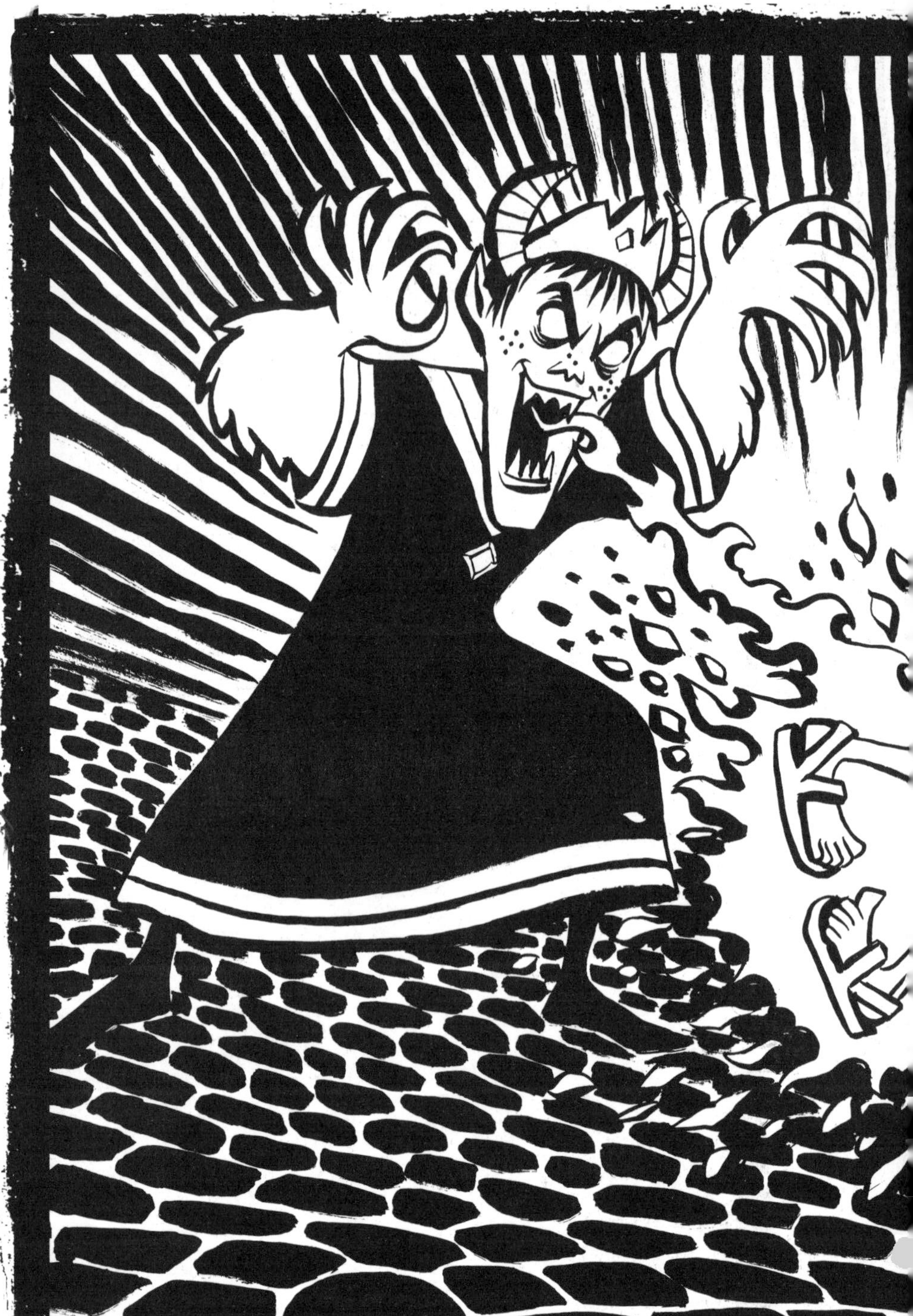

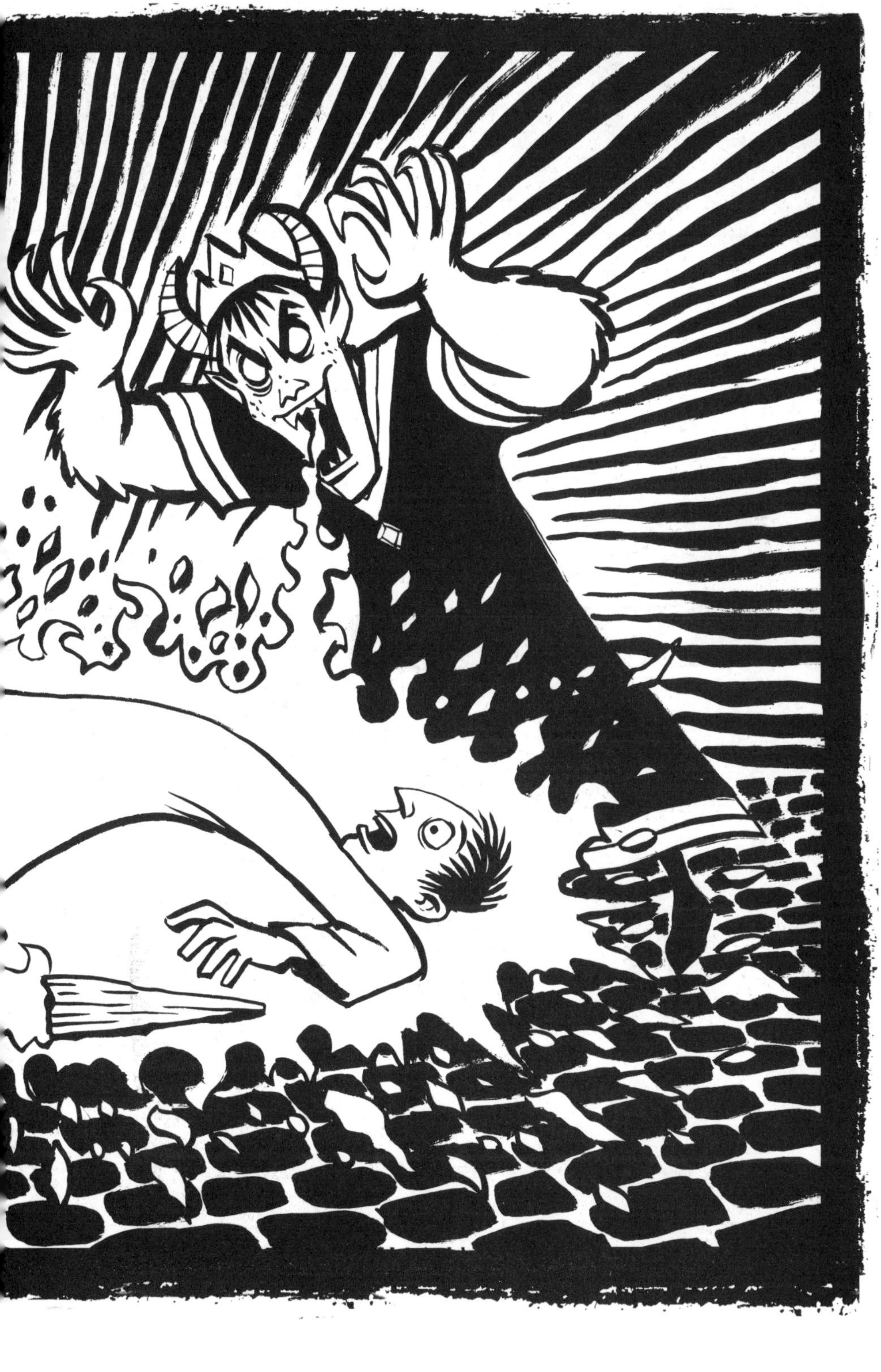

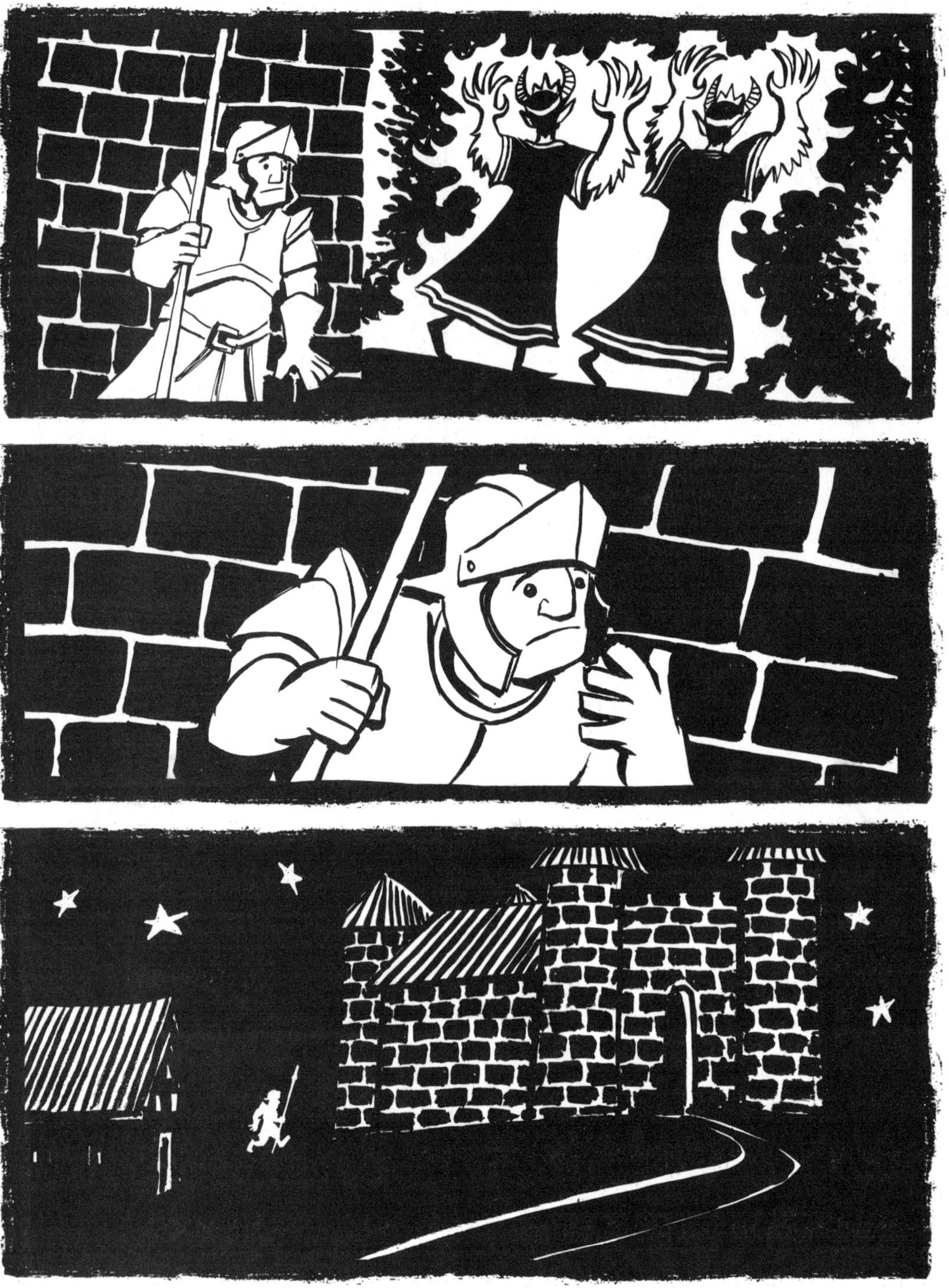

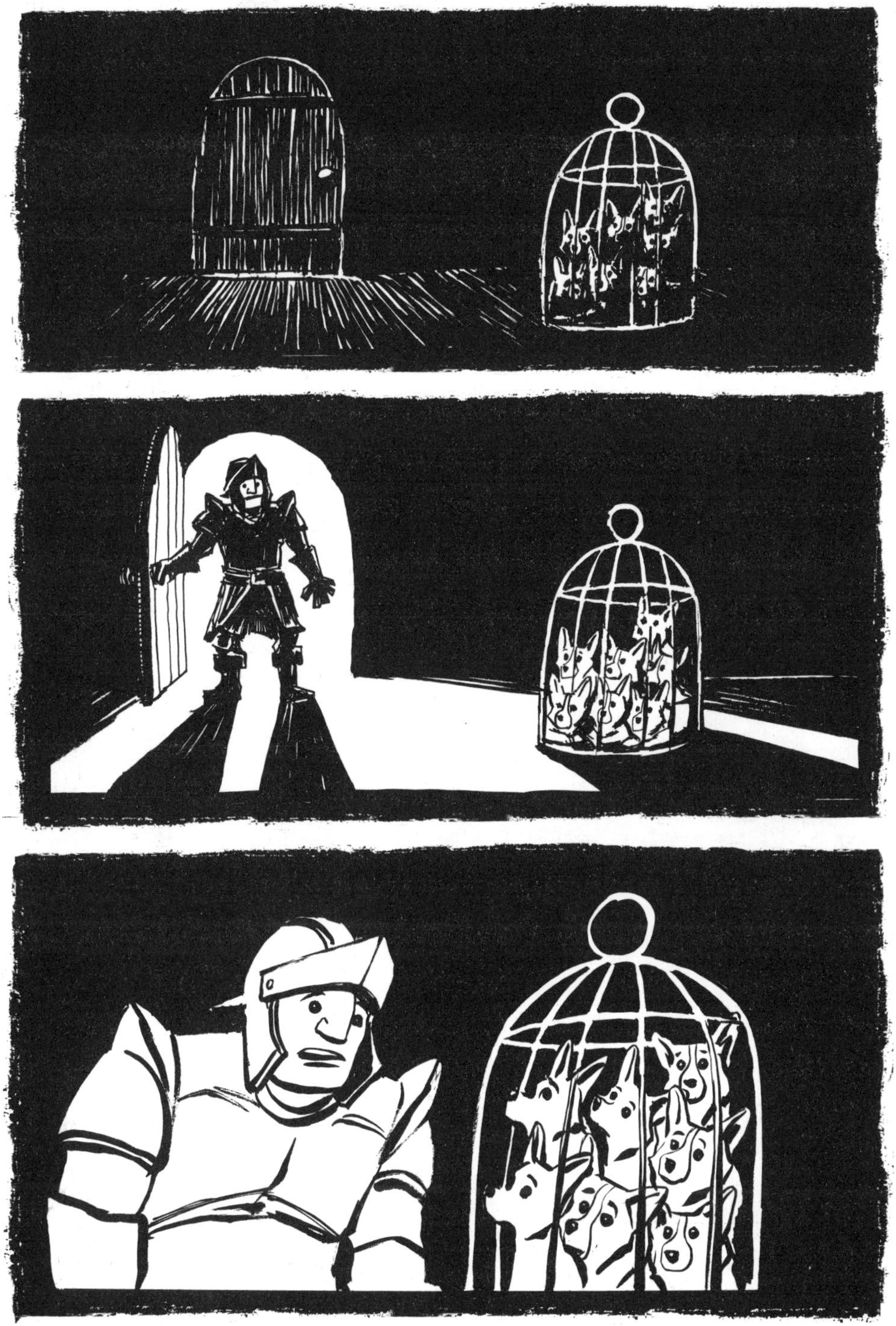

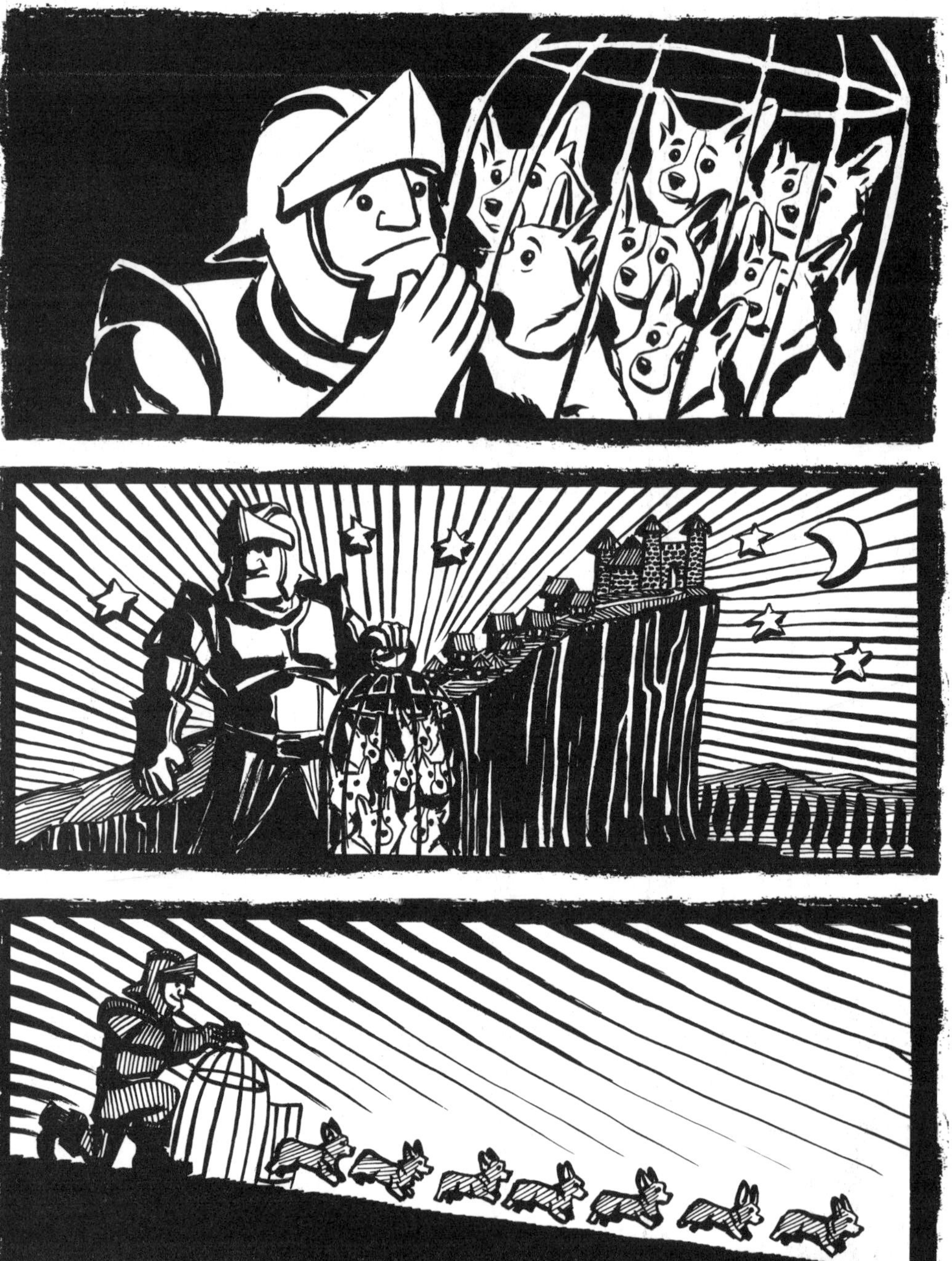

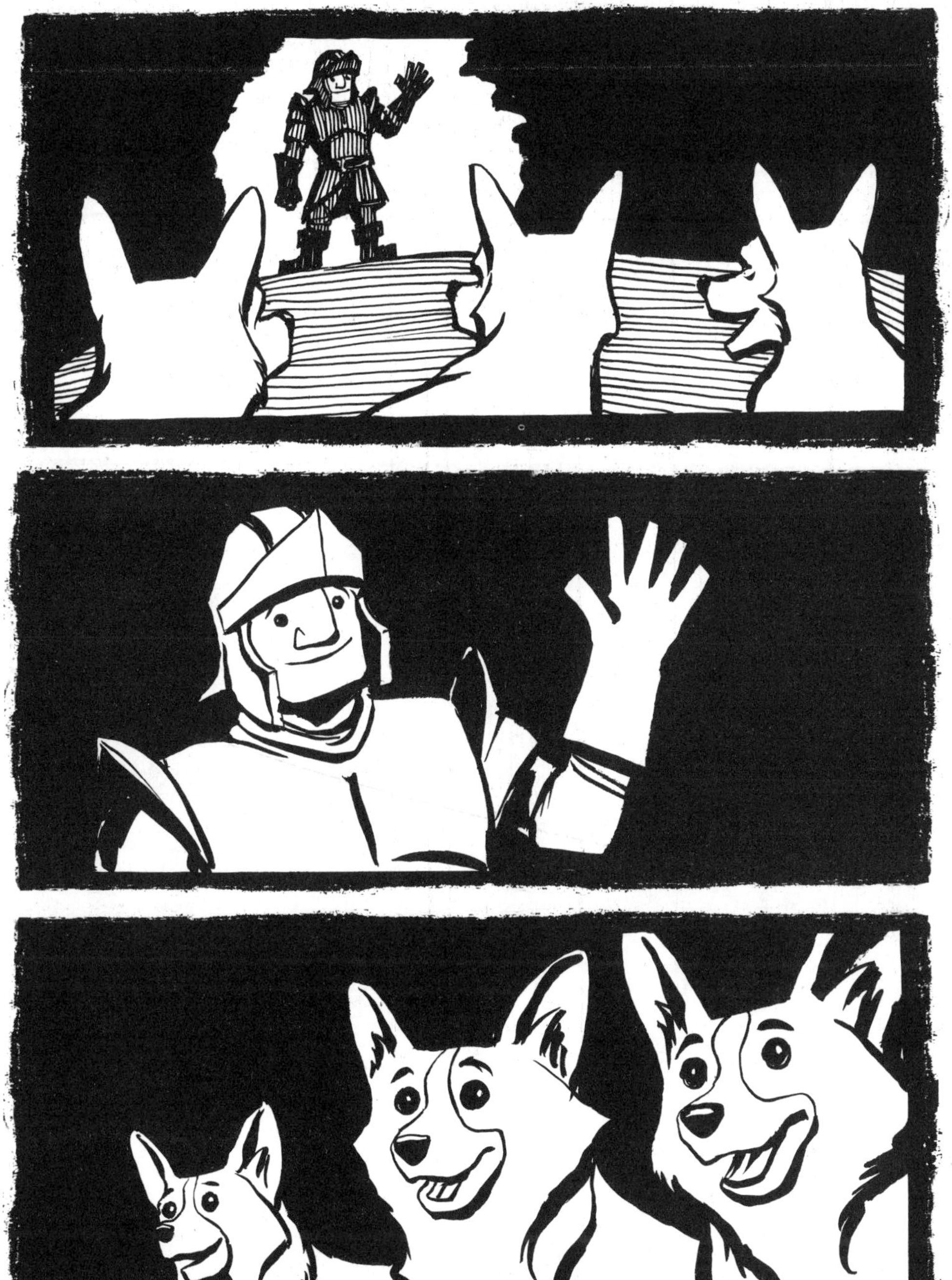

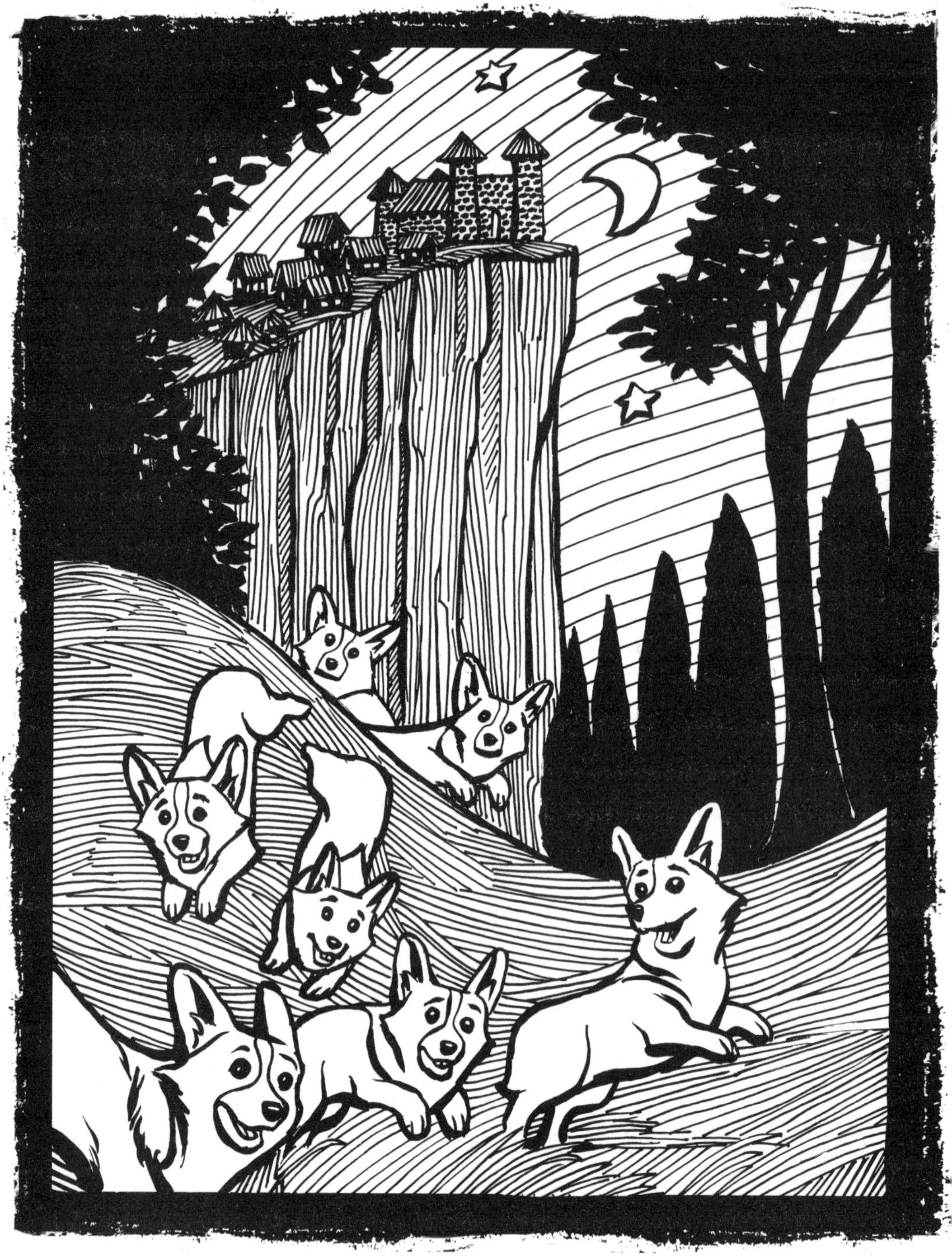

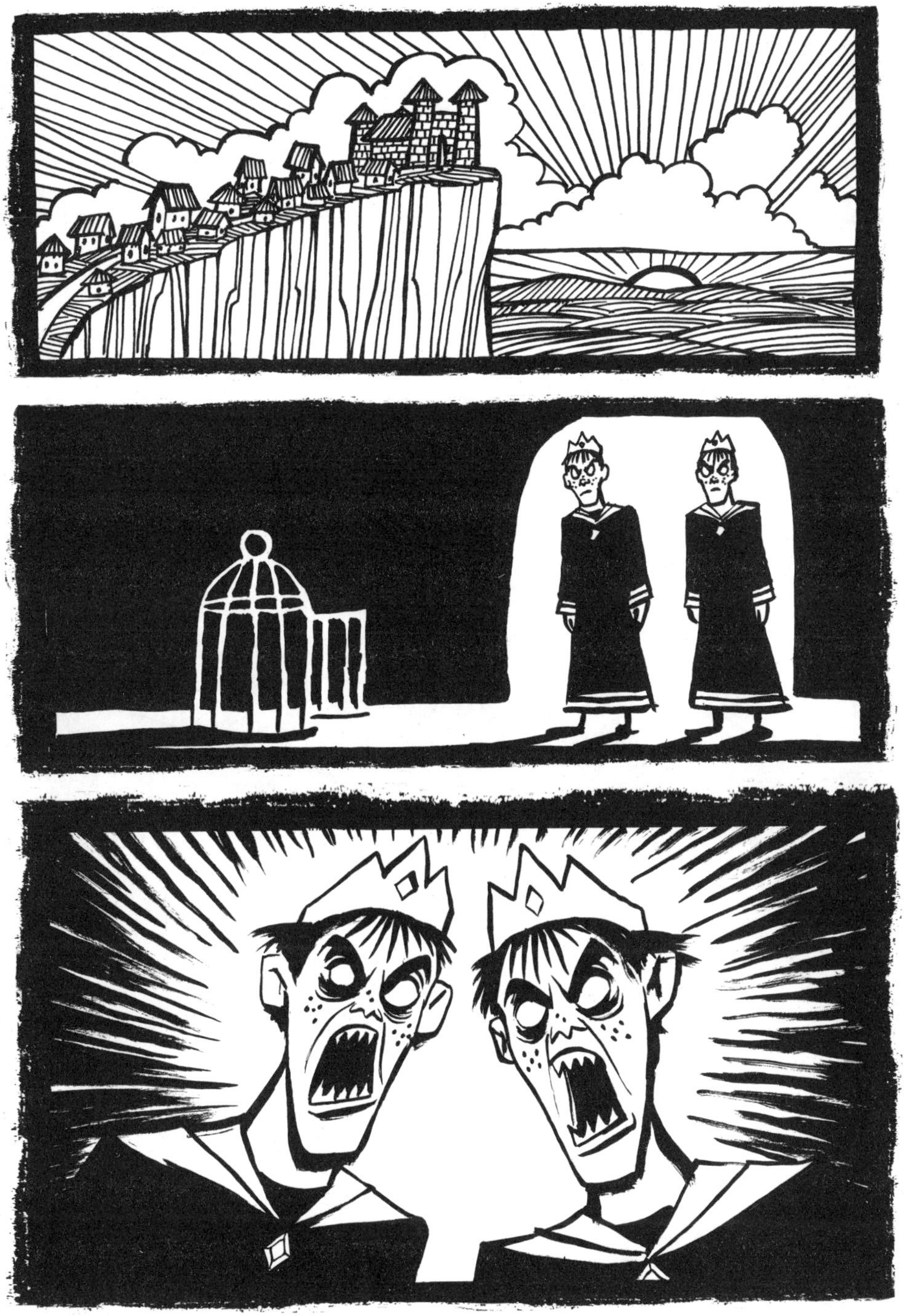

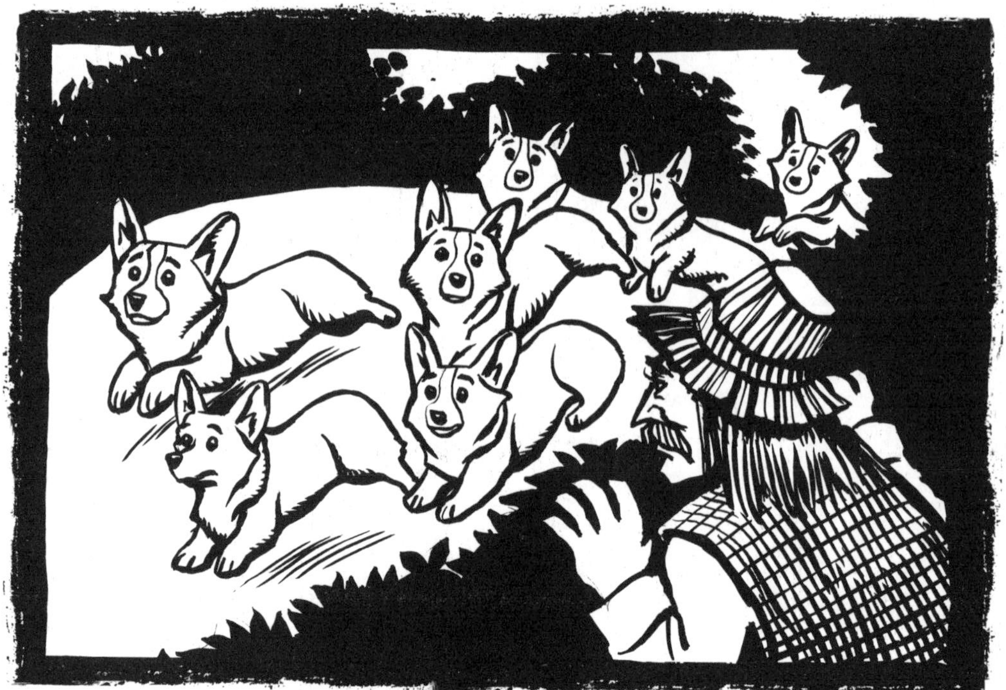

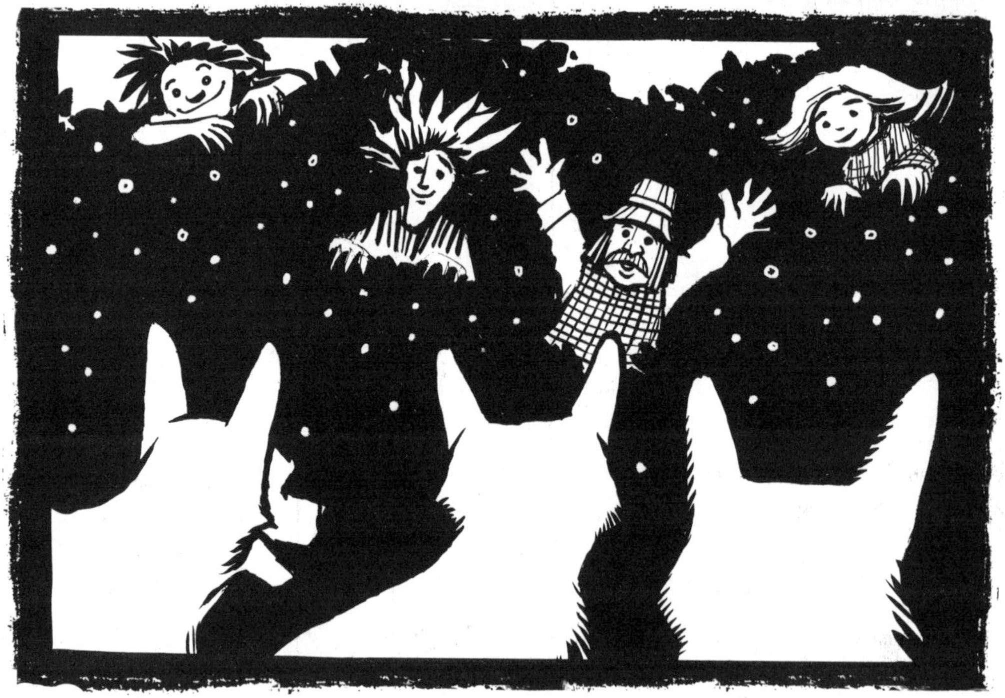

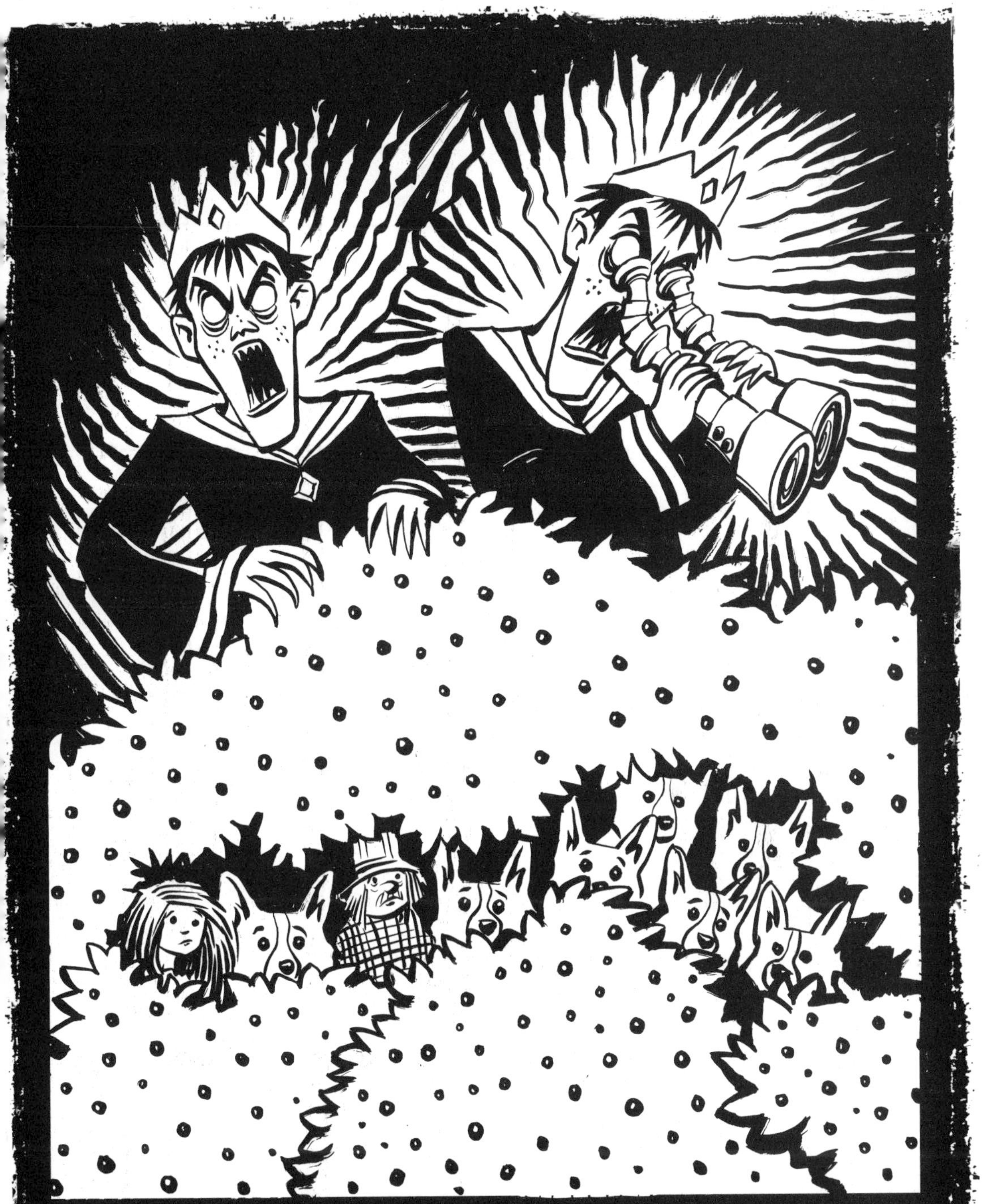

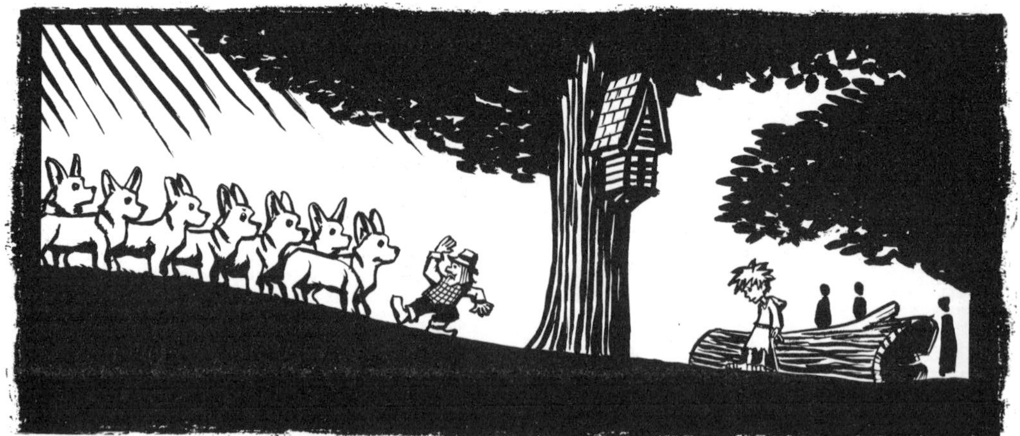

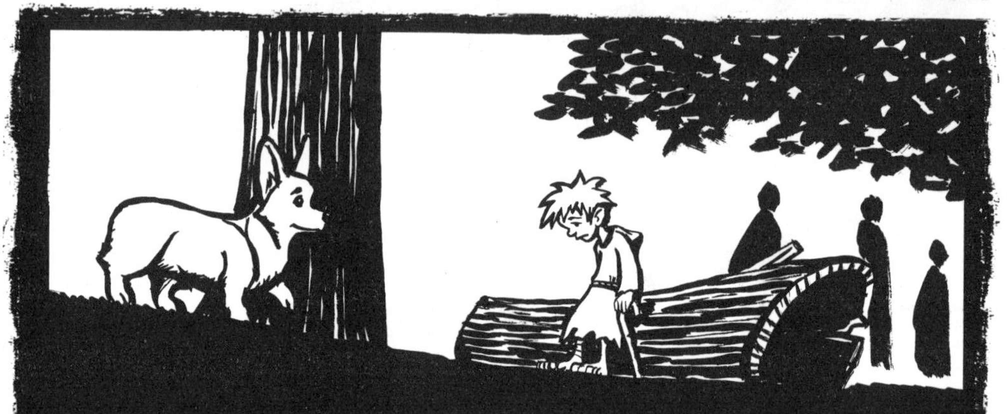

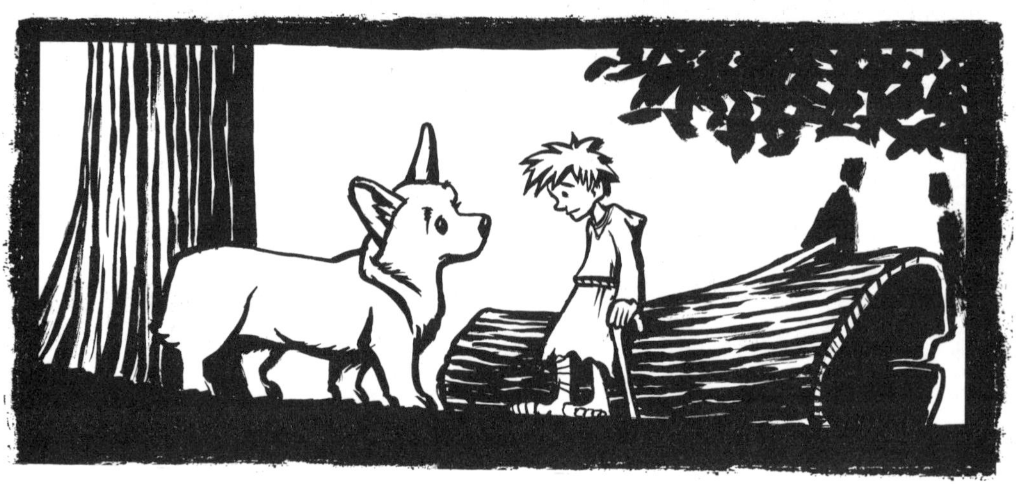

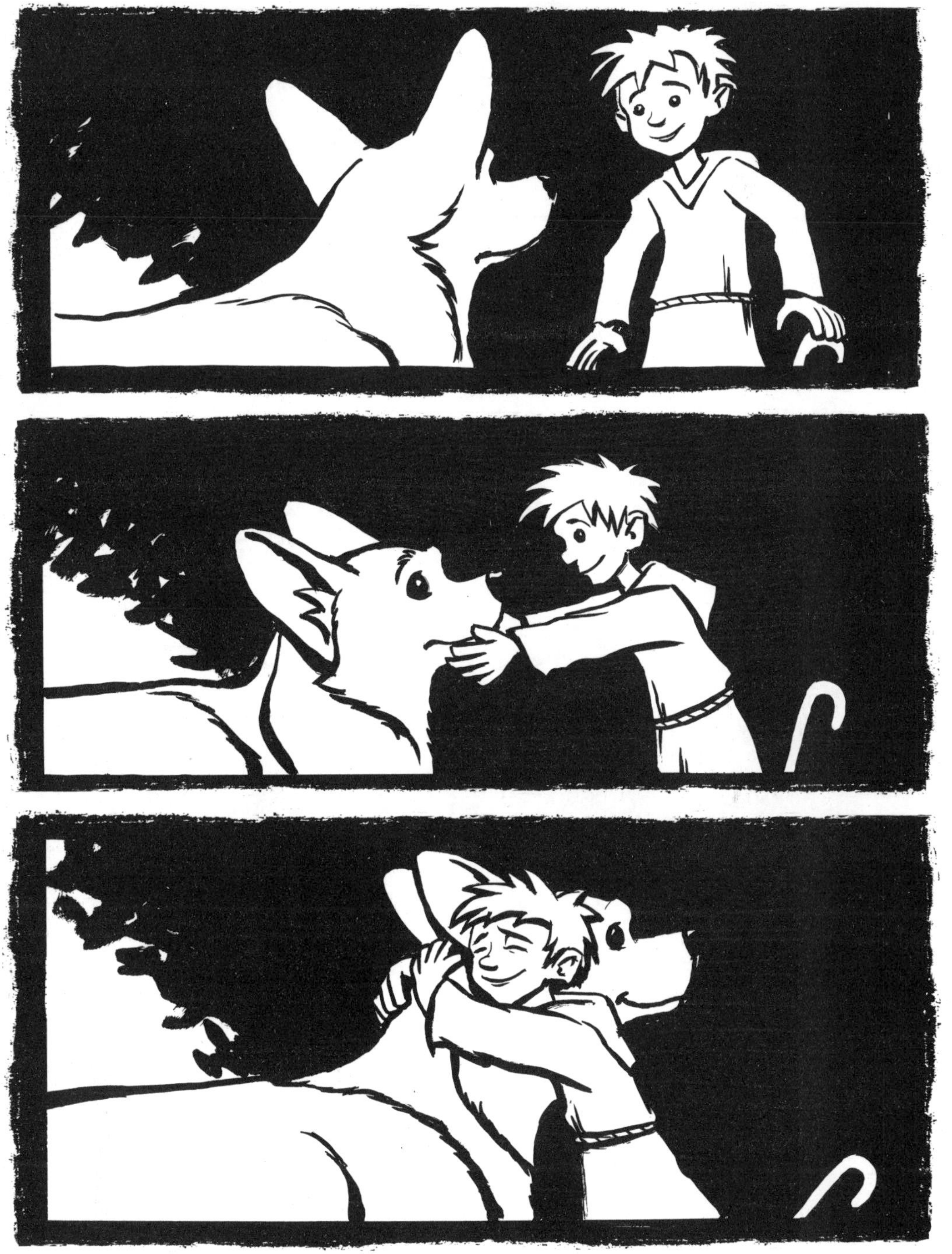

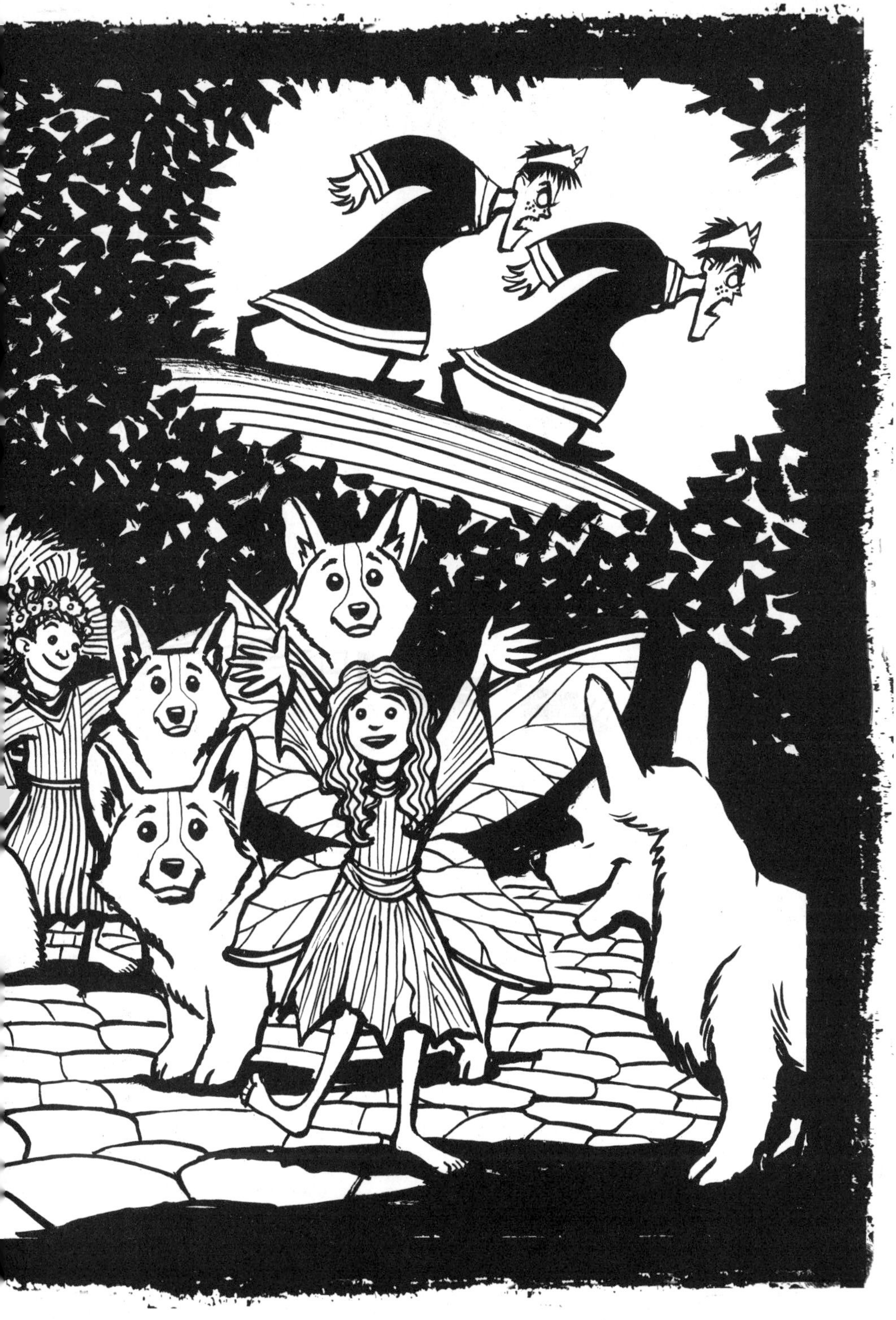

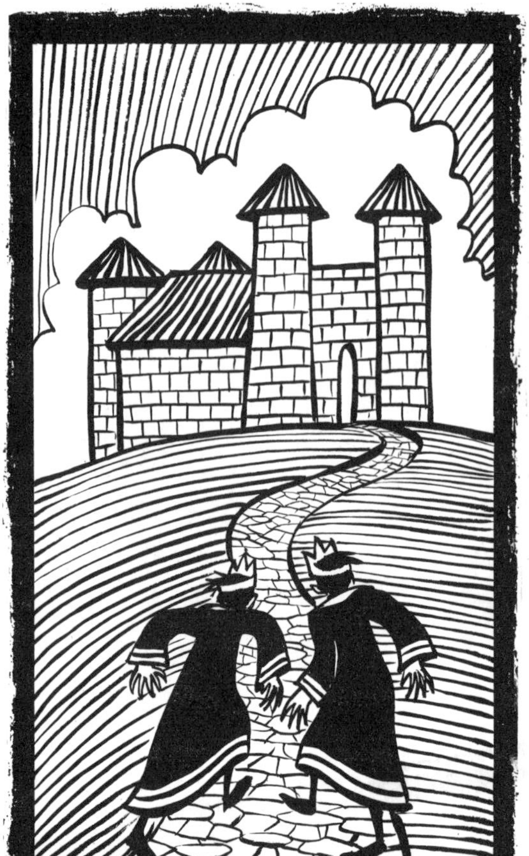

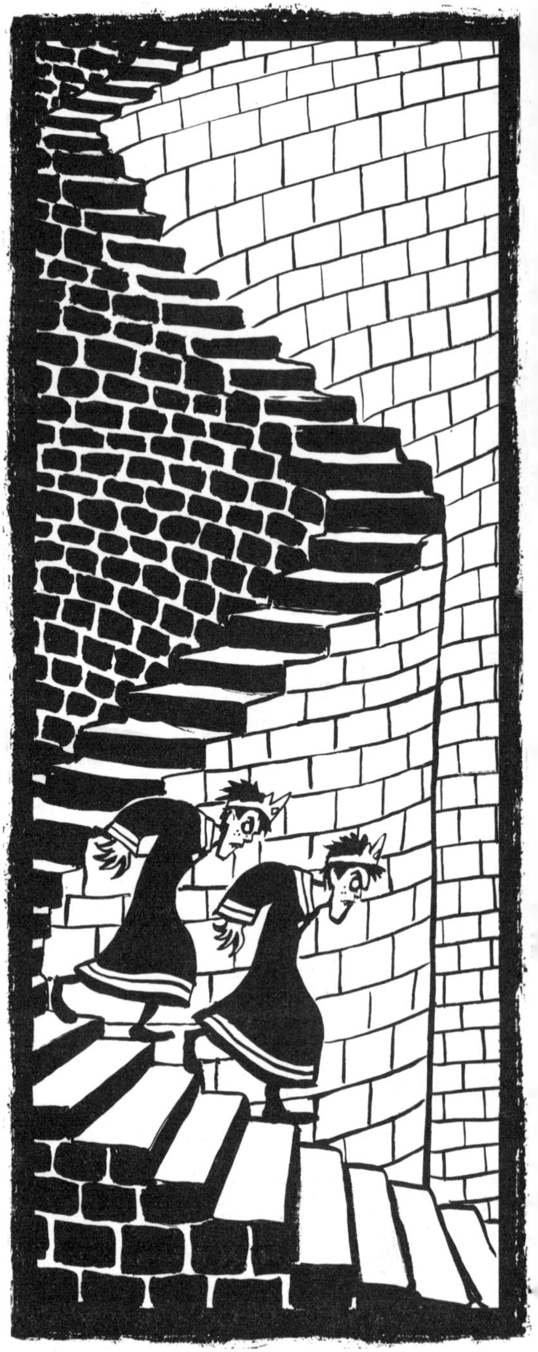

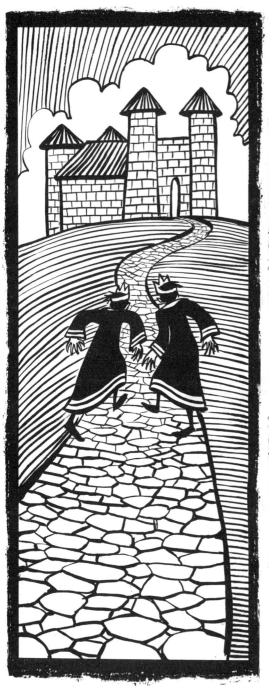

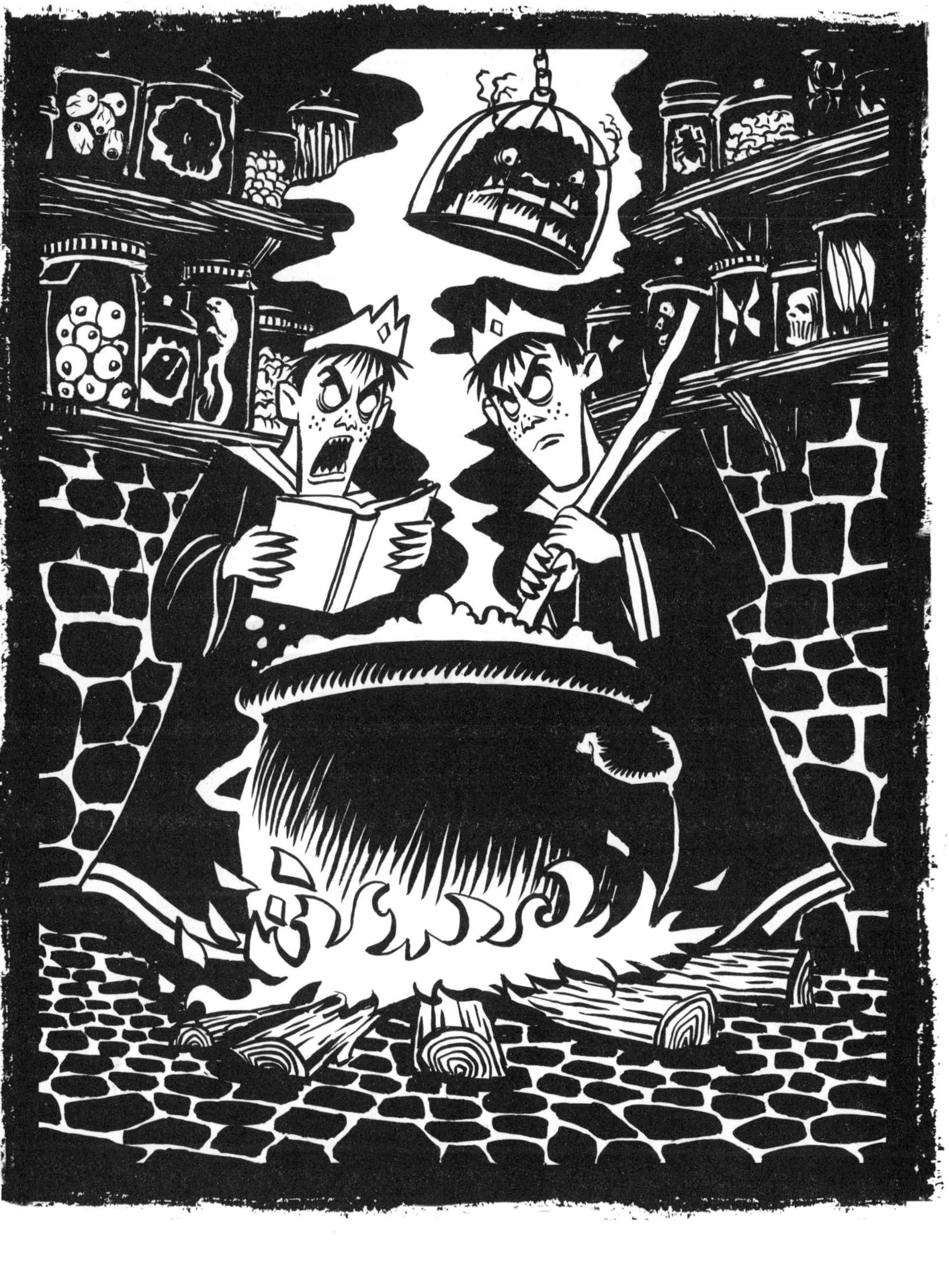

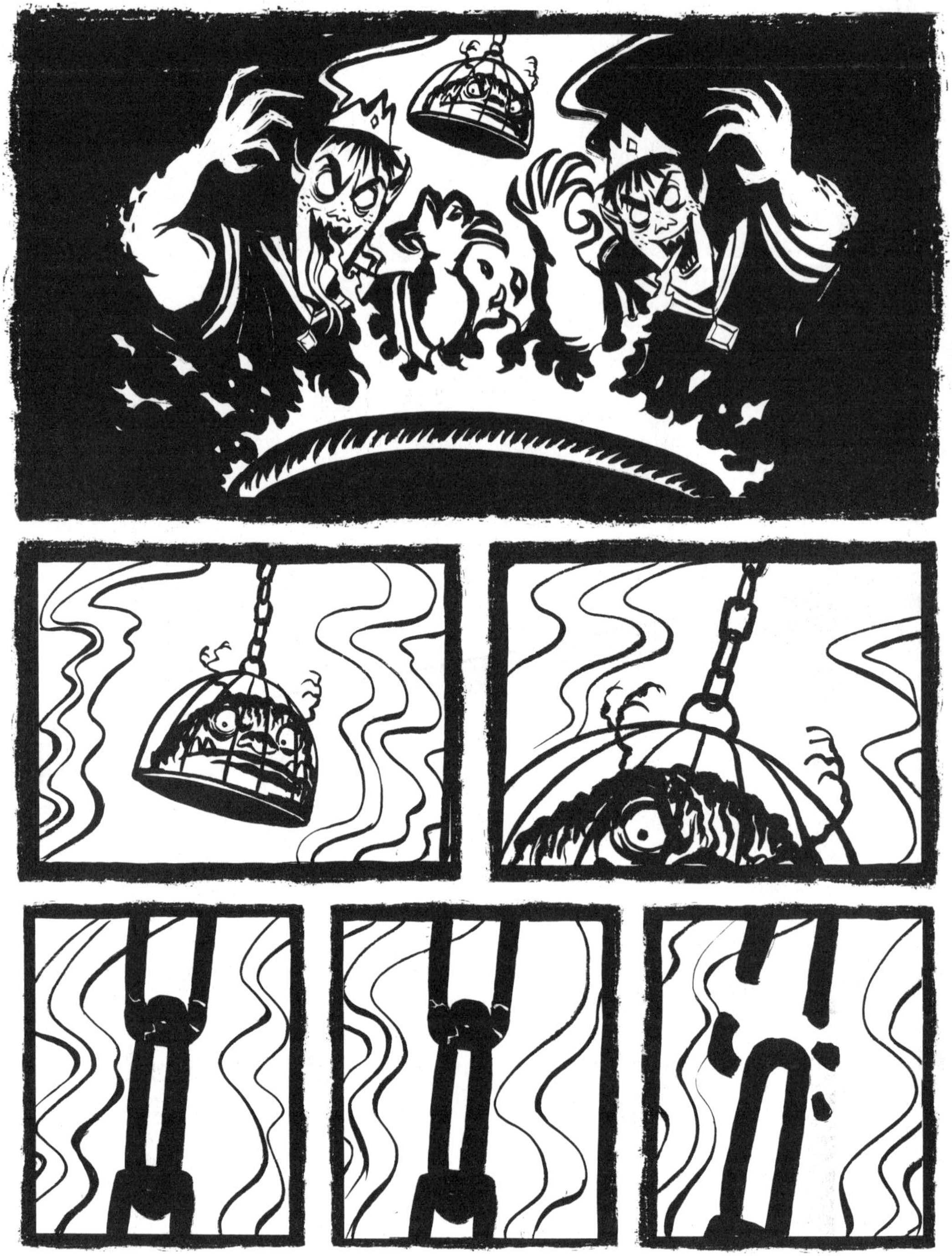

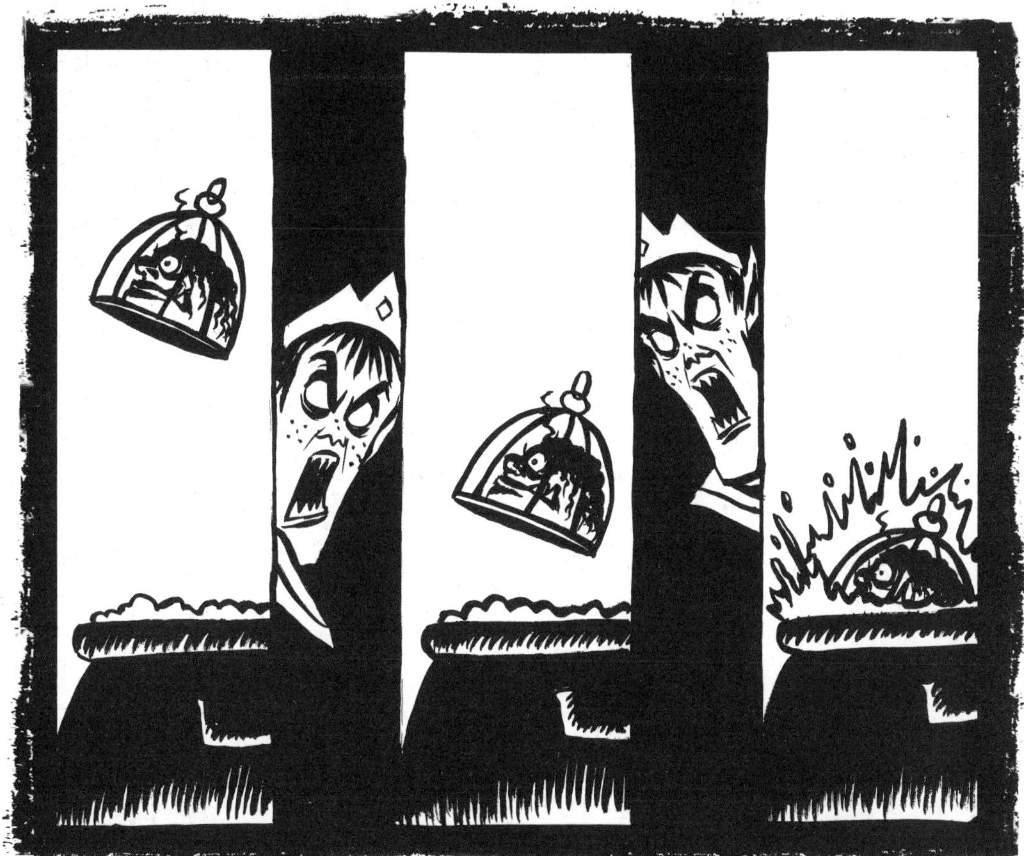

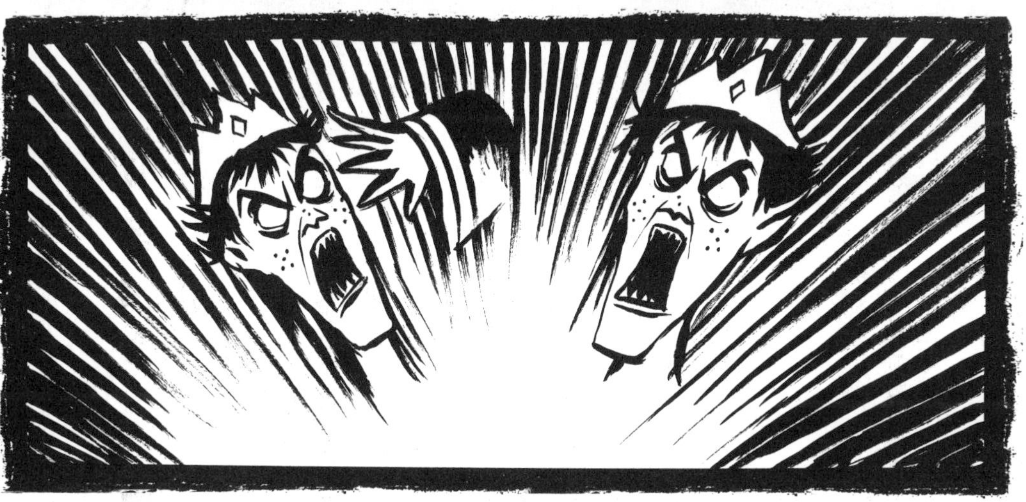

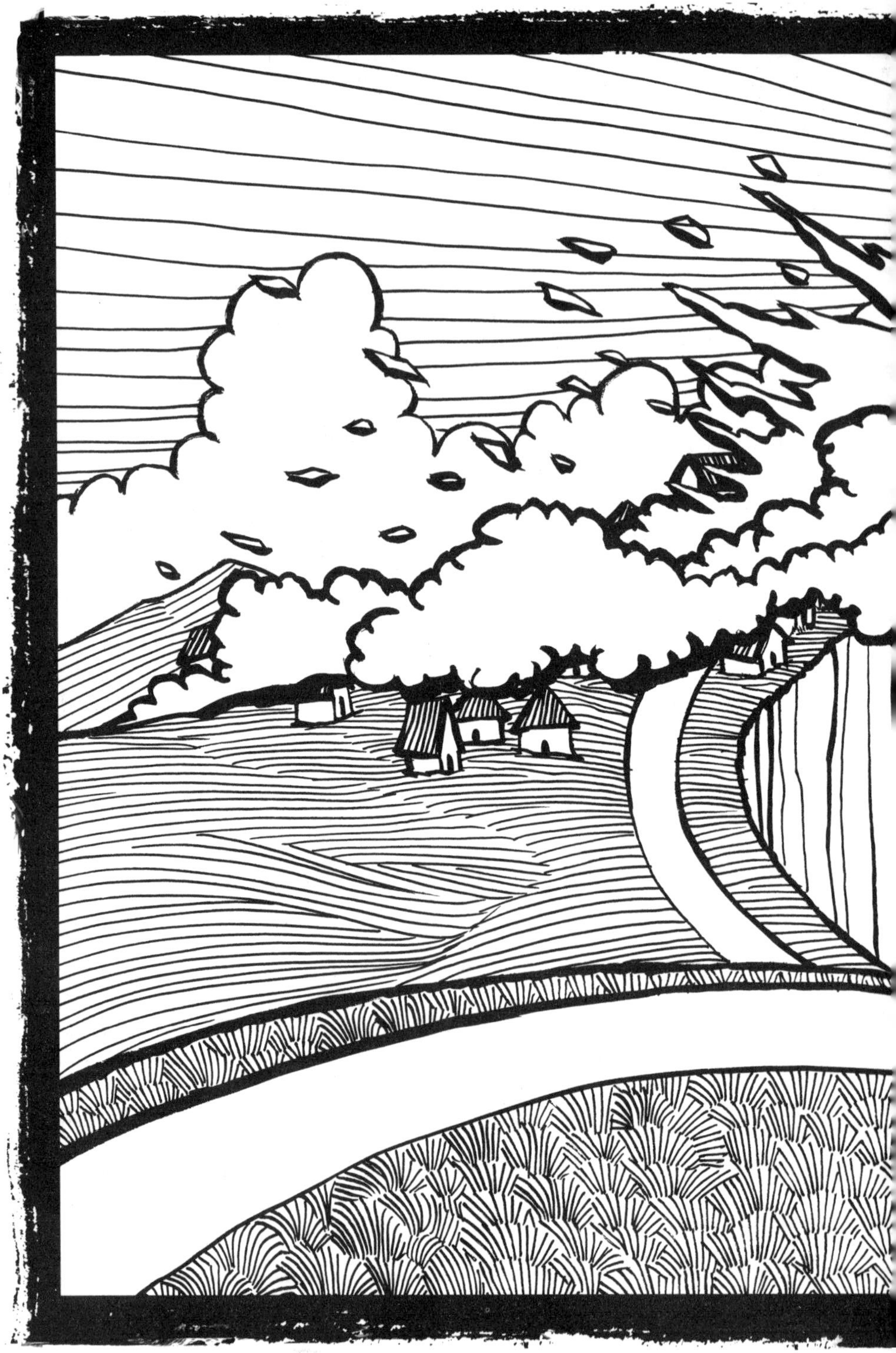

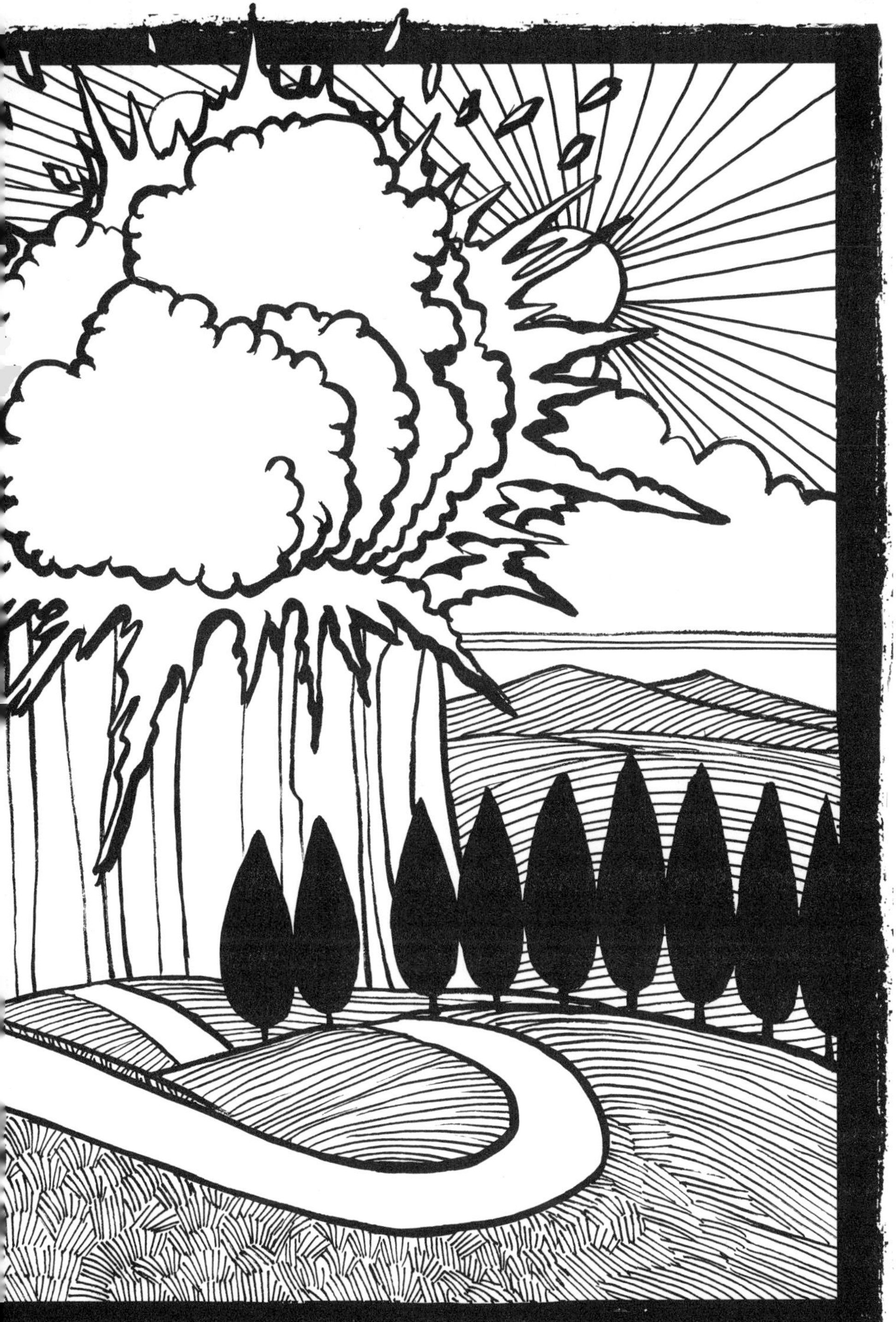

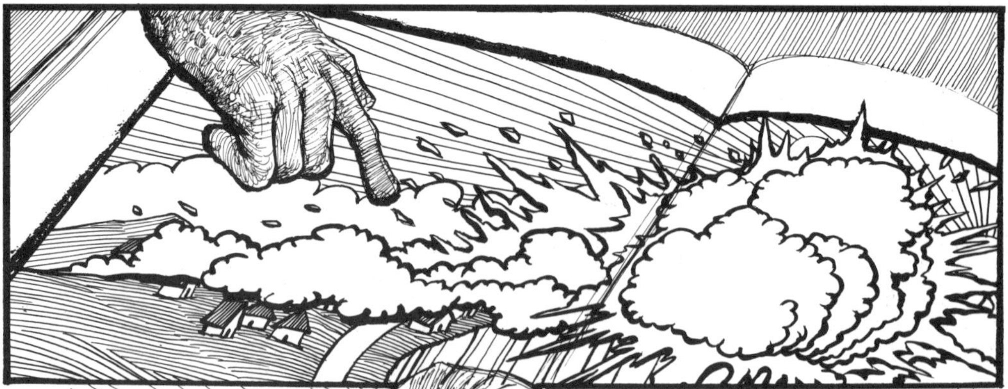

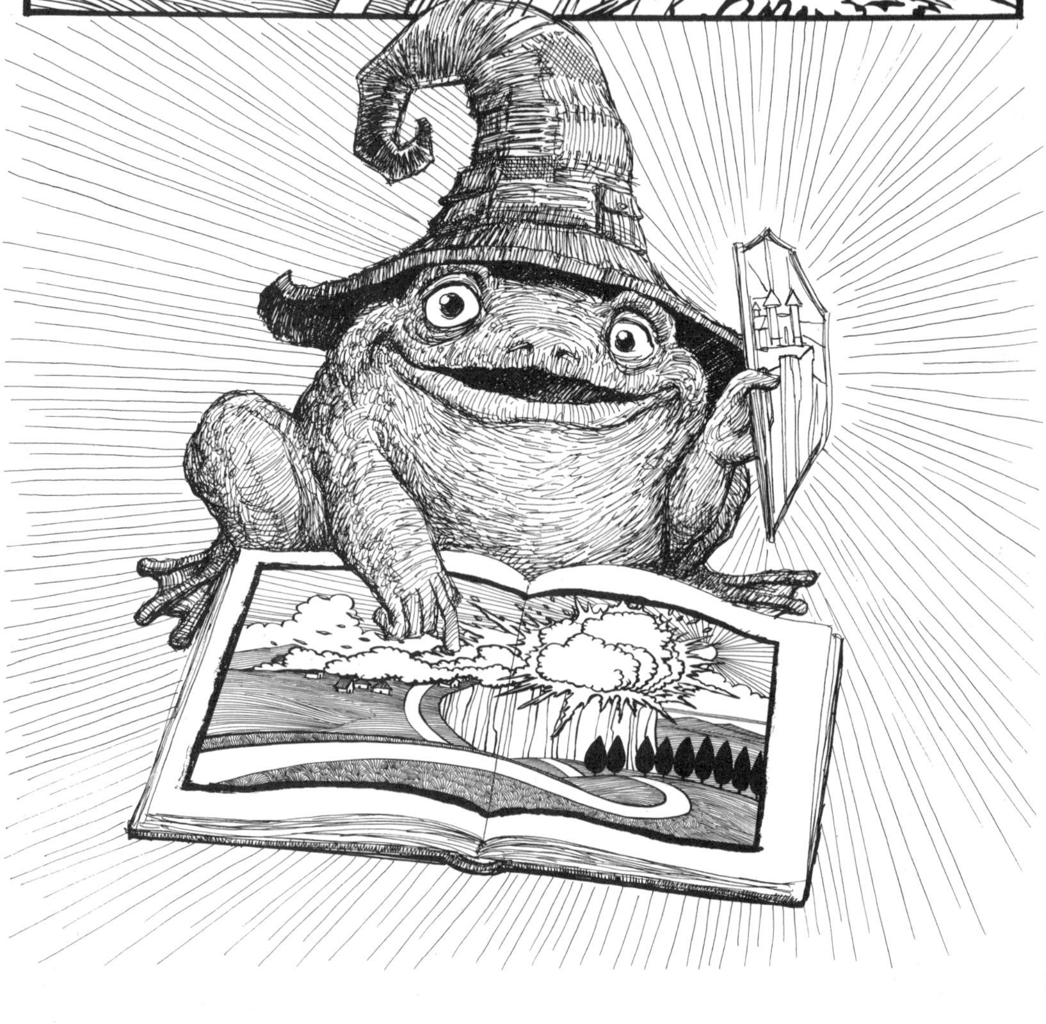

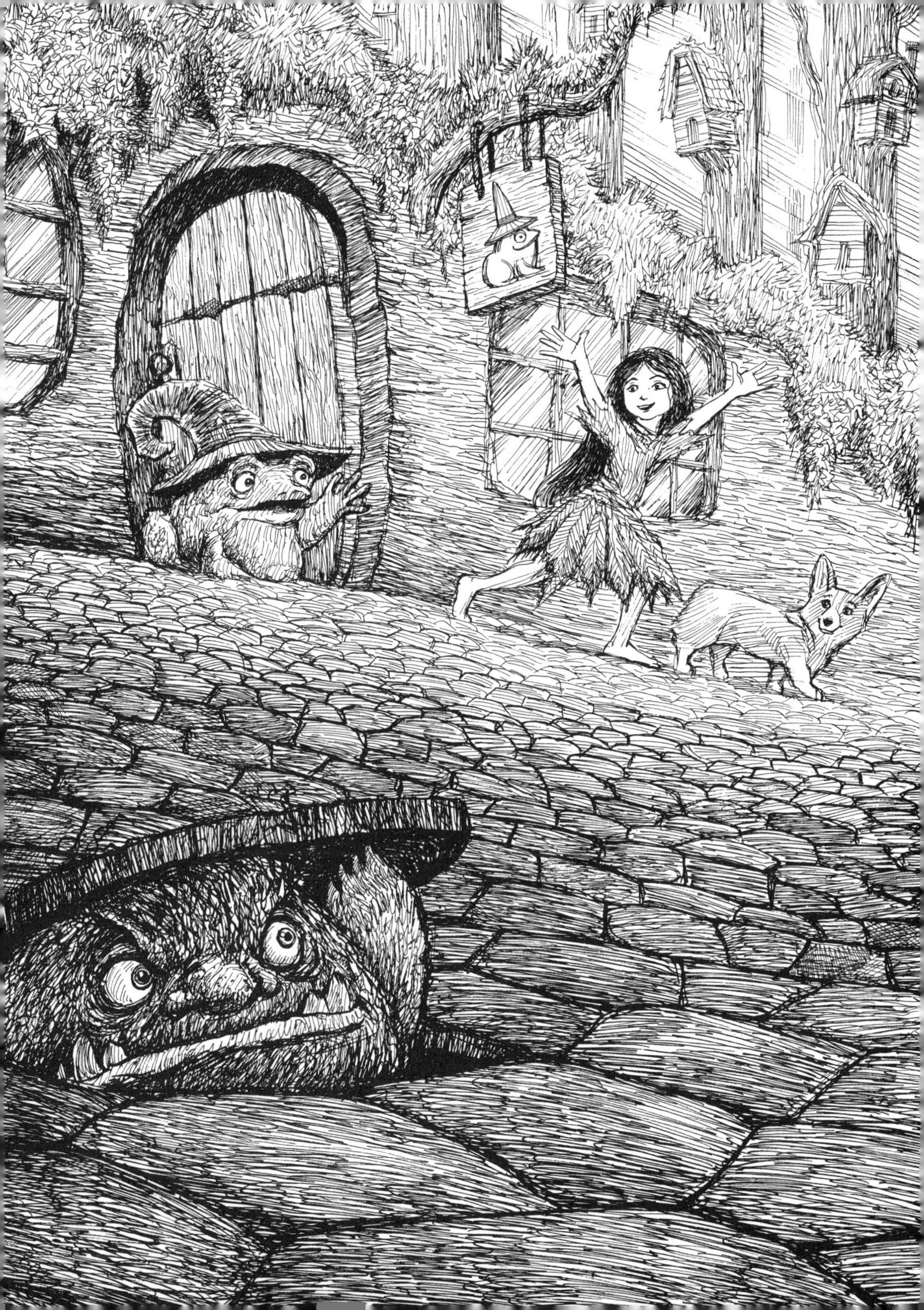

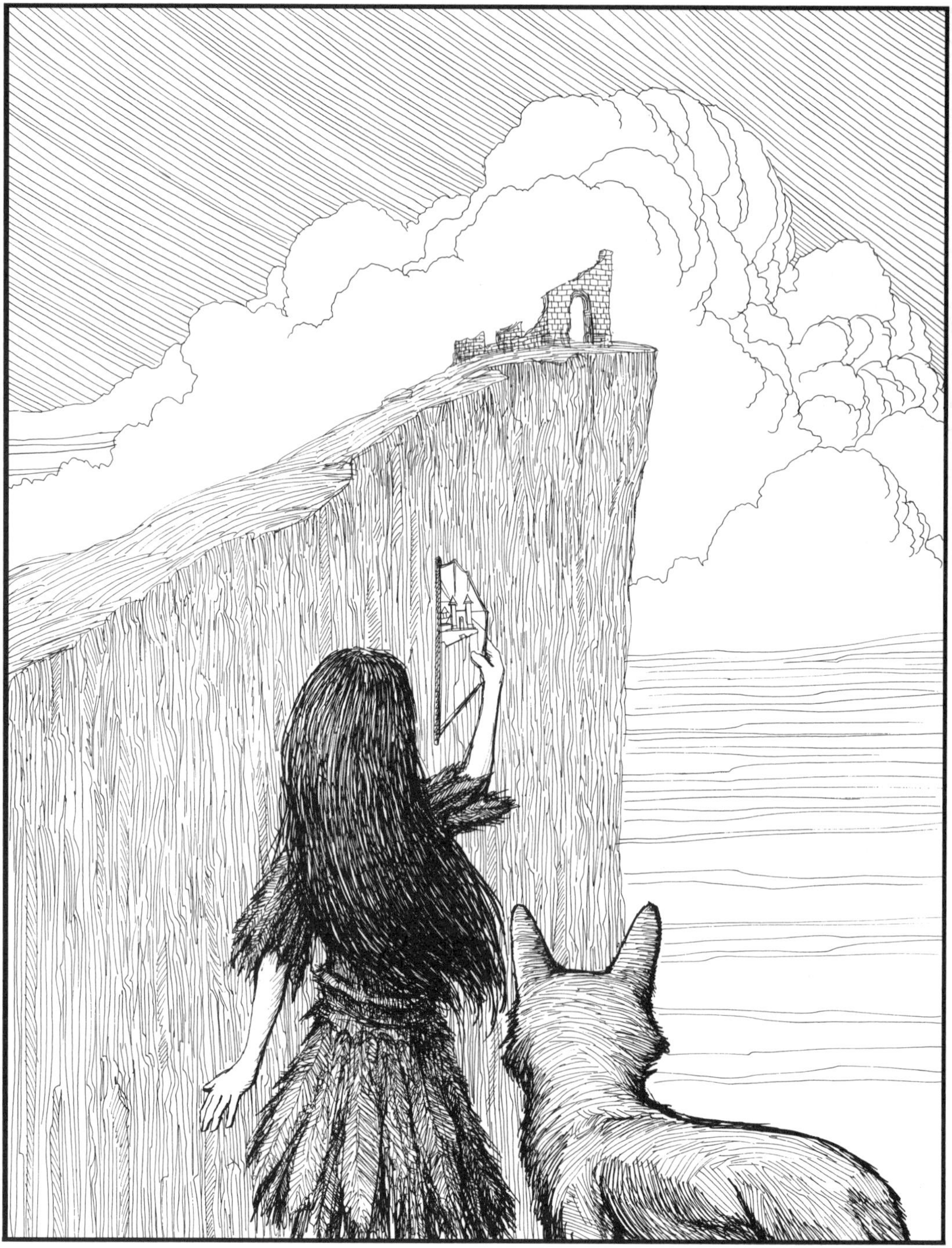

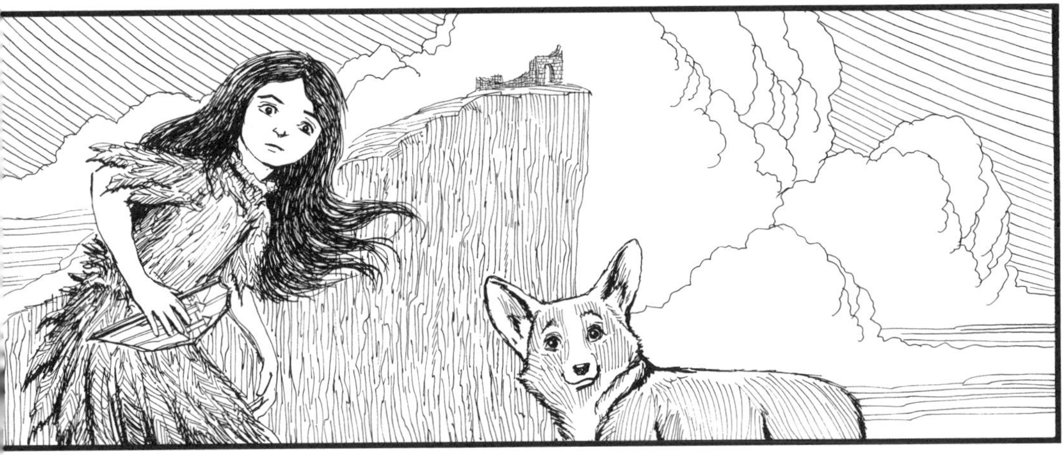
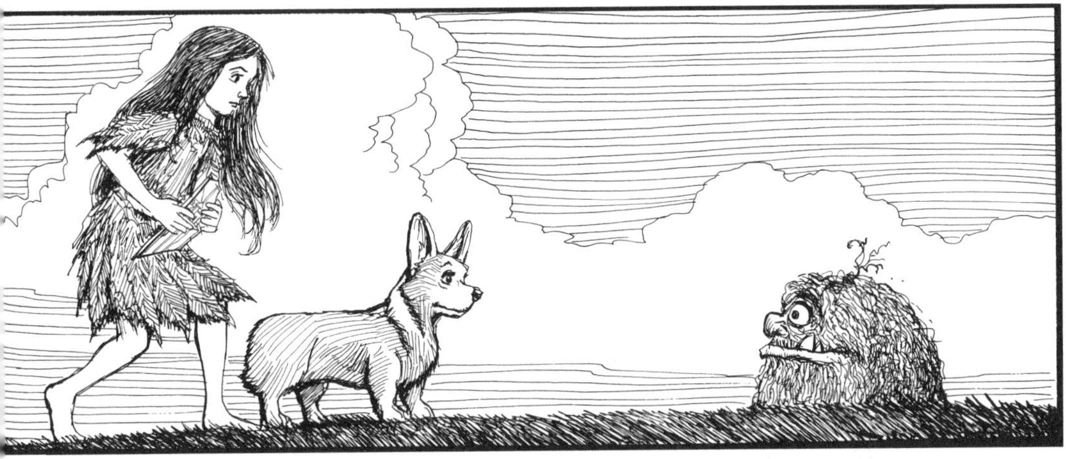
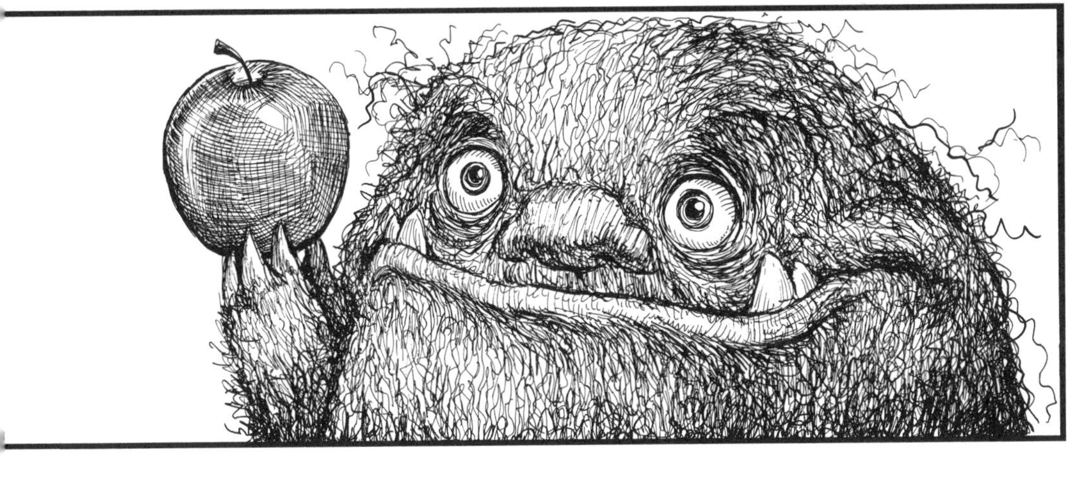

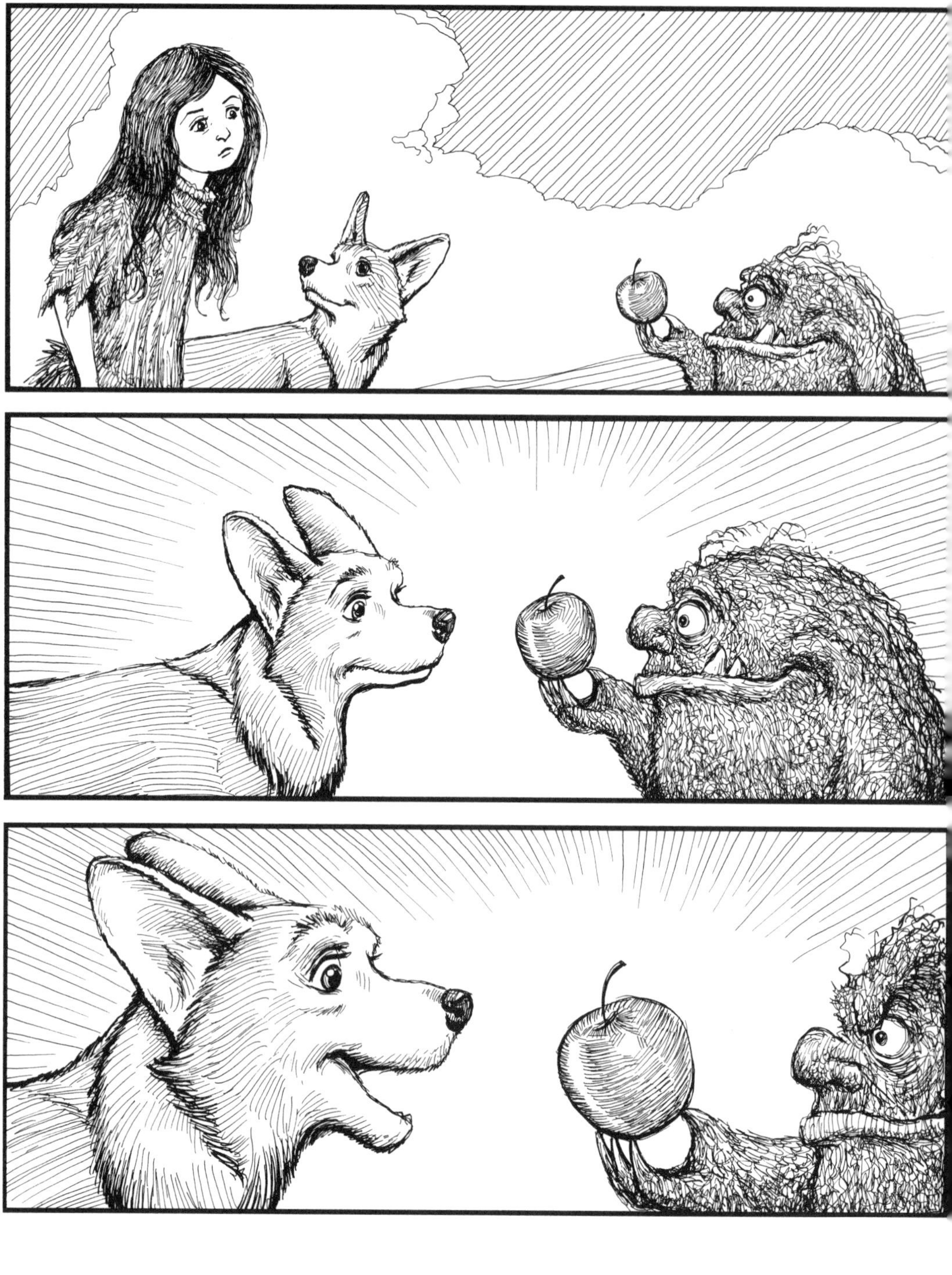

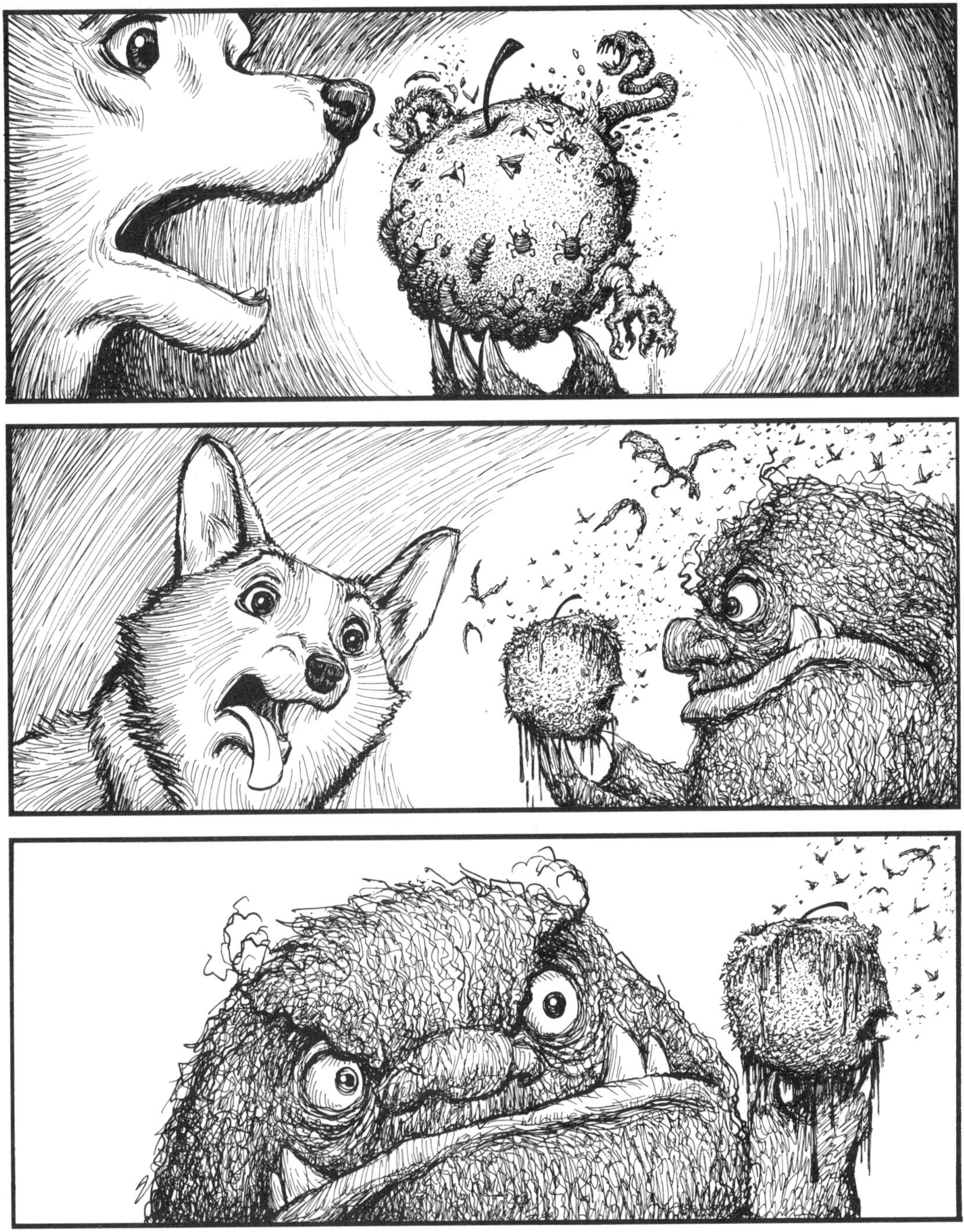

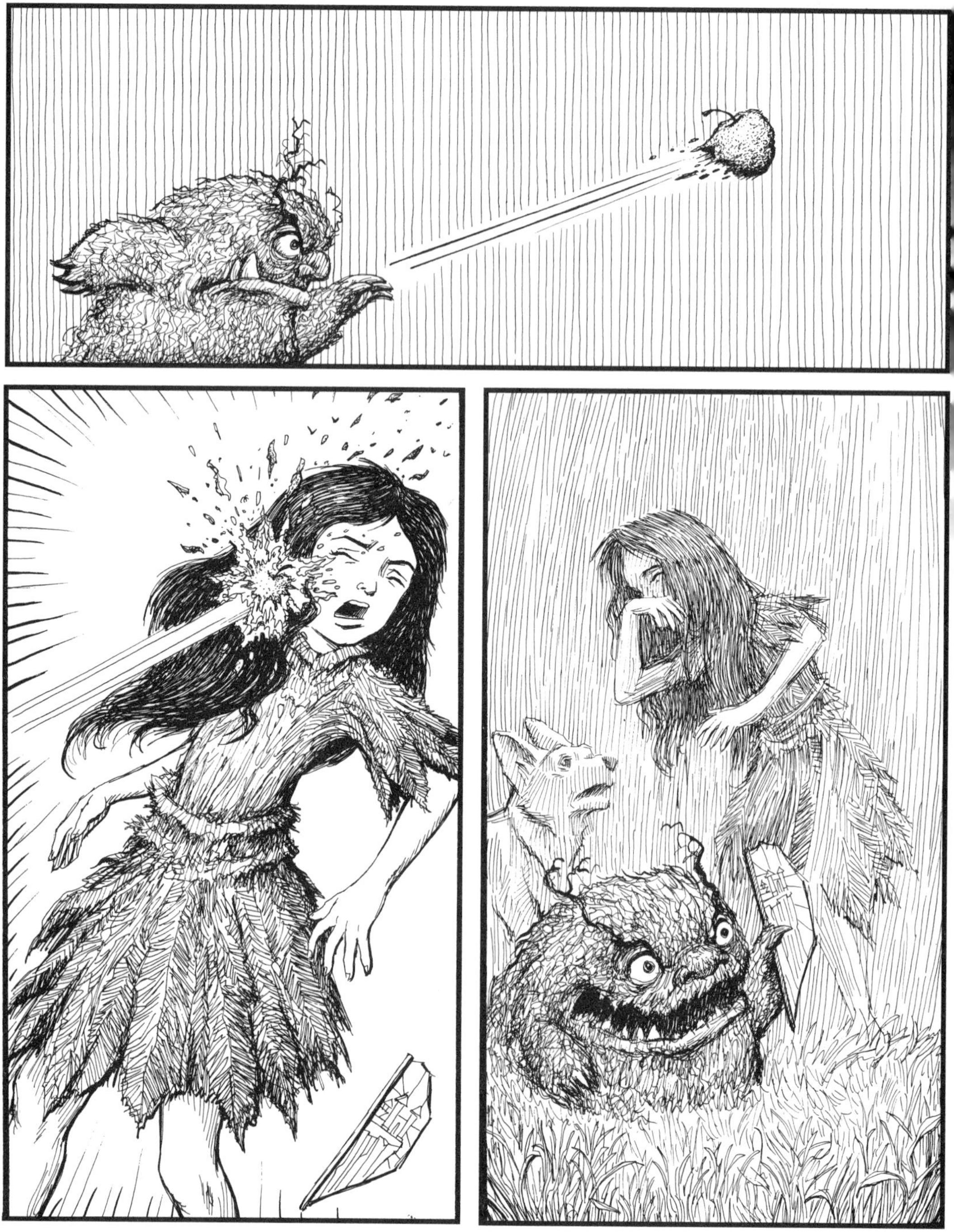

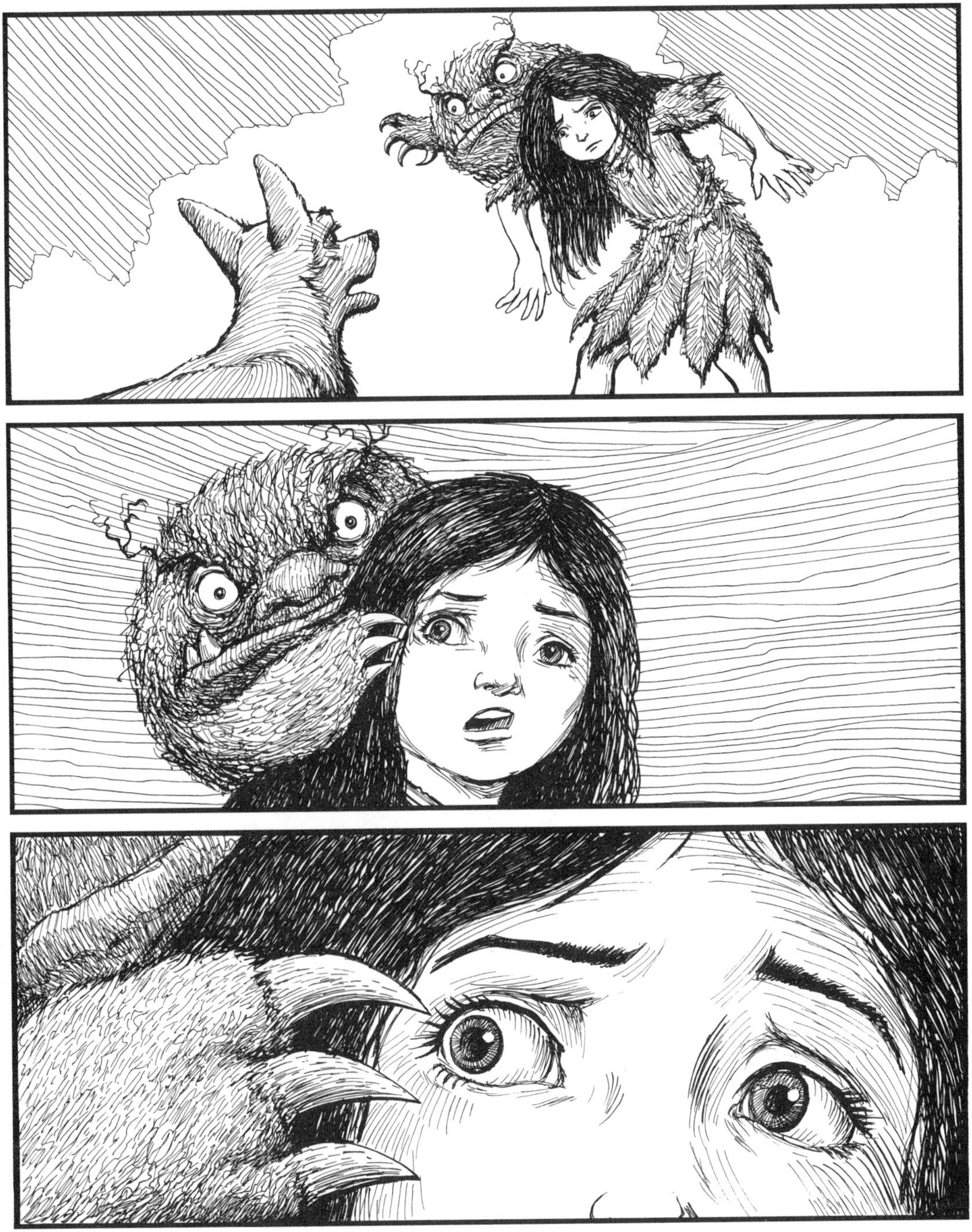

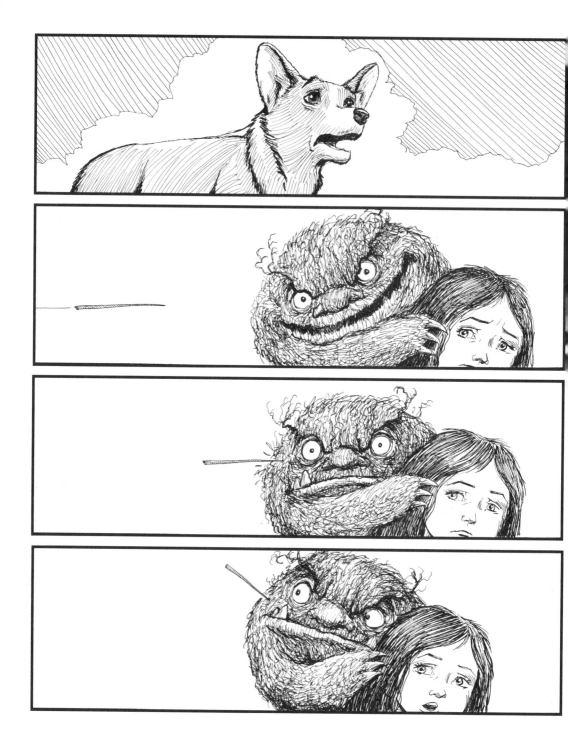

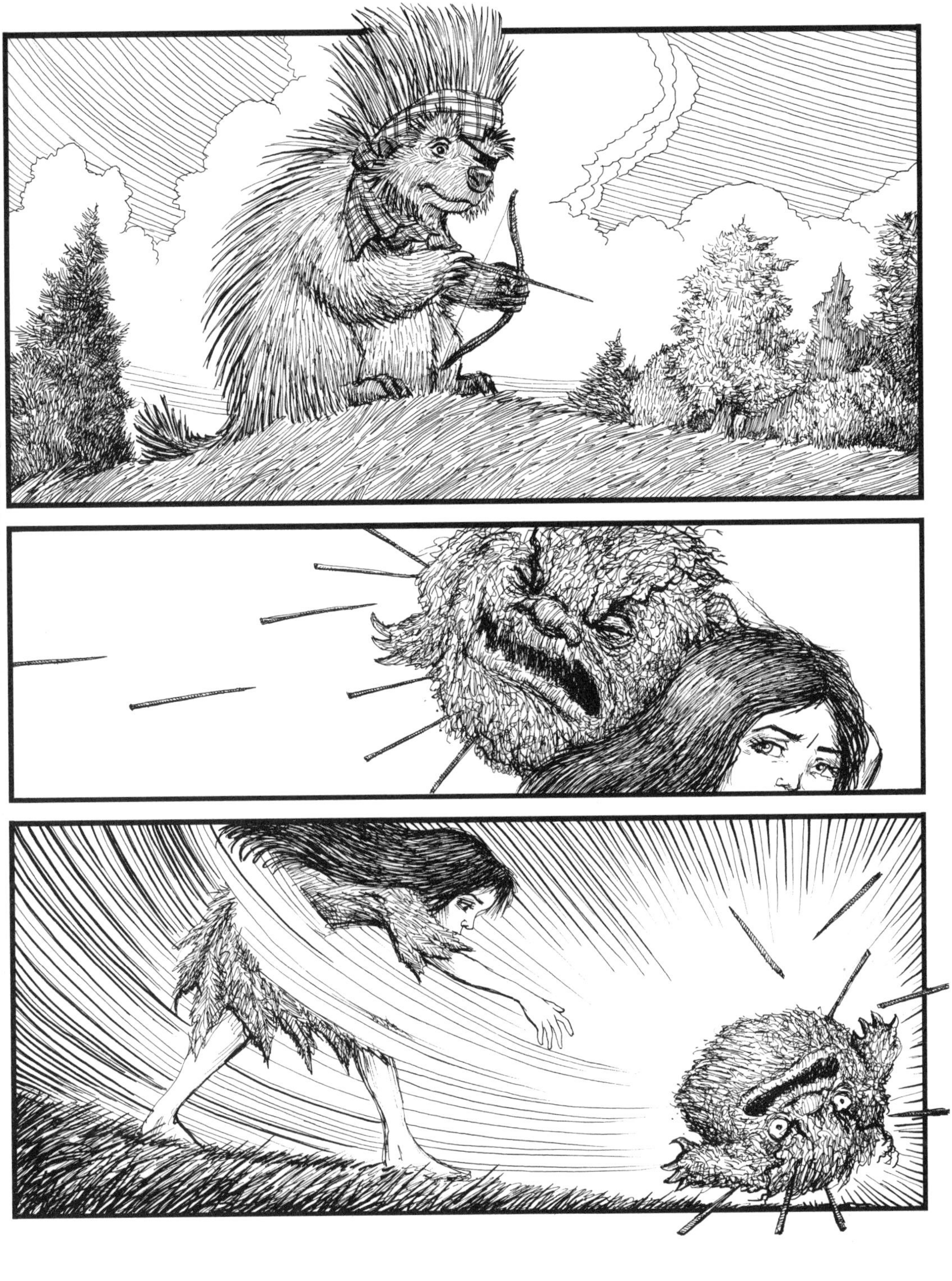

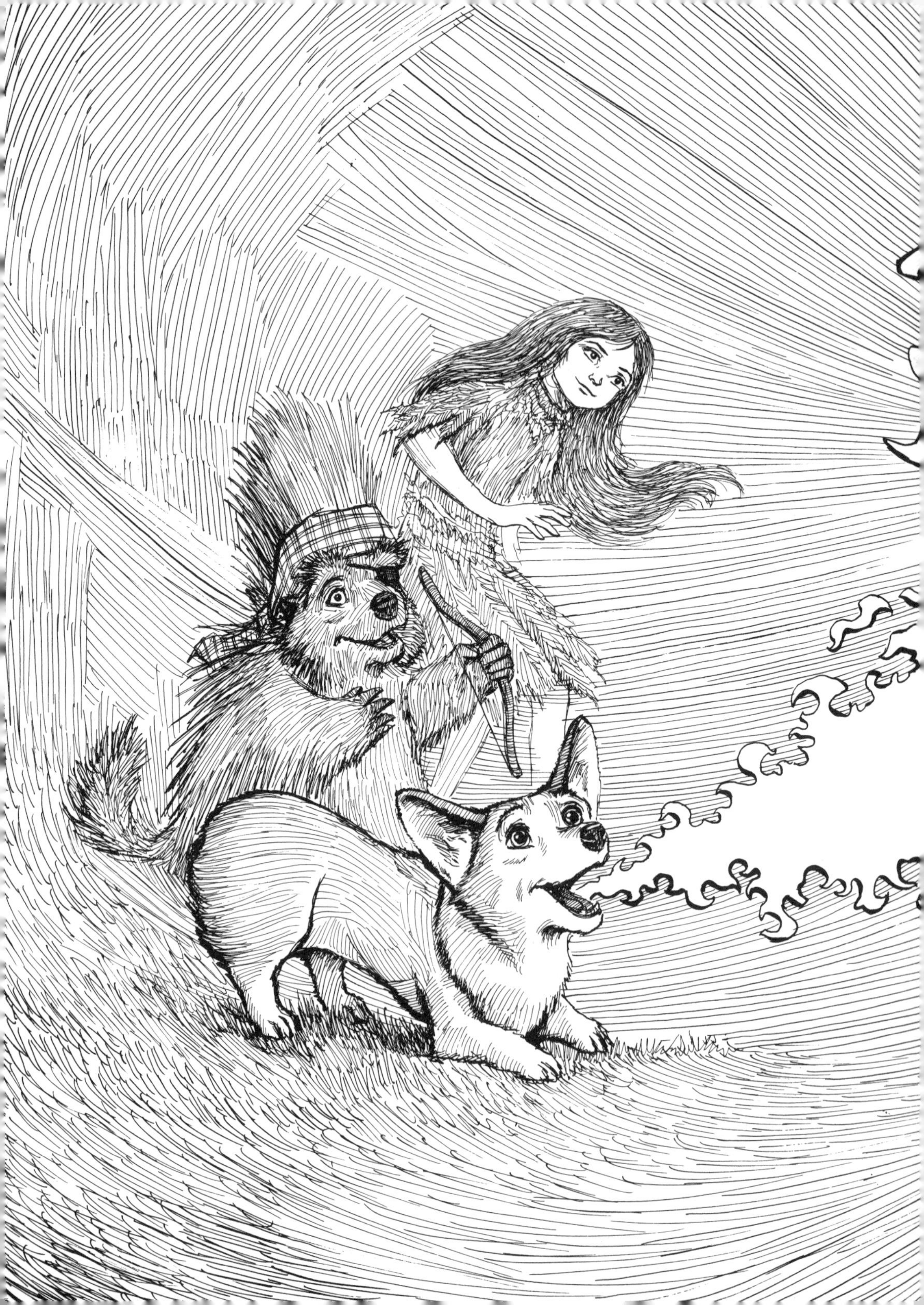

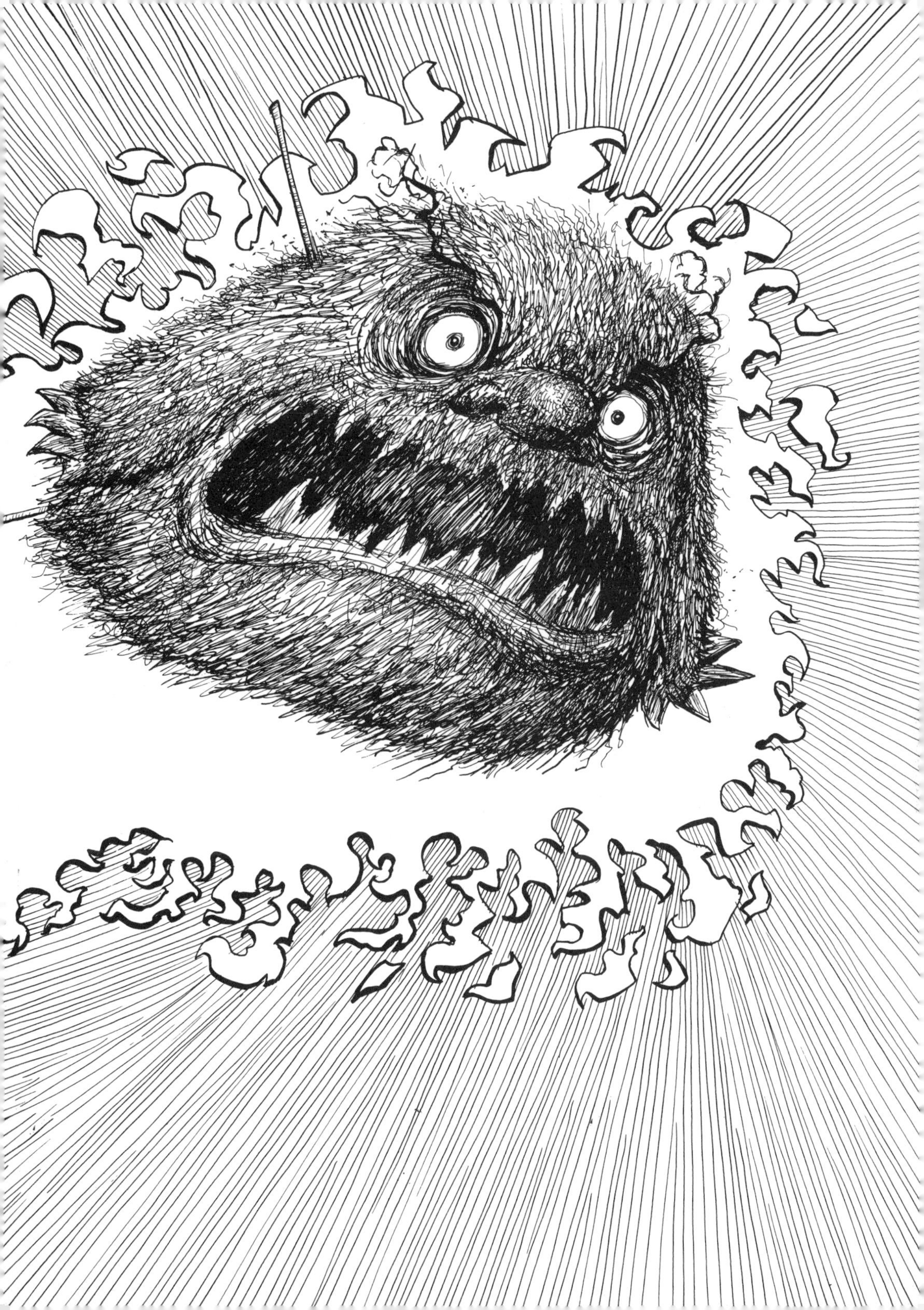

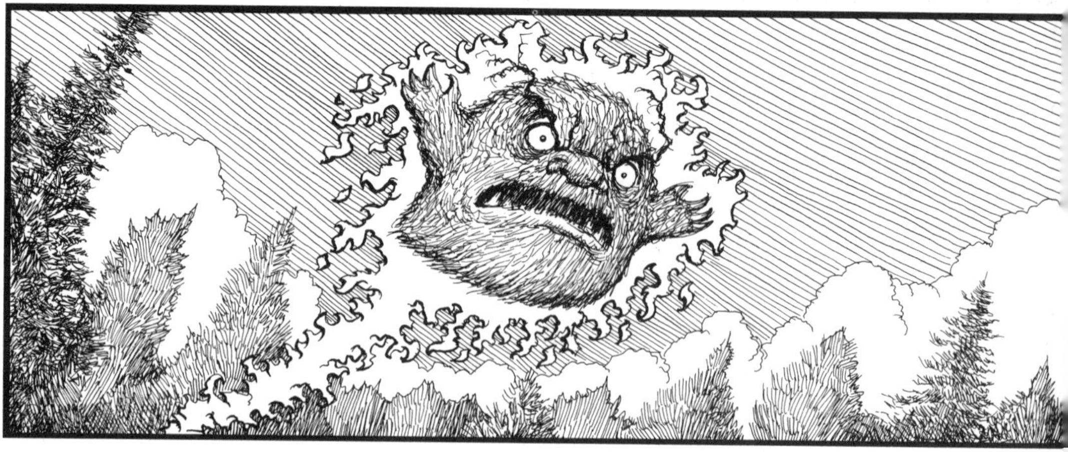

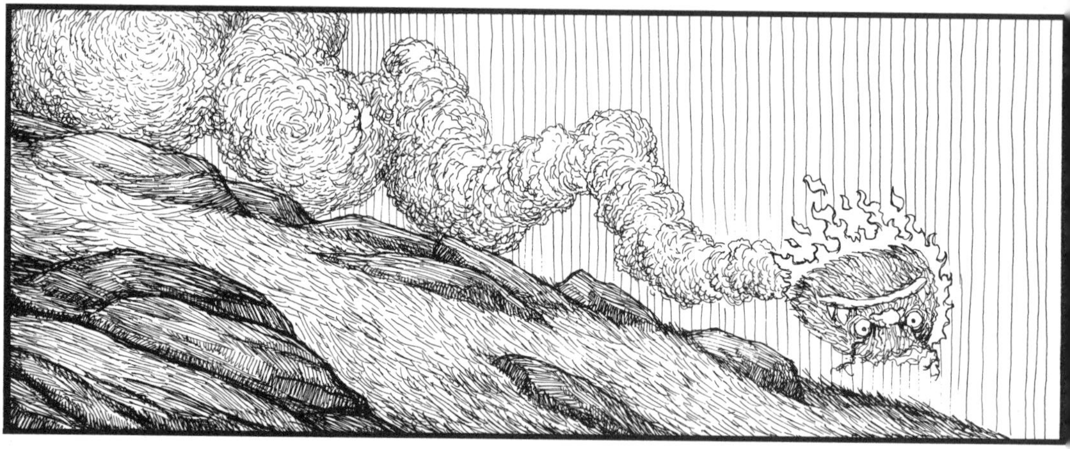

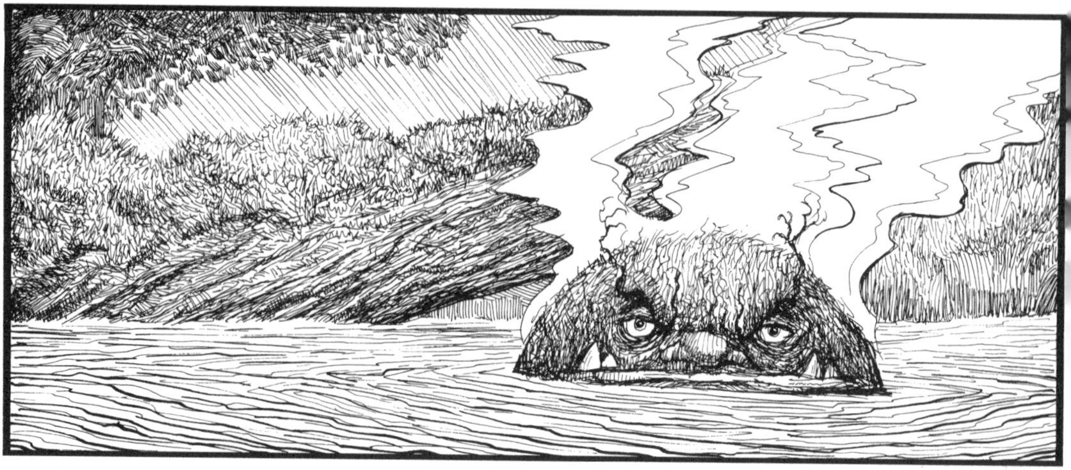

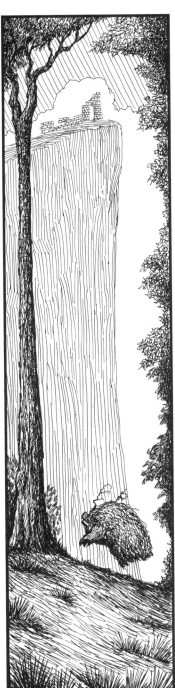
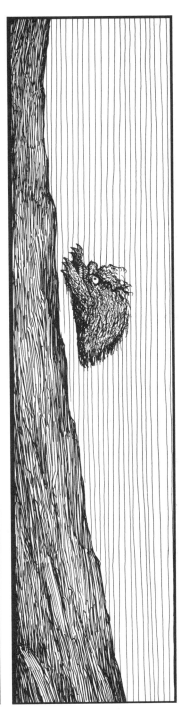

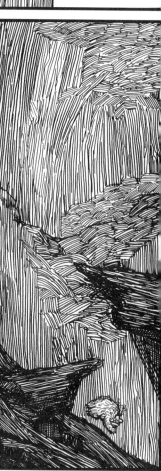

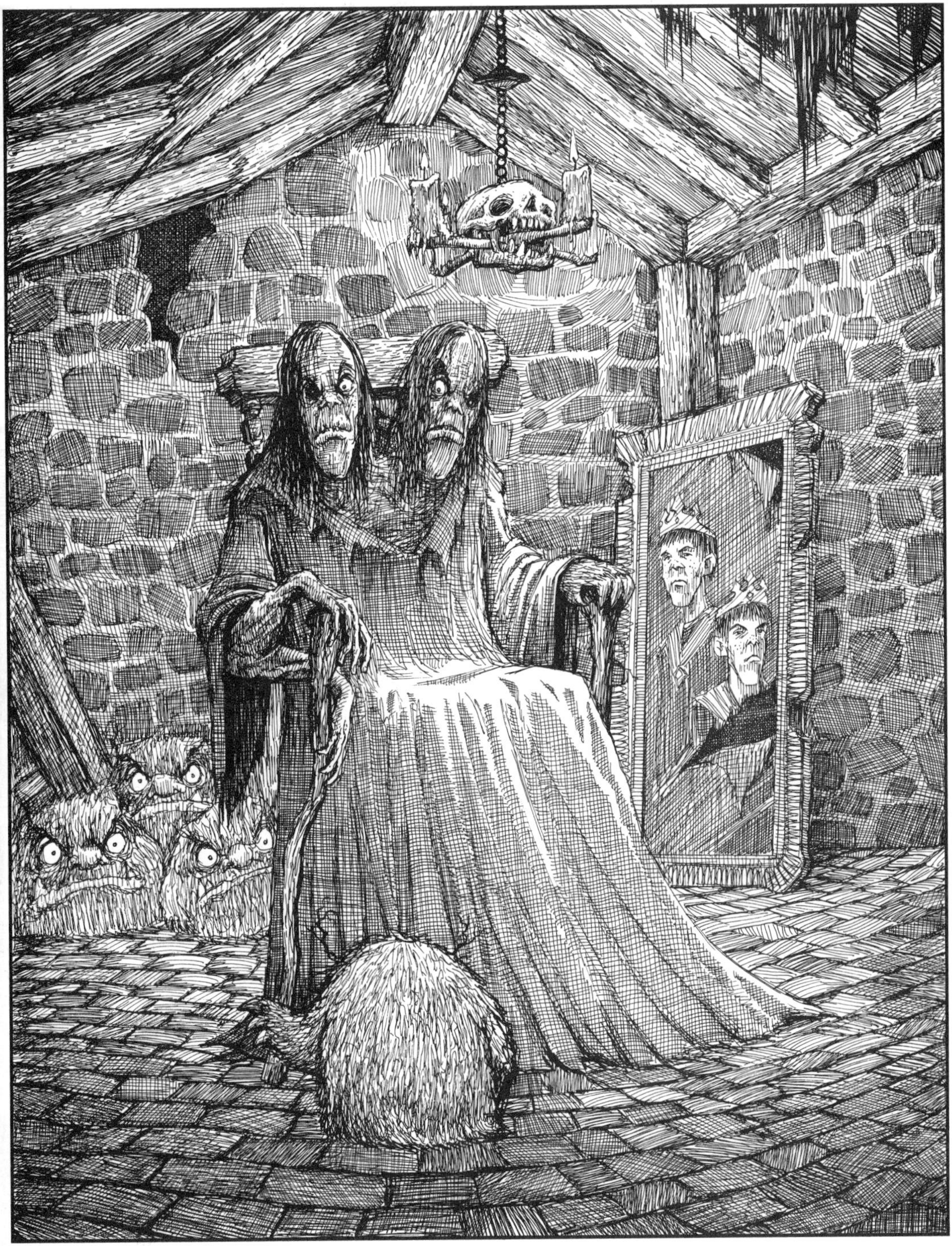

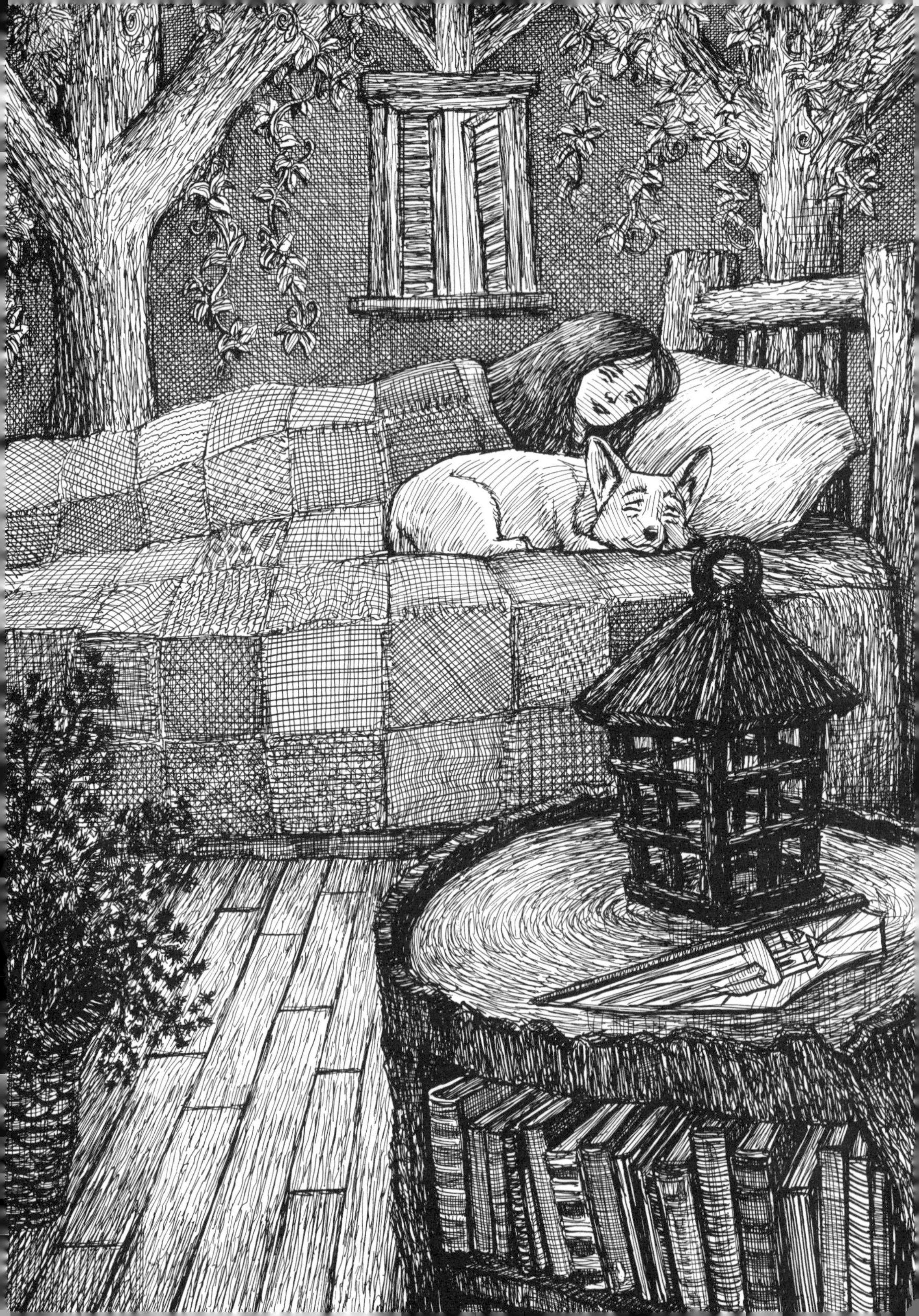

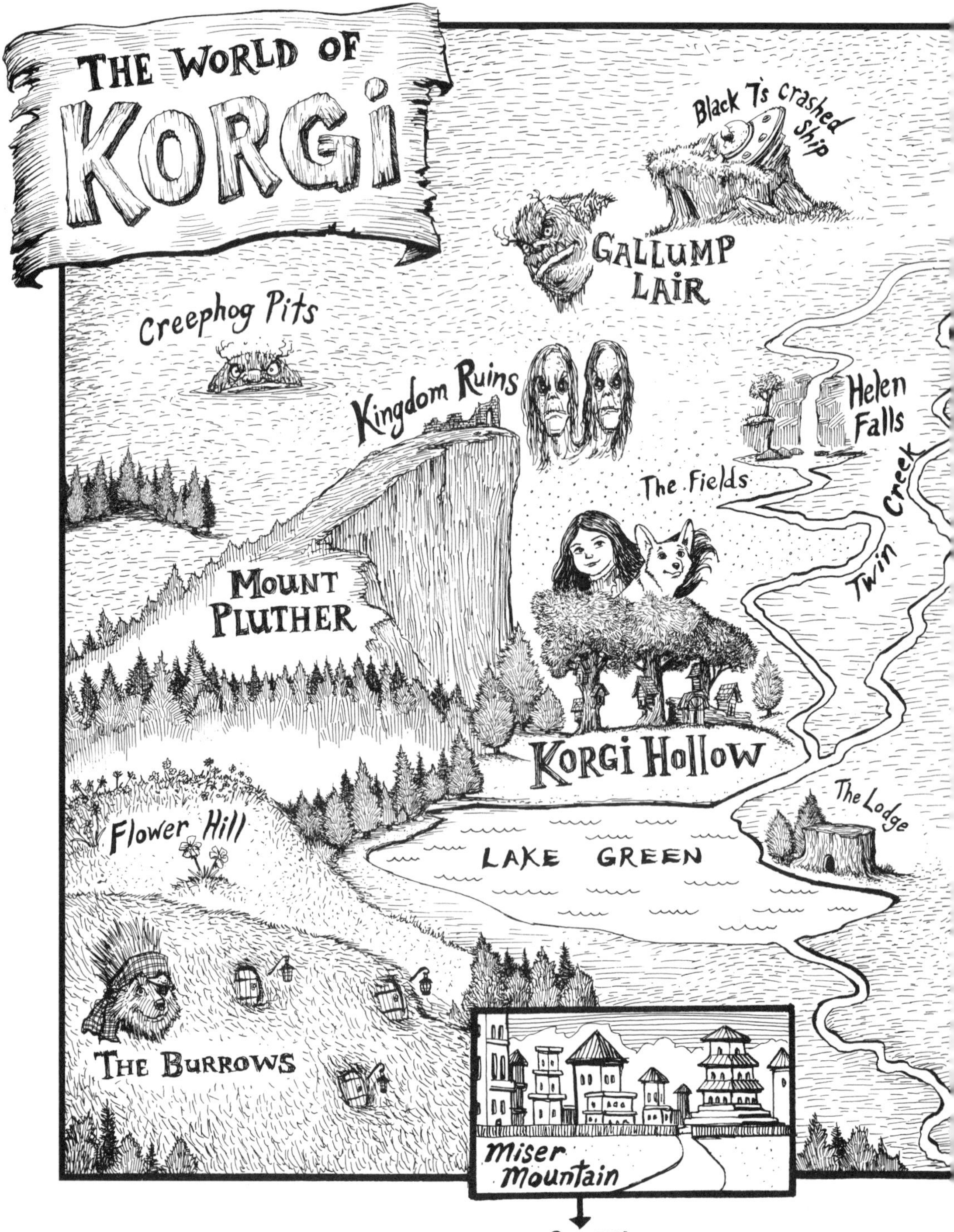
THE WORLD OF
KORGI
Black 7's crashed Ship
GALLUMP LAIR
Creephog Pits
Kingdom Ruins
Helen Falls
The Fields
Twin Creek
MOUNT PLUTHER
KORGI HOLLOW
The Lodge
Flower Hill
LAKE GREEN
THE BURROWS
Miser Mountain
SOUTH

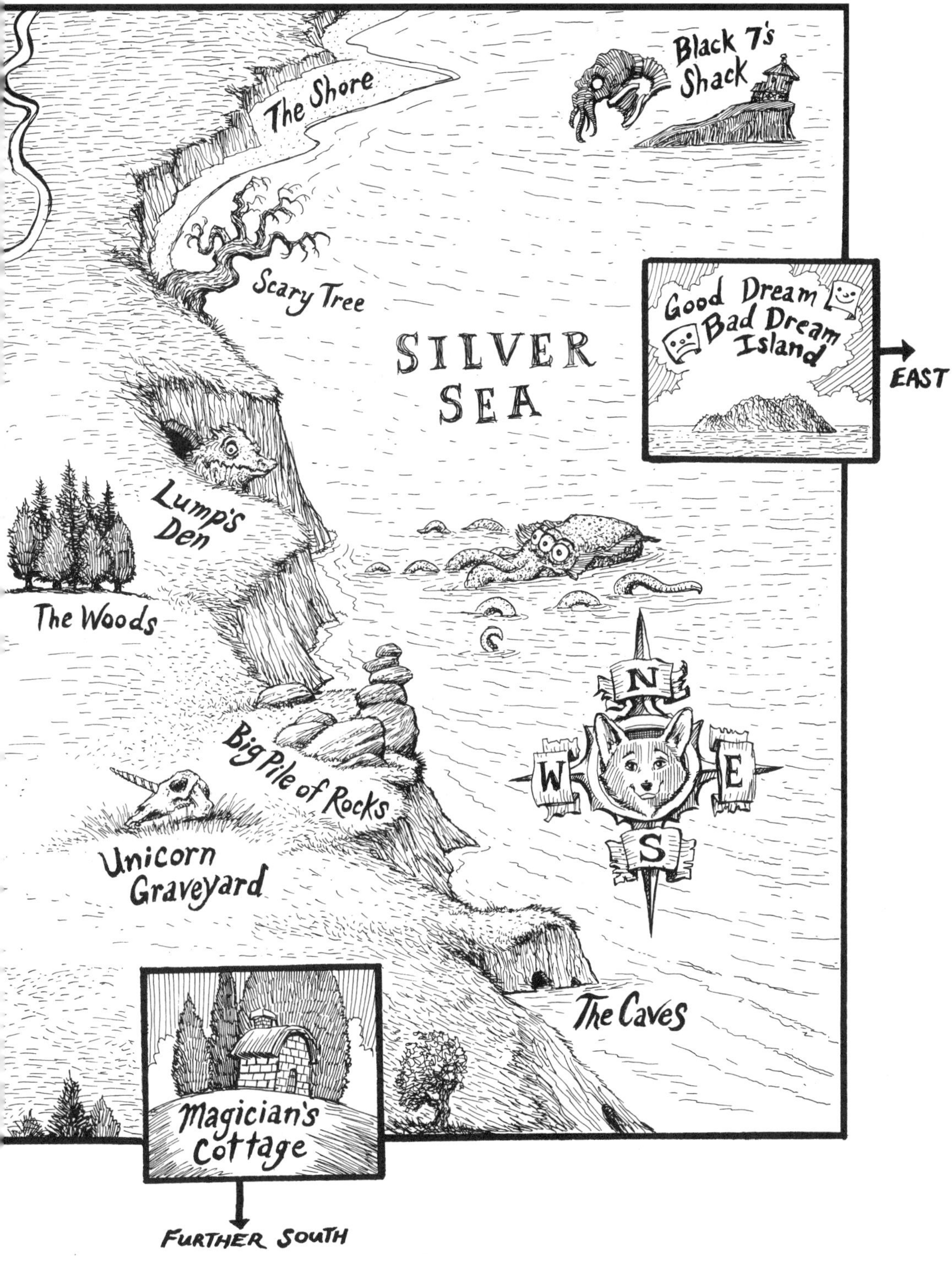
Black 7's Shack
The Shore
Scary Tree
SILVER SEA
Good Dream Bad Dream Island
EAST
Lump's Den
The Woods
N
W
E
S
Big Pile of Rocks
Unicorn Graveyard
The Caves
Magician's Cottage
FURTHER SOUTH

Characters

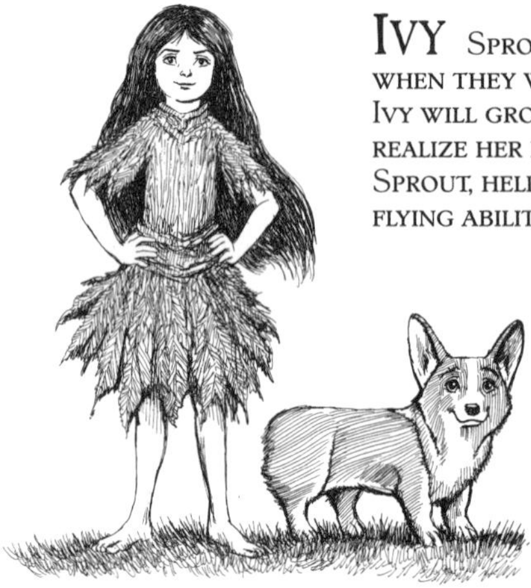

Ivy Sprout's best friend and caretaker. Ivy found Sprout when they were both very young. As with many Mollies, Ivy will grow up alongside her Korgi cub, who helps her realize her potential. Ivy spends a lot of time caring for Sprout, helping out in the Korgi community and using her flying ability to patrol the outer edges of surrounding lands.

Sprout Ivy's Korgi cub and best friend. Even though Sprout is young, he possesses the great talent of fire breathing, a rare skill that has not been seen in a Korgi for many generations. Sprout is a curious cub who enjoys exploring the lands surrounding Korgi Hollow with Ivy. He also has a great passion for food!

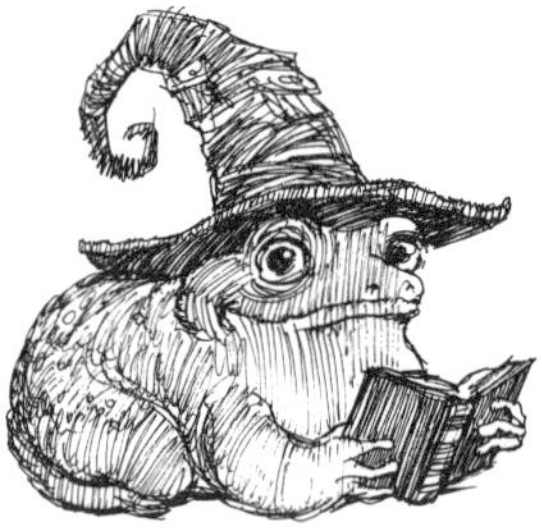

Wart Having lived in Korgi Hollow for a long time, Wart collects books and is the town's historian, scroll keeper, and librarian. He also counsels many of the Hollow's leaders, advising on important matters that concern the growth and safety of the village.

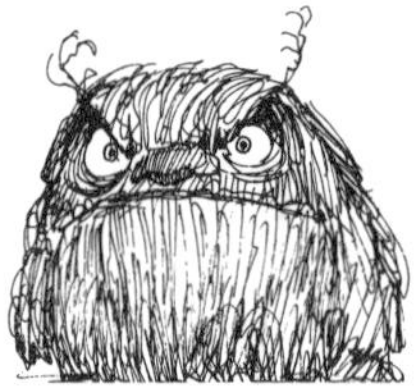

Creephog Dirty, stinky and, well… creepy are a few of the words to describe these creatures. Creephogs like to dwell underground or be partially buried in dirt, which they also like to eat. They are natural diggers, which makes them tough to spot. They are excellent spies. That said, their small brains and constant bickering get in the way of retaining much information.

Otto Living just outside the border of Korgi Hollow in the Burrow community, Otto practices his archery skills every day. He has a history of playing practical jokes with his good friends Ivy and Sprout.

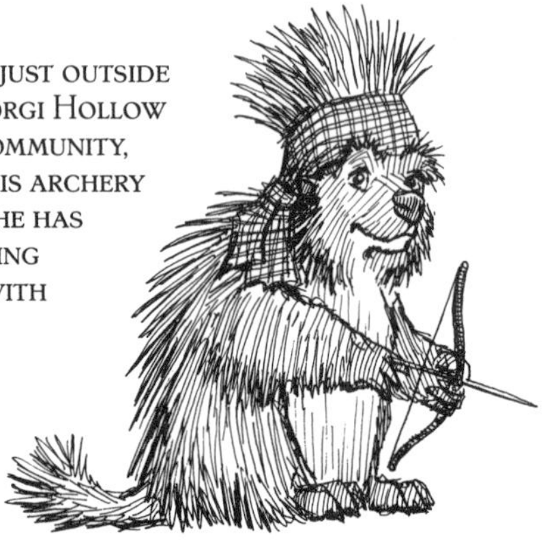

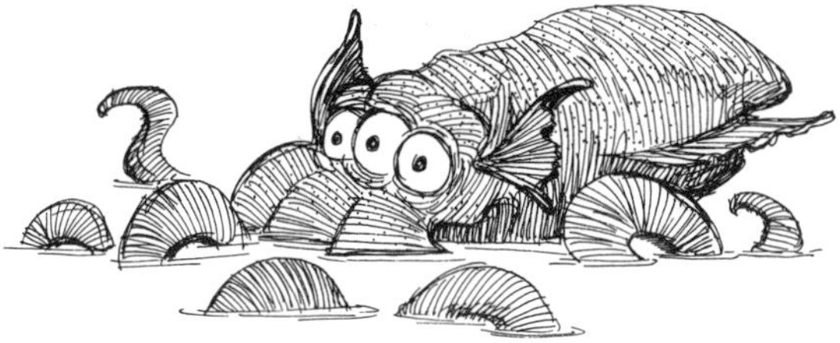

Scarlett A friend of Lump who enjoys singing. She is older than Lump and helped look after him as he grew up in the oceanside cave.

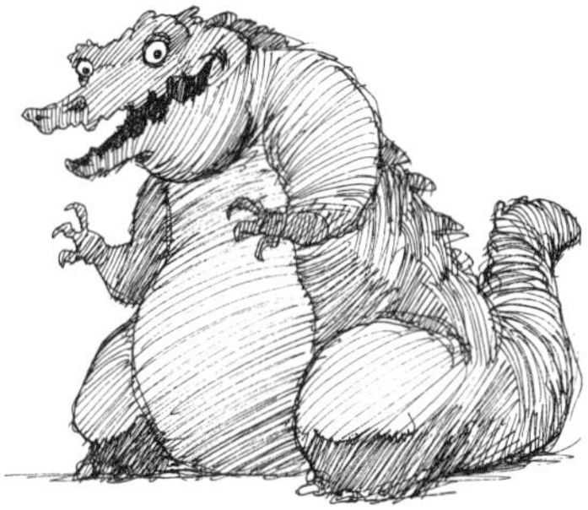

Derog-Glaw This two-headed monster is the result of two evil princes (one named Derog, the other named Glaw) whose cauldron went awry and exploded when they were using potions that would help reveal their escaped Korgi prisoners. When the magic backfired, Derog and Glaw were fused together into a hideous creature buried in the dungeon below the collapsed kingdom. Over many, many years, Derog-Glaw have used their mind control over the Creephogs, who have no choice but to serve their master and help it recover. The only way Derog-Glaw can split and become two again is by drinking the blood of a fire-breathing Korgi.

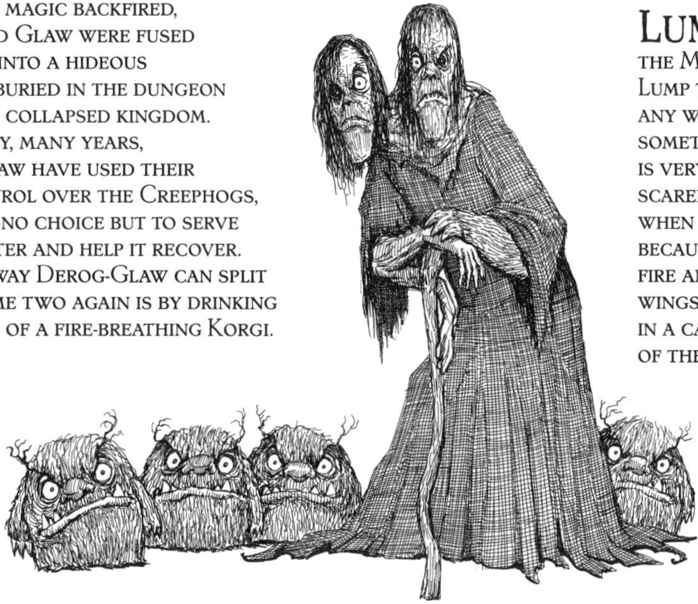

Lump A friend to all the Mollies and Korgis, Lump tries to help them in any way he can. This is sometimes difficult, as he is very clumsy and easily scared. Lump was abandoned when he was a young dragon because he cannot breathe fire and doesn't have wings. He grew up living in a cave along the coast of the Silver Sea.

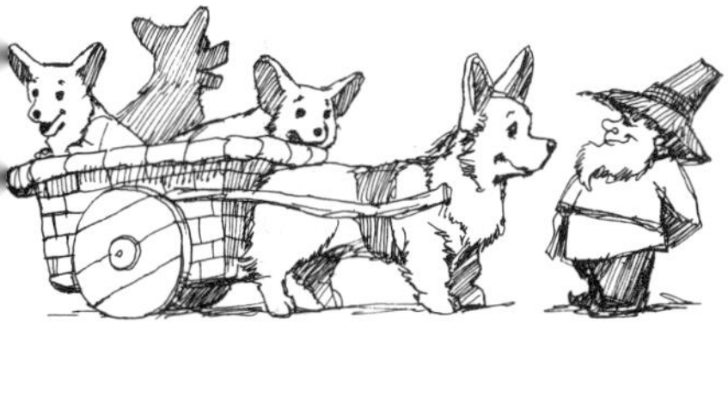

Mollies & Korgis Mollies used to be a tiny, lazy group of woodland folk. This changed when the cute and fuzzy Korgis came to live with them. Since then, the Mollies, while still small, are full of life and energy. Korgis are fuzzy animals with big ears, big smiles and even bigger hearts that have the special ability to help those around them by their very presence. Often, those in the company of Korgis discover powers they didn't know they had, such as the ability to fly or build elaborate things.

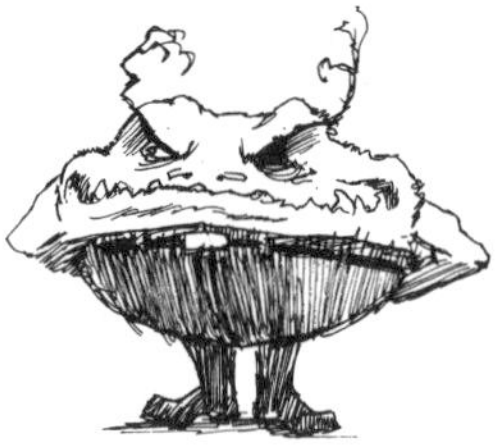

Gallump

A sad monster who lives underground and attacks all who fall into its lair. Other creatures live with the Gallump, and they have formed a sort of community who fear the outside world and sunlight.

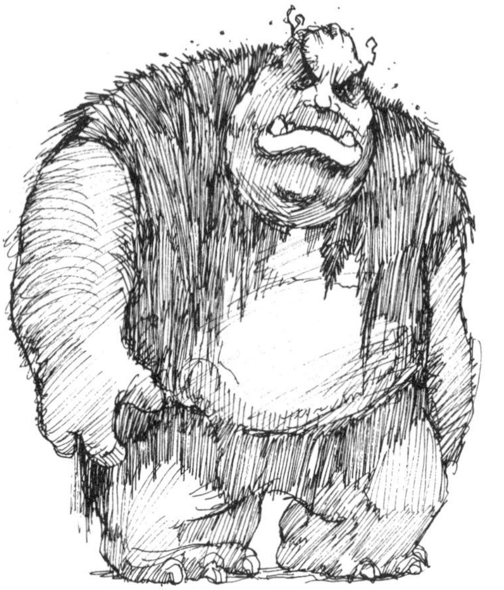

Lieutenant

A creature who often keeps company with the Gallump. He got his space outfit by looting the crashed alien ship that looms above the Gallump's lair.

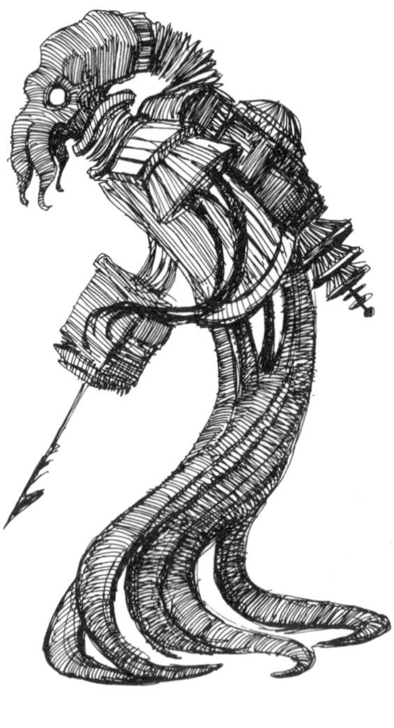

Knick & Nack

Small twin snails who are often seen around the Hollow. They like racing each other, rowing boats along the creeks and telling scary stories.

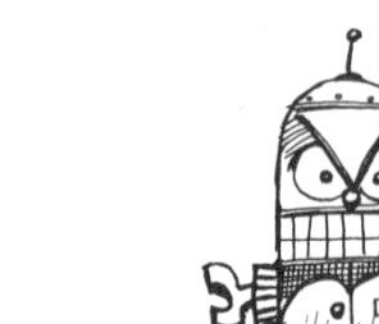

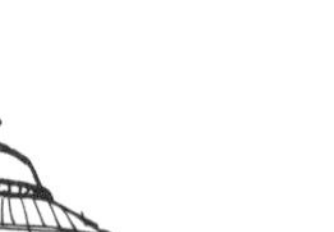

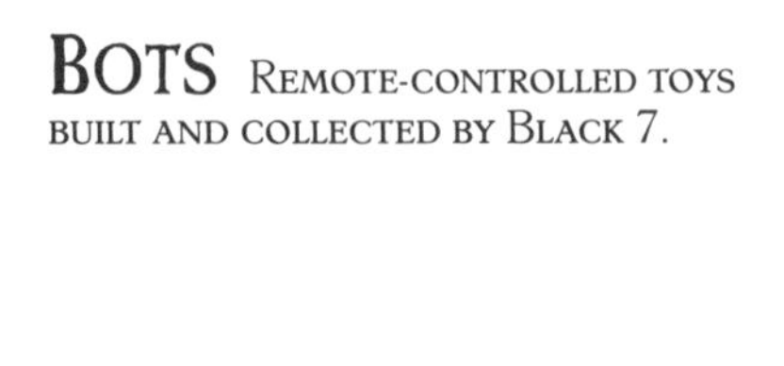

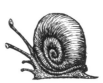

Black 7

A marooned alien whose ship crashed long ago on the bordering lands of Korgi Hollow.

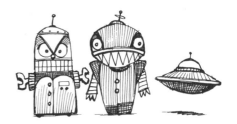

Bots

Remote-controlled toys built and collected by Black 7.

FLASHBACK CHARACTERS

MAGICIAN & KORGIS

IN A DISTANT LAND LONG AGO, THE MAGICIAN LIVED IN A COTTAGE WITH A HERD OF MAGICAL KORGIS. THESE SEVEN KORGIS WOULD EVENTUALLY BE THE FIRST ONES TO LIVE WITH MOLLIES AND FORM THE COMMUNITY THAT WOULD BECOME KORGI HOLLOW.

AUNTIE PLUTHER

OF THE ROYAL PLUTHER FAMILY BLOODLINE. AUNTIE IS A CRUEL WOMAN WHO GIVES THE KORGIS TO HER TWIN PRINCE NEPHEWS, DEROG AND GLAW, FOR THEIR THIRTEENTH BIRTHDAY PRESENT.

King and Queen Pluther

A kind royal couple. Their rule is peaceful and the kingdom has never been happier.

Nicholas

Head of the Royal Pluther Guard.

Vulchant

This unscrupulous character spends his days peddling trapped creatures at the marketplace in the city of Miser Mountain.

BANDITS

THESE VILE THIEVES TRAVEL DISTANT LANDS,
STEALING AND TRAPPING RARE CREATURES
TO SELL AT MARKET.

DEROG & GLAW

UNKNOWN TO THEIR PARENTS, DEROG
AND GLAW ARE TWO EVIL PRINCES WHO
ARE PLOTTING TO DESTROY THEIR PARENTS
AND ENSLAVE THE PEOPLE. THEY OFTEN
EXPERIMENT WITH THE DARKEST KINDS
OF MAGIC AND USE THEIR POWERS FOR
CRUEL AND SINISTER DEEDS.